2/18/12

For Elaine —
a sailor's delight,
and good on the "bridge."

Jack

Guantanamo Remembered

[A collage of short stories drawn out of Naval Air,
Water-fronts of Cuba, and the Forgotten War]

by

Jack K. Campbell

Jack K. Campbell

authorHOUSE®

AuthorHouse™
1663 Liberty Drive, Suite 200
Bloomington, IN 47403
www.authorhouse.com
Phone: 1-800-839-8640

First published by AuthorHouse 6/12/2008

ISBN: 978-1-4343-5894-3 (sc)

Library of Congress Control Number: 2007910100

Printed in the United States of America
Bloomington, Indiana

This book is printed on acid-free paper.

DEDICATION

These *flights of fiction* are dedicated to the officers and men of the heavy cruiser, USS Macon, and utility squadron, VU-10, but are not takeoffs on any of them.

TABLE OF CONTENTS

A FOREWORD

I GAVE MY wife the word on Guantanamo Bay! *"Gitmo,"* I told her, "was that naval base where I sweated out the Korean War, marooned on the underside of Cuba, a friendly Cuba in my day."

We'd been watching the evening news viewing Guantanamo Bay as a "holding camp" for suspected terrorists! "Guantanamo Bay only *holds* memories for me," I said, looking away from the hooded detainees on screen.

"Thought you felt like a prisoner of the draft," my wife looked at me in surprise, "let those memories go."

"A prisoner of patriotism," I now preferred to remember, firing-up my pipe and a glow of my naval past, "did time at Gitmo in service of my country."

"Do any time in service of off-base Cuban girls?" My wife was more interested in Cuban women than Islamic terrorists. She switched off the television, turned on a smile, asked if I held any "prisoners of love" in my *"Gitmo* memory?"

"Made war, not love," I claimed, even though some really *off-base* escapades were flying back to mind. "The Fleet Training Command always kept my squadron on the wing," I claimed, "towing targets for the whole fleet to practice shooting at!"

"Wish I'd gotten a shot at you, back then, in your cute sailor suit!"

"Wish it still fit," I mused, settling down in my smoke and memories, "and this old boy could fit back in with squadron mates of half a century ago."

"Take to the Internet," my wife suggested, "cast around for those old buddies, fish 'em up before they get away, and all their stories of Gitmo."

▪▪▪ ▪▪▪ ▪▪▪

A RETURN OF THE EAGLES

WHAT REALLY HAPPENED to Lieutenant Lazerov and Plane Captain Mann? Their aircraft took off one night from the American naval air station at Guantanamo Bay, Cuba, and never came back! That's all we remembered when a few of us squadron mates got together in Miami, half a century later, to plan our outfit's first reunion. Lazerov and Mann were the only casualties our naval air squadron ever took and ought to be remembered at our get-together, but we couldn't remember much about them, their appearance or disappearance.

Who were Lazerov and Mann? What really happened to them? The six of us who'd gotten together to work out our squadron's reunion hardly knew what happened to each other, except that we weren't flying high anymore, the gravity of time having pulled us down. We could barely hold our belly tanks up, or landing gear, and our memories were really dragging! We only knew our utility squadron was decommissioned

1

long ago and our base at Guantanamo Bay converted into a "holding camp" for suspected terrorists! Miami was as close as we could get to the tropical breezes and waving palms of Guantanamo Bay, and we couldn't get anywhere close to the flyboys we used to be. Our youths had flown off, disappeared, like Lazerov and Mann.

We'd been called together by a host of former squadron mates who designated us to get a reunion off the ground. Six of us huddled round the table in a Miami hotel suite, soaked up old times, coffee and smoke, called plays for the reunion. Our missing men came out of the blue.

"It's a bitch, dying young," one of us thought, tapping fingers on the table.

"It's easy to die young," I said, "hard to live old."

"Who says they're not growing old, somewhere?" one of us suggested.

"You think they're still up in the air?"

"What happened to them is still up in the air!"

"They spun out in the Caribbean, oceans of time ago!"

"Went down with their flaps up," someone piped up from the other side of the table. It was an old enlisted man we still called, "Woogie." He still had a guitar stuck to him, strummed it up, sang out, "went down with their flaps up!"

"Woogie" Woodrow Woods, the guitar player, had gone from Navy clean-cut and crew-cut to unkept and uncut, from the pink of youth to the gray of age. "Went down with their flaps up," he sang again, his stringy mustache rising and falling to the shape of his words, his gray ponytail going up and down to the rhythm. The ponytail was strung down his back like the guitar was strung down his front. Every time he struck the guitar his ponytail struck his other side.

"That little bit of flap," he sang out, "was the refrain in the requiem I wrote for those boys' memorial, back when we were young." He kept plucking at the strings, trying to pick out the rest of the melody.

"Can't even remember the memorial service," I said, barely able to recall the guitarist. When we got together I had to be reminded he was a grease monkey out on the line. I couldn't imagine the black-stained fingers of a mechanic plucking out a requiem. It was hard to believe he'd gone from grease monkey in Navy blues to soloist in New Orleans blues, all the way up to the top of pop? That's what he'd let us know as soon as we got together. Back on the flip side of his life, after the Navy, Woogie cut a disc that hit the charts, and even had his own radio show, *"Boogie With Woogie."* The ponytail must have been his passport to the world of blues and swing, but the world of Rock got too fast for him, he'd let us know. Phonograph records slowed over the years from 78's to 45's to 33's, but music went from fast to faster and left him behind. He'd complained about being "gigged out," but promised to "swing" our reunion back to the Fifties.

"Went down with their flaps up," Woogie was still singing, shaking his head, and ponytail. "Can't come up with the rest of it," and dissonance came out of the soundboard.

"Love songs are easier to remember," another voice rang out.

"This guitar's been my sweetheart since Cuba," Woogie said, tightening the strings, "got myself strung to a string of wives, but always kept in tune with this old *guitarra*, my Cubanita!"

"Maybe if you touch her right," I thought, "she'd let you have your requiem back. We could use it at the reunion."

"Maybe I should write us a new requiem," Woogie said, plucking at each string as he talked, "a dirge for all the dead days we buried down there at *Gitmo*."

"If you hated it so much," someone piped up, "why'd you take on this reunion gig?"

"Dead days make for good blues," Woogie said, nodding his head and ponytail.

"Duty in a land-based squadron at *Gitmo* was choice duty, after cramped-up on a ship."

"Hell, *Gitmo* was like a ship that never hit port."

"A ship dead in the water!"

"How we gonna get our reunion off the ground with talk like that?" I asked.

"Let's face it," somebody interrupted me, "times down there were pretty lonely, and we lost a lot of career time."

"Think of all the time Lazerov and Mann lost."

"Maybe they're still somewhere out there?"

"You think their time didn't run out that night they didn't come back?"

"Who knows?"

The man who kept questioning the fate of Lazerov and Mann was our host, name of Lyon, a big man lounging around in a flashy red smoking jacket. I didn't drag his memory along with me, not even his name. Some of the former enlisted men among us called the old boy "Slick," or "Slim," but he wasn't slim anymore. I only knew he was another airman, like Woogie, who'd gone up in the world. He had his own Cadillac agency near Miami, had a diamond on his little finger, booked us in the hotel, welcomed us into his suite, the "Lyon's Den." Now I had to look up to an enlisted man.

"You know something we don't know about Lazerov and Mann?" I asked the man in the red smoking jacket. I was still trying to place him in my shaky memory. I knew he was now the joker in our pack, going for laughs, kidding around. He still looked like a kid. His dark hair must have been touched-up with boot black. His face may have taken a tuck or two. He was in good shape, must be working out.

"Just a *Slick* hunch," Lyon said, playing with a pun on one of his names. He started rolling a cigar between his fingers and aimed it at his mouth. "Navy might have pulled a *cover-up*," he spoke, making room in his mouth for an unlighted cigar. "Navy might have laid a smokescreen down. Weren't we on some kind of hush-hush Cold War mission when our boys dissolved in thin air?" He struck a match, disappeared in his own smokescreen.

"We sure were up to some covert reconnaissance," someone remembered.

Lyon waved off his cigar smoke. "A million things could have happened," he piped-up. "Our boys could have gotten fished up and salted away on some island in the Caribbean, or maybe they just wanted to take leave of the Navy, set themselves up for a fall, got themselves hid out somewhere?"

"Rotting on a tropical island 's a better way to picture them," someone said, "better than bones rusting at the bottom of the Caribbean, along with dog tags."

"Or, maybe worse than death," the big man named Lyon resumed puffing out theories and smoke, "they were downed by the Commie gunrunner we were on the lookout for. They could be in a Russian Gulag, somewhere in Siberia, worse than death."

"Maybe they got carried off by mermaids?"

The man who scoffed at Lyon's theories was our elected president and spokesman, an old pilot known as *Dutch*. "Let's get back on the beam," he commanded.

"We are on the beam," Lyon talked back, aiming smoke at the shiny bald pilot, "are homing in on the men we want to honor at the reunion?"

"You're homing in on ghost signals!"

"They could have ditched their plane," Lyon's voice rose above the pilot's. "They could have paddled off to some enchanted island."

"Yeah, faked an accident, went AWOL," another one of us alleged. "A lot of guys were dying to get out of the Navy!"

"Dying's how they got out," Dutch Decker interrupted, tapping his Annapolis ring on the table. Unlike the rest of us, Dutch was regular Navy, had retired a full commander. I remembered him as an ensign, a high flying New Yorker bragging about his New Amsterdam blood lines. He had a Dutch look, too, a solid build, bristling blond hair, sky blue eyes. We called him "Dutch" and the old boy still carries it around. Except for the name, he's all different! Time took the old pilot down, left hardly a recognizable body part amongst the wreckage.

"Dump the bullshit about our boys rising alive out of an oil slick and debris field," Dutch kept speaking with authority. "They're at the bottom of the sea, dog tags and all, and we'll never get to the bottom of it!"

While he talked I was looking him over. He was a bright blade in my memory, a withered old leaf in my eyes, all wrinkled except for the shiny top of his head.

"God knows what really happened," Dutch kept talking and shrugging, "engine failure, pilot error?"

"From my sunset point of view, it was moon death," I said, referring to moonlight's distortion of sky and sea. It always made me question my instruments when I was flying at night.

"Moon Death, that came up in my requiem!" Woogie broke in with a rip at his guitar strings. He worked at a melody, started singing something about a last breath, and a moon death, a winging on moon beams to moon dreams, a *ride* on moon's borrowed light, to unending light on life's other *side*. He finished with "going down with their flaps up." He looked up, said the old boys were coming back to him.

"What if they really did come back?" Lyon asked, blowing smoke in the direction of his old superior officer. "What if they picked up our web page or our notices in *The Legion Magazine*? What if they show up at the reunion? What if they knock at our door right now?"

"Knock it off," Dutch said in his commanding voice. "The Board of Inquiry found them officially dead, lost at sea!"

"They could be unofficially undead," Lyon shot back, aiming the cigar at his open mouth again and screwing it around with his words.

"We're not in the middle of a paperback mystery," Dutch reprimanded. "The book on Lazerov and Mann is closed!" Dutch spoke with the authority of a naval officer. We'd elected him president, figured he was the best man to hold our new veteran's association on a steady course. He was a career man in the Navy, outranked us all, and kept up with his Navy connections. Dutch never married, flew solo, had time to work on the squadron reunion.

"We can't raise Lazerov and Mann from the dead," our president insisted, slapping the tabletop, "but we can raise a glass to their memory at the reunion."

"What you want in the log?" I asked, assuming my role as recording secretary.

"How you want to raise a tribute to our fallen comrades?" Dutch asked, turning his bald head round the table like a searchlight, glaring in every eye.

While his shiny head was beaming round the table, I kept reflecting on the disappearance of Lazerov and Mann, started picturing the whole squadron up in the air, searching high and low. Lazerov and Mann flew out of our lives, I remembered, but left an oil slick! I caught a memory of myself dropping the memorial wreath over the water where the oil slick had appeared. I remembered the wreath hanging in space, circling down, diminishing into a white zero, around and around, into nothing.

Around and around my thoughts kept carrying me back, around and around, back to my naval life and the Ensign Dutch Decker I used to know. Why hadn't he married? He loved women as much as flying, loved snuggling in wind and sky, and "fluffy females." When he talked about "getting it off," he wasn't talking about his plane. We were throttle and stick pilots in those days, and he talked about getting women off with his joy stick. "You have to gun her up," he used to brag, talking about thrust, acceleration, power. Sex and flying were the only ways to hit a high, he used to say. He thought the world tried hold us down to earth. Maybe he thought a wife would hold him down?

It was the guitarist, Woogie, who snapped me out of my thoughts with a chord on the guitar. "Our missing flyboys deserve a memorial," he was saying, plucking a string and tossing his ponytail around. "Our missing boys ought to get a musical liftoff."

Father Roy, sitting next to Woogie, came up with a "spiritual" note for a memorial. It was the first time he'd spoken up at the meeting. Father Roy had surprised the hell out of us when the kid we remembered as "Roy Boy" showed up as a priest in the Archdiocese of Miami. He said he came as a Bluejacket, not a man of the cloth, but none of us felt completely at ease in his priestly presence. "I'll get the memorial underway," he offered.

"I'll go for Woogie's music, and a touch of *Father* Roy's spirit ," I agreed, remembering Roy Boy as a young yeoman in the squadron office. I was the Personnel Officer, remembered his youthful, unfinished face. It was now well set, firm, trimmed in speckled-gray sideburns. He was distinguished, even without collar or cassock. I didn't know it back at Guantanamo Bay, but he was the best of us.

"Along with the service for Lazerov and Mann," Father Roy said, "we should hold a memorial for all the squadron mates taken down by time."

"Let's go for it," I said. "From my sunset point of view, I see a memorial service as the highlight of the reunion."

"How's that fly with you boys?" Dutch checked around.

"Sure would make a good wrap for the reunion," Woogie said, with a touch at the guitar, "a memorial ending."

"You know," I said, "it's coming back to me, the memorial service we had on base! I was the pilot who dropped the memorial wreath off the coast where we found the oil slick."

"Chaplain said the oil slick was their shroud," Father Roy remembered.

"Why put a religious spin on our reunion?" Ponzio's voice came out of the smoke. He was an old pilot buddy of mine, full of high spirits in the old days, but hadn't cracked a smile since we started talking about Lazerov and Mann.

"We're not on a pilgrimage to some sacred past," Ponzio kept spouting. "Quite the opposite!"

I wondered why the old pilot had dropped his carefree ways. He was full of play when we flew and hung out together in the bachelor officers quarters. He answered to "Touchdown," either for carrier landings, or football prowess, I forgot which. Now he was just "down," mostly scowling, tapping at the table or scratching at the armpits. Gone were the high spirits of his flying days when a football was a thing to airlift, and a plane was only a plaything. His body used to be made for pushups and passing footballs, but his quarterback form had bulked-up, and football padding seemed to be under his Hawaiian shirt.

"Our squadron reunion's not the occasion for getting up on a pulpit," Ponzio insisted, tapping his fingers on the tabletop, scowling.

"Why shouldn't the squadron reunion go up on *a wing and a prayer*?" Father Roy smiled, alluding to a World War II song we all remembered from our youths. Humor hadn't shown up when Roy Boy was a yeoman filing service records in my office. When I was just clocking-in flying time I offered to take him up, give him a "God's-eye view of Guantanamo Bay," but he refused, said he didn't want to tempt God. I used to think he was out of place in the Navy.

"I'm for it," Lyon spoke up, squinting through his own smoke. "A memorial service would lift our spirits."

"A shot and a beer would lift us faster," Ponzio thought, still tapping at the table.

"A rum and coke sure would zing us back to cha-cha-cha land," Lyon agreed, chewing on his cigar, moistening his words.

"Your feet were wired to the *cha cha cha*," Woogie remembered, and picked at a Cuban rhythm.

"Back in the barracks, you pulled the strings," Lyon remembered, toying with his cigar, "and my feet did their duty. Your music kept us grease monkeys from going ape-shit."

"Barracks was a zoo," Woogie thought, moving to the sway of his own music. "We were caged-up, wanting to get back home. I called it *The Gitmo Occupation Blues*," and he tapped his foot and remembered the tune of another one of his old songs.

"We were at war," Lyon said in tune with the music, "but only fought the blues! Boredom was our enemy."

"Still is," Ponzio grumbled.

A few licks of Woogie's *Gitmo Occupation Blues* snapped Lyon up to his dancing feet. He bent his knees, gave the hips a twist. "Your guitar helped shake those *Gitmo* blues away," he said, out of breath, sitting back down. "In the good old days I could fill my shaker with Cuban booze, shake it all up and get fluid like the music."

"Those Cubans lived to a different beat," Father Roy contributed.

"They danced their troubles away," Lyon thought, getting to his feet again. He gave the back of his silky red smoking jacket a swish with his butt.

I thought Lyon was a storybook character, but still couldn't quite look him up in my memory book. He might have prepped my plane, kept me in the air. He was keeping me laughing.

"Woogie's Cuban music can beam us back to *Gitmo*," Dutch called us back to attention. He turned to me. "Log-in a memorial, schedule a time and place, get Woogie and Father Roy on the stick."

"I'll commit Lazerov and Mann to the deep with the sailor's prayer," Father Roy spoke up as I was making my notes. "I'll "take them up on a psalm or two, the wings of the morning, and let them dwell in the uttermost parts of the sea forever."

"And I'll put it all to music," Woogie promised with a flip of the strings.

"But how can we really bring their memory back?" I looked up. "I can't even remember what they looked like,"and I started lifting a shaky cup of coffee up to my words, my hand trembling. Everyone stopped talking, and I caught their stares. They must be remembering I'd been diagnosed with Parkinson's, was on a downward course, getting pulled down by what I called "the grave in gravity." They seemed to be thinking more about the state of my cup of coffee than the state of the reunion. My mind was on the state of my memory. It was receding like my hairline. Memory lapses were coming like little strokes, cutting me off from the past like Parkinson's was cutting me off from the body. "What can we say in memory of boys we can't remember?" I asked everyone, getting the cup of coffee safely down.

"Lieutenant Gordon's hit the bulls-eye," Lyon spoke up for me. "We need something to trigger our memories."

"I can hardly get a memory of myself back then," Woogie said. "My youth's been missing a lot of years, gone AWOL I guess."

"Our youths are all missing," someone thought. "That's what a reunion's for, to hunt 'em up, bring 'em back alive!"

I mentioned that we hadn't brought back a single living memory of Lazerov or Mann, and still don't know what really happened to them.

"It's no puzzle, the facts of their disappearance," Dutch answered me, fitting on his glasses. "It's all here in this clipping I kept from the base newspaper, *The Indian*."

"*The Indian* covered the base like sunshine," I shared my memory of the paper's slogan with everyone.

"No sunshine in an obituary," Dutch said, unfolding the clipping out of his pocket New Testament. "This old book used to be Government Issue," he said, starting to read the article: "Their plane was reported overdue, 0315, Sunday morning, May 23, 1954." He peered at us over his glasses, looked down again. "A fuel tank was found, part of a JD-1 landing gear, a water-logged flight officer's manual, and a life jacket." He paused to scan ahead. "The Board of Inquiry pronounced them dead in the line of duty,"and he shook the clipping at Lyon, read on. "Their memorial service at the Naval Base Chapel was Friday, May 28," and he flipped off his glasses. "That's all we need for the memorial."

"That brings it all back," Woogie looked around at everyone, giving his ponytail a good swing. "I was sleeping off a Saturday night liberty, got blasted out of a boozed-up dream, sirens blowing my head off, bunkmates hitting the deck! We thought the Korean Conflict was tuning-up again."

"We got mustered in the barracks," Lyon kept it up, "bussed to the hangar. Night crews were winding up the planes by the time we got dumped on the runway."

The Old Man had me looking for Navy regulations governing sea and rescue missions, I mentioned, remembering round the clock flights of search missions. Every plane was in an "up" status, every sector covered. "The fleet was called out," I let myself go on, "destroyers kicking up whitecaps all along the coast, and one of those airship dirigibles hanging low over the waters."

"Everything quieted down when the oil slick was found," Father Roy said, "and we took in a memorial service."

"It was outdoors on Chapel Hill," I remembered. "The wind was dead, flag limp, palms dangling, the chaplain stirring up the hot air with words about Lazerov and Mann getting called to a higher duty station. There were rifle shots, and the sound of a guitar, and the mournful sound of taps.

"I was flying their relief," Ponzio's voice cut me off, "picked up their operational data, radioed them to head back to base. It was all routine for me, but all over for them."

"It was the only excitement our squadron ever got," Lyon rushed to comment with a blast of cigar smoke. "Planes all scrambling, all us mechs losing sleep to keep those legacy World War II crates patched up."

"It was the only shot our little old utility squadron ever got at history," Dutch said, "but our mission was classified, never made the history books."

"Not even a footnote," I said, remembering my college courses in American history, and the history homework I helped my kids with.

"It's not classified anymore," Woogie sang out, with a fanfare on the guitar. "It's an open book, starting to all hang out."

"What's hanging out?"

"Our intervention in Guatemala!" Woogie explained. "Secret CIA files are going public, spilling the beans. Our intervention was all about bananas."

"How did our squadron intervene in Guatemala?"

"We were looking for a ship suspected of carrying guns to the Communists in that banana republic."

"It was a minor incident, a footnote to the Cold War," Dutch shrugged. "You should have been in the squadron when the Cuban Missile Crisis came along!"

"Now's the time to stick our footnote into history," Lyon said, "and put a good foot forward for the squadron's reunion."

"Are we the heroes or villains in that footnote?" Woogie wanted to know.

"We were following orders," Dutch insisted, tapping with his Annapolis ring. "Our planes weren't armed, and no suspicious ships were ever spotted. Nothing happened."

"Did you pilots know you were up against the freedom of the sea?" Woogie asked, snapping sounds of discord out of the guitar. "Enlisted men on the ground never got the official word, only scuttlebutt, and a whole lot of extra duty-shit."

"We knew the squadron was on a covert reconnaissance," Dutch Decker said. "It was the Cold War, for God's sake, and we just got out of a hot war in Korea, thousands of men died!"

"It was good we helped stop Communism in Guatemala," Father Roy judged with a shake of his head. "We should have stopped Castro in Cuba before he took hold. We'd have saved the Cubans a lot of grief, and saved the world from that Cuban Missile scare, that time the world went face to face with Armageddon!"

"Our little memorial service doesn't have to hash all that up," Father Roy said, "but we need to hash-up some good-buddy anecdotes to remember Lazerov and Mann."

"Those boys still don't pass muster in my memory," I said.

"They went through our lives like water through a sieve."

"All our lives got poured down the drain of time," I made another point. "Death's a waste!"

"We're wasting time now," Woogie thought. "It's time to bail out, drop down to the hotel bar and get ourselves wasted!"

"I'm for bailing out, too," Ponzio started to get up.

"And leave the memory of Lazerov and Mann up in the air?" Father Roy protested.

"We might find the spirit of them at the bottom of a whiskey glass!"

"I need a memory of them that will fly at the service," Father Roy pleaded

"How would each of us like to be remembered?" I wondered, thinking about my own time running out.

"My life won't be remembered for anything I did in the Navy," Lyon picked up on my question.

"You gonna be remembered for all the times you came off liberty and landed in the quack-shack," Woogie reminded him.

"You got your stacks blown out over there, too!"

Suddenly, we all felt embarrassed, looked uneasily at the priest.

"Well, I was a sailor, with human urges, like you," the priest said, trying to get down to our level. "There was a convent girl over in Cuba I'd have given my soul for."

"Que paso, padre?"

"Nothing came of it. Both our souls were saved." Father Roy tried to smile, "but I would have married the girl if my request got through official channels," and he looked at me, the personnel officer. He paused, said something about another sailor trying to get married to a Cuban national, getting turned down, too. He brightened. "I'm beginning to think that poor kid was Mann, the missing plane captain!"

"I got it!" Lyon yelled out in a shot of cigar smoke. "I remember a kid shacking up with a *mamacita* in Caimanera, wanting to get married! He was one of us mechs, a kid we called Manny, not Mann. He didn't hang out in the barracks much, was busy brown-bagging it to Cuba on weekends, living with a woman over there."

"Both our requests to marry Cubans got locked up in the chain of command," Father Roy remembered, looking at me again.

"It was my job to make it hard for boys to hook up with Cubanitas," I tried to exonerate myself. "There were hookers looking for a meal ticket to the States."

"I'm not blaming you," Father Roy eased my feelings. "Marriage for me wasn't in the Book, and not for Manny either."

"Now we got a bead on one of our missing men," Lyon said. "He had a woman off base in Caimanera. We could say he lived it up, before going down."

"I'm not sure he'd want to be remembered for living in sin," the priest thought.

"What shall we remember him for?"

"Wasn't he on the baseball team?"

"That he was," Lyon mused, "got time off the line for practice. I think he had a cross tattooed on the meat of his arm. Padre can make something religious out of that."

"Yeah, he was branded like a piece of meat," Ponzio came up with another memory, "but the tattoo was a plane, not a cross."

"Maybe a winged plane is the cross we all had to bear at *Gitmo*," I said, smiling, knowing I was remembered as "Crash" Gordon, a bumbling and reluctant naval reserve pilot who always bellyached about getting called up for active duty. Time had changed my view, made me more proud of flying in the Navy than teaching literature in the university. *Pilot* was the only word on my personalized license plates. I guess that's what I'd like to be remembered for, a pilot in the Navy!

"Let's remember his tattoo as a cross," Father Roy suggested. "I could say he bore a cross on his arm, and Christ in his heart."

"I think I remember the tattooed Mann as a cross I couldn't bear," Ponzio said. "I wouldn't have him for a plane captain. He didn't take to orders."

"Is that a sin?" Lyon asked, rolling a cigar around his mouth, "not taking to orders?"

"Not taking orders was the first Sin," Father Roy answered for Ponzio.

"You could give a sermon on the fall of Mann," Lyon quipped, "a long fall."

"I was in charge of Mann's seabag," I suddenly came up with another recollection. "I was on the Inventory Board, had to supervise the collection and sorting of everything the missing enlisted man left behind, get it packed for shipping to next of kin. I think the seabag went someplace in Texas."

"Remember pulling anything memorable out of his seabag?" Father Roy asked. "There could be a sea story or two for the memorial."

"Surely some drunken mementoes were among Mann's souvenirs?" Ponzio thought, tapping his fingers on the table.

I was reminded of pills among his personal effects. I think they may have been controlled substances, got reported in my inventory, but not in the official letter to his next of kin.

"There were some drugs in his possession," I mentioned out loud. "Can't remember what kind."

"Looking back to that war in Korea," Dutch got to thinking, "I don't remember anyone doing drugs. We just did alcohol, back then, and also kept ourselves lit-up like smokestacks."

"You suggesting Lazerov and Mann did drugs, doped-off, lost control of their plane?" Ponzio wanted to know. "That's a rotten memorial to lay on them! Laz wasn't into drugs!"

"Laz? You know something about Lazerov?" Dutch asked, focusing on Ponzio.

"Laz and me, we logged-in good times together, wing to wing, buddy to buddy. He was a bone of my bone."

"Why in hell didn't you come out with it, give us something good to remember him by?"

"Let his bones lie."

"We only wanted a bone or two," I said, "enough to reconstruct him in our memories."

"Remembrance won't bring him back."

"Remembrance is communion," Father Roy thought, looking at each of us in turn.

"Remembrance brings back their death all over again," Ponzio kept scowling. "Some things need forgetting, need to be covered up, buried, period!"

"I'll be damned if I'm not parting the veil on Lazerov!" Lyon was waving his cigar around to command our attention. "Wasn't he a snappy little officer, punk-size, always yakking about being small, but well-packaged?"

"You got him, *well-packaged*," Ponzio shrugged, "short and sassy, Hollywood good looks!"

"That's the short stub of an officer who checked out of bachelor officers quarters when he got his wife shipped down to *Gitmo*," I spoke up as though getting a flash on the evening news. "I did the paper work myself, got him set up in married officer quarters."

"Nobody saw much of the old boy after he got the wife on board," Ponzio said. "Not even his best buddy."

"I'm picking up signals on that little flying dude myself," Dutch thought. "He was a good pilot, played a cool game of poker, but moved out of the BOQ before we got the full hang of him. Yeah, I can picture the dude hopping in the cockpit, hooking himself in, jerking off a salute."

"That's Laz, all Navy."

"All regulation Navy!" Woogie piped up, trailing his fingers across the guitar strings. "Sorry men, but I'm picking up different vibrations. *Lieutenant Chickenshit*, that's what the men in my crew called him. He was always making out squawk-sheets, getting us all in trouble. Don't get me wrong, no one hated his guts enough to screw up his aircraft."

"Laz could be a pain in the ass," Ponzio nodded. "He lived by the book, but flew by the seat of the pants, had more than a thousand flight hours under his belt."

"Looked like a glamour boy movie actor," I was remembering. "Didn't he have a great wave of hair he was always brushing up?"

"Yeah, great hair," Ponzio finally came up with a smile, "always fussing with it, saying he couldn't get the wave out. You know, he married a Wave."

"You trying to tell us something about his marriage?" Lyon wondered, aiming a puff of cigar smoke at Ponzio. "You say he wanted to get the Wave out of his hair? Maybe he really did ditch his plane, left an oil slick to cover up. He wanted to get a new life."

"He *was* getting a new life," Ponzio said. "He had a kid on the way."

"The kid would be middle-aged by now," Dutch calculated. "Is there a way we could get in touch? What a bonanza to have Lazerov's wife and kid on board for the reunion!"

"I drew the escort duty, convoyed the widow back home," Ponzio said. "Dropped her off in Crawfordsville, Indiana."

"We never thought of locating dependents in our Internet searches," I mentioned, thinking of more ways to build up attendance at the reunion.

"The widow was a basket case, carrying an egg," Ponzio said, eyes sparkling with a far away look. "She got a boy,

Lazerov's son to raise. Got Christmas cards from the little lady for a couple years."

"She was a slick character," I spurted out as soon as I got another flash of memory, could almost see a tightly shaped woman in hose and heels dancing at squadron parties, fitting neatly in the arms of a wavy-haired pilot.

"First class woman," Ponzio said, smiling again, smiling at a memory. "I could have gone for her, but she wouldn't give up on Laz, thought he'd turn up someday, said she'd set a place for him at her table and keep a space for him in her bed, until that day came."

"That's the kind of woman I'd go for," Dutch said. "This old flying Dutchman was looking for a woman like that."

"He got a lot of love out of life, if not a lot of time," Father Roy was saying out loud as though phrasing an idea for the memorial service.

"Why not just say Lazerov was a pilot," Ponzio said, "lived fast, got it over with. And Mann was an enlisted man, like any man."

"Why not speak of them in music," Woogie suggested, accompanying his words with a twang of guitar strings. "Lives are measured in time, like music."

Lives measured in time! It sounded like something our musician might have aired on his show, *Boogie With Woogie*. I asked him what music would best measure their time.

"We're all the same in music," Woogie said, "in tone and pulse, a little different in melody. Music doesn't lose tone or pulse, not ever." He picked at the strings. "Music sounds the same whenever it's played again. Wonder why we run down, come to an end?" He felt around for the right notes as he talked, found the melody of "Tenderly." "What do you say to that?" he asked the priest.

I heard no answer. Woogie's music was spinning my head back to jukebox nights of college, and lovesick dates. Music ages, I considered, gets old with old times.

"Music's in time," I spoke up, "and everything gets old in time."

"My requiem's coming back to life," Woogie said, his fingers catching hold of a solemn melody. His eyes closed and he nodded his head and ponytail, taped his foot, sang out: "To drown and not to be, dissolve into a salt, and sterilize the sea."

"That's a helluva low note," Dutch interrupted, shaking his head, "too heavy to fly at the reunion."

Woogie paid no attention, let his music drown-out the dissonance of the old officer. *"Dissolve into a salt,"* he kept repeating, *"and sterilize the sea*! *But soul immiscible, a misty miracle, drifts on eternally."*

As Woogie's words were dissolving in my mind, I wondered what it was like for Lazerov and Mann when their measure of time was up? What went spinning round their heads when they flew out of control? Noise? Silence? Panic, pain, peace? An instant playback of their lives? A holy vision? The flash of a shark's grin?

I came up with my own bubbly blue memory of hitting water, going under, the time I was a student pilot working on my wings, the time I bobbled a carrier landing, went through the barrier, roared over the side, crashed into a breathless, blue silence. There was a gulp of what I thought would be my last living thought. My mother would miss me, that was the thought, but I burst back up to life, noise and air and pain, got myself hauled out of the drink, soaked, scared, and not thinking of my mother anymore. I was saved for another death, had to live with the call name of "Crash" Gordon.

"What are we supposed to do with life?" I heard myself asking.

"You asking if life has a mission?" Father Boy asked me.

"We can do anything we want with our lives," Lyon interrupted, "after we're out of the Navy."

I made myself a naval officer, I thought, a pilot, husband, father, college professor. I played all the roles, acted and reacted on cue, but is life just theater, play acting? I'd been wondering about that since I came down with Parkinson's, and knew the curtain was coming down.

"Maybe we could make more of our life," Dutch carried on, "if we could run through it more than once. I sure would like to crank up my past, get my youth flying again."

"I think we want to have a *renewal*," I said, "more than a *reunion*!"

"Far out!" Woogie struck another chord, "a renewal reunion!"

Father Roy raised his voice over the banter of talk, spoke of a Psalm that urged us to renew ourselves *like the eagles*. "Why not promote our reunion as a return of the eagles?"

"We were no eagles," Ponzio scoffed, "no birds of prey. We were stuck in a utility squadron, flew turkeys, leftovers of World War II."

"We rated two cougar jets a little after Lazerov and Mann went missing," Dutch reminded us. "I got checked out on one, never went back to props."

"We were called the Mallards," Ponzio insisted, "sitting ducks for ship crews to track and shoot at the targets we towed."

"We never killed like eagles," Dutch acknowledged, "but we sure took to the air like eagles, and can fly back to a reunion like eagles."

"We can't fly back," Ponzio tapped the table. "Life's a one way flight, no round trip."

"Another Psalm tells us the way of the eagle in the sky is too wonderful to know," Father Roy got our attention back. He talked about the eagle leaving no trail in the air, no tracks. We don't know where the eagle comes from, or where it goes. "It's God's mystery," the priest pronounced. "Where the eagle came from and where the eagle goes, it's a mystery."

"One day we'll be having a big reunion in the sky," Lyon suggested, trying to make light of it all, blowing smoke rings in the air.

"Far out!" Woogie said, watching his perfect circles of smoke dissolving in the air.

"A far out *surprise* party!" I thought out loud, keeping to myself the memory of life taking me by surprise. My first memory was being surprised by life, accepting it, but wondering what it was all about. Why not be surprised by death, find out about it?

"We've been looking back long enough for one day," Dutch announced, checking his watch. "Let's regroup after dinner."

As we were getting ourselves up to leave, I thought we may have been off our bearings all day, looking in the wrong direction. We were looking backward instead of forward, reckoning full astern instead of full ahead, *dead ahead*! It wasn't so much what happened to Lazerov and Mann that had us all strung out! It's what was going to happen to us when we fly out of time, disappear, leave no trail behind!

REMEMBER THE MAME!

WE REMEMBERED THE Mame. We'd forgotten a lot about each other, even about ourselves, but we remembered the Mame! We'd gotten together for the first reunion of our old squadron that winged over the naval base at Guantanamo Bay, in the Cuba before Revolution. We remembered "Battleship Mame," big and brassy, the "flagship" of a fleet of Cuban women on the lookout for liberty boats. The Mame fired off "business cards" that directed every liberty party to the *Mame's Domain.*

We drank to the memory of the Mame as we stood around the hotel bar. Her "*muchachas*" came up in the aftertaste, called for another toast. We remembered her "girls" were promoted on those printed cards as the "cleanest" in Caimanera, "inspected monthly." We remembered our fantasies about being the inspector. We remembered her girls teaching us the mambo on a dance floor quivering above shallow bay waters, and we remembered other things the girls taught us in the back rooms of the *"Mame's Domain"* in the "District" of Caimanera.

Caimanera was a backwater town named for the alligator, five miles from the open sea. It lay sunning itself on the inland shore of Guantanamo Bay, bottled-up by the American naval base. It was a sailor's only outlet, only escape hatch from the regimented life.

After Caimanera we let fly a toast to the old naval air station we called the "Rock." It reminded me that I used to be known as "Rock," or "Rocky," not because I was dull and hard and set apart like the naval base. "Rock" was written on me! My initials, ROC, showed up as the laundry mark on my uniforms, dungarees, white hats, skivvies and socks, everything. There were too many Roberts and Bobs in my maintenance crew, so the boys hit me with "Rock."

The men still remembered me as "Rock," and raised their glasses to me. The flow of time had watered down our memories, but the Mame came back in more toasts undiluted, in full strength. We celebrated her red-rouged face and mop of red-dyed hair. She sure was no "pinup," but held her place as the centerfold in our Cuban memory books. I could still see her bustling round the bar in floppy red dress and slippers, fat arms rattling with seashell bracelets. Broken English came out of her mouth to the accompaniment of clicking false teeth. Her bad fitting dentures clicked together like castanets, click, click, click.

All the toasts to "our" Mame made her go to our heads, and stay there, even into our general meeting the next day. After the business of electing officers and agreeing on a time and place for a second reunion, we broke into small groups, waited for our pictures to be taken. The wives had taken off for Miami shopping and sight-seeing. My wife had stayed home, didn't trust her arthritic knees to the cramped seats of an airplane. Thus, we were left to "manly affairs," and manly memories.

We reminded each other of the scarcity of women at the naval base, and our craving for the female touch! Women dependents were mostly out of sight, confined to the civilian side of the base. There were a few nurses to see in Sick Bay, but the only women most of us got a crack at were the Cuban "housemaids." They rode our buses around the base, but went to the end of the line to work in one of the civilian housing units. Some of those women looked more like houses than housemaids.

We remembered the poker games in the barracks. We faked each other out about the cards we had, and the women we'd had. We really didn't know much about women in those days, but pretended we did. Our poker or drinking talk went back and forth between the boredom of the base and our hunger for women. In the barracks we fed on talk of breasts and thighs and legs. At the "Picolo Beer Garden," close by, we sorted women into bottle shapes and sizes. There were coke bottle women, beer can women, fancy liquor bottle women! We drank to women of every shape and size, loved them all. We got the real thing at the *Mame's Domain.*

"How about the Mame's stable of females?"

"Got me a souvenir off one of 'em," someone volunteered, "a dose of *Gone-to-Korea!*"

I remembered "Gone-to-Korea" was what we called "gonorrhea," during our service in the Korean War.

"Never caught it," someone piped up, "and never got to Korea, either."

"Tom-catting in Caimanera was a sight better than dog-fighting in Korea," a pilot assured us. He'd served in Korea before landing a billet in our land-based squadron at Guantanamo Bay.

"We only had to play war games with the fleet," I said of our utility squadron, "and love games in Caimanera."

"Rocky, old boy, you got rocks in your head," someone laughed at me. "No games at *Gitmo*, no war, and no love."

"When those bar girls started looking good," one of us kept up the pace, "we knew we'd been away from home too long."

"Can't remember the looks of any one of them females," complained someone else.

"Some things we don't want to remember," I mused sadly.

"Some things never came down the way we remember," our old parachute rigger spoke up. "We don't have a full seabag anymore!" The big guy had gone up in the world, from parachute rigger to psychologist, but I'd always looked up to him. He still towered over us but had come down a little with a stoop. He'd turned gray, too, and put on weight, and a trim beard.

"Some things we had to remember in history never really happened," our former yeoman, a retired high school history teacher, contributed. "History is a jigsaw puzzle, with pieces missing."

"That's why I helped put this reunion together," I said, "to find missing pieces."

"We only been remembering pieces of hot tail!"

"Anybody remember *Zombie Girl*?"

"The one who only went through the motions?"

"Didn't we think she was raised out of the grave by Voodoo?"

"Didn't the Mame's Voodoo drinks make zombies out of us all?"

"Some guys really went for that Zombie Girl," another one of us kept the Mame and her girls in focus. "The Mame had a tart for every taste!"

"Quite a pastry shop!"

"Those were the days women lived to make men happy, like Marilyn Monroe," our yeoman-history teacher reminded us. "That's history!"

"Women sure have gone through the change," another man piped up, through a puff of smoke. He was an old boatswain's mate we remembered as "Popeye." He complained that "ships and planes used to be for men, like the whole damn world."

"World's gone through the Change!"

"Cuba's really gone through the change," our big parachute rigger reminded us, "gone Commie!"

"We can't go back to Cuba, or the past."

"*Gitmo* must have gotten pretty stuffy after Castro kicked the door shut," our retired history teacher speculated. "How could we have made it through a tour of duty there if we couldn't let off steam in the hot spots of Caimanera?"

"What you think happened to the Mame, after Castro cut off Cuba?"

"Battleship Mame would be scuttled, and sunk!"

"Castro outlawed prostitution," our yeoman-history teacher let us know.

We didn't want to think about the fate of Battleship Mame. We quieted down, but seemed to be taking on ammunition for the next round.

■■■ ■■■ ■■■

I was thinking our celebration of the old squadron had turned into the celebration of the Mame, couldn't get her out of my mind. You could get anything you wanted at Mame's *Domain*. You could get anything except the Mame herself. She could take on a whole ship's company when in "fighting trim," but by our day in Cuba she was "decommissioned." She was still stacked like a two-stack cruiser! She still had a battery of big guns up front that any sailor would like to get a load of, but she kept her "gun-house" locked, kept herself for herself. She only handed out drinks for a dime and samples of her life history for free. Sometimes she'd read the palms of our hands, turn up our futures. Endowed with the gift of divination, she called herself a "soothsayer." When she wasn't busy at the bar pushing her drinks and stories she'd grab a hand, flatten it out like a map, tell you where your life lines were headed. She told me my four years in the Navy were almost up, and she was right on. She told me I had a long life ahead, and I'm still in the swim of things, treading water in retirement. She told me I'd land a blue-eyed girl for a wife, and I did. She told me I'd come up with kids, and I did, two boys and a girl. She saw the future in a lot of hands, but never got a line on Fidel Castro or the Cuban Missile Crisis! She did predict a really bad time for Cuba, and bad times between Cuba and the States.

■■■ ■■■ ■■■

"The Mame liked to predict the future," our history teacher opened the book on the Mame again, "but she took us into the past most of the time. She told us Columbus discovered the inlet at Guantanamo Bay, lay claim to the very land we marched over! I found out that was true, but it's not in the history books that Columbus discovered the charms of one of her Indian ancestors, and got into her family tree!"

"Didn't you discover the charms of some Cuban girl in Caimanera?" I asked the history teacher, remembering him always with the same woman in a Caimanera bar.

He ignored me, kept to the Mame's saga. "She was also right about George Washington's older brother coming to Guantanamo Bay on a British military expedition, but I doubt her claim that she had the seeds of Washington in her. The Mame would have us believe," he finished, "she came from the first man to discover America, and the first president of the United States."

"Yeah, and she was first rate at leading us on wild goose chases," the boatswain's mate growled, "like getting us to look for pirate treasure buried around the base. We only dug up the shards of beer bottles."

"Claimed a pirate's *family jewels* also got buried in the roots of her family tree,"our history teacher added to the Mame's genealogy.

"She sure kept her motor mouth running."

"And false teeth grinding in the wrong gear."

"And both hands stuffing big bucks down her chesty cash register."

"She sure had a treasure chest."

We all started to cash-in our stories about the Mame, spiced them up with the Mame's Cuban accent, and clicked our teeth.

Most of her stories, it seems, were about the Spanish-American War. She called it the "War for Cuban

Independence." She even claimed she had the inside dope on how the USS MAINE got blown up in Havana, but had to keep it close to her chest. Our history school teacher said the blowing up of the *Maine* in Havana harbor was the "main" cause of the Spanish-American War.

We all recounted her stories about giving herself to the cause for Cuban independence, giving her all to the sailors and soldiers of the American Expeditionary Force! She said Teddy Roosevelt really was a "rough rider!"

Some of us thought the Mame could hardly hide a smile as she poured out some of her stories and filled up our glasses at the same time. Some of us had swallowed every word. Not me. I always figured she was too young to "take on" the American Expeditionary Force. When we knew the old girl, she said she was "salty, sexy, and *sixty*!" The Spanish-American War was a bit more than fifty years before we got to Cuba, and that would have made the Mame about ten years old, much too young to mount those big guns up front! Now that fifty some years have passed since we were in Cuba, I'm thinking sixty isn't so old. She could have been well over sixty, just looked old to young men. She could have been seventy when we knew her, plenty old enough to have excited the boys of 1898!

We liked to hear her stories about the war that put the United States in the front ranks of world powers. We were proud our country let Cuba go free after a brief occupation, only held the "coaling and naval station" at Guantanamo Bay. Some of us wished we hadn't held to that!

The Mame claimed she remembered when the American flag was raised over our old base. She remembered the Great White Fleet, and other American fleets, war after war. We remembered how her mouth kept clicking.

We remembered her complaining that Americans were too rich, and too free. She'd push her *Cuba Libre* drinks on us, tell us there was no *libre* for Cubans, only freedom for "landowners and bandits!" She told of Cuban governments going up and down with the price of sugar cane, but nothing changed for Cubans. Common men and women kept on "scratching for food and sex, like chickens and goats."

We didn't have to be told that life in Cuba was hard, except for Havana and the other end of the island. Our end of the island had few roads. Caimanera was mostly of unpaved streets that ran wild with barefoot kids, and chickens and pigs. House-fronts in Caimanera kept their doors open to the streets, used the streets for living rooms, and latrines.

All at once someone remembered we'd forgotten something about the Mame. We were forgetting her ghosts!

■■■ ■■■ ■■■

The Mame believed in ghosts, and knew some of them by name. She reserved a back room for sailors who'd gone down without ever "living it up with a woman." Each of her girls got the "ghost watch" once or twice a month, after work hours. Each girl had her turn to sleep alone in that room and pleasure any virgin ghost-man who materialized. The Mame herself relieved the watch from time to time and bore witness to "spiritual couplings!" She felt things in the dark, she'd tell us from the other side of the bar, things that came from the other world. One time she even picked up the smell of a man's sweat, and breath. He'd been into garlic.

She believed ghosts gave her a hand in pulling back the past and divining the future. Ghosts came to her through the incantations she got from "Mother Africa." All life came out of Africa, she said, and the soul of life was in the rhythms of Afro-Cuban cha-cha-cha. We are only a step away from ghosts ourselves, she said, a step ahead of our shadows.

"I think I had a ghost between the sheets," one of us said, trying to lay his own ghost story on us. "I married a widow! Ghost of her old man wouldn't go away for a night or two." He raised a laugh among us.

"Ghosts may be a laughing matter," another one of us thought, "but who really knows what's out there?" He was a mechanic in our memory, now a retired mechanical engineer. "The universes are masses of *matter-energy*, waves and particles." He suggested that an aura of our unique energy might hang on after death, might be perceived by people with special senses. He mentioned *anti-matter*, figured there was something beyond the material world.

A former radioman amongst us came up with what he called "ghost signals," said he picked up a World War II naval message during our time in the Korean War. He tried to convince us that radio waves never die, only keep radiating with less and less intensity. They can die down in molecules of air, in the wrinkle of a cloud, get preserved in some envelope of atmosphere. The vibrations can be retrieved by a wireless if it's set just right.

"Maybe the words of Christ are still somewhere in the air!"

Most of us didn't go for ghost signals, but thought our soothsaying Mame figured she was wired for them. The only "spirits" around the Mame's *Domain*, we agreed, were all in bottles!

Someone reminded us that the Mame believed in *two worlds*, and communion between them. We knew there were seances at the *Mame's Domain* after the shore patrol ran sailors out. She opened her door to a different kind of clientele, and to another world. None of us witnessed one of her spiritual sessions, but she liked to tell us about them, and the other world.

One of our pilots said he imagined a parallel world when coming in for landings. Sometimes he'd see the shadow of his plane alongside, mirroring his every move. Maybe the shadow had its own existence, its own pilot just like him, in a parallel world?

We laughed at the shadows and the parallel worlds, but our mechanical engineer said the parallel universe was lined up in the theory of *anti-matter*! It had science on its side.

We agreed there was more to the world than we could ever know, but most of us thought the only parallel world came in double vision, after too many of the Mame's Voodoo concoctions. We also agreed the Mame had no parallel! There could be no one like her.

■■■ ■■■ ■■■

We had to let go of the Mame, let her fall back into memory. Our reunion photos got snapped in a flash. Wives were "materializing," returning from the world of shopping. There was a reunion timetable for us to follow. After lunch we were in for a bus tour of Miami and Miami Beach. In the evening we got a taste of Cuba at a restaurant in "Little Havana," and I was recognized as the one of the first to call the men together for a reunion.

■■■ ■■■ ■■■

It was a long time before I got back to my hotel room for the night, a long time before I could reach for the phone and dial back home to Rockford, Illinois, speak with my wife. I told her I missed her and hadn't yet connected with any good buddies. I assured her I saw no former girlfriends among the Cuban refugees in Miami.

She whispered through the phone that she missed me, wished she could pull me through the telephone wires. I wished the same, and said that the Florida sunshine and seashore might have been good for her arthritis. She said her bones were in the good care of Robert the third.

I told her I was honored as the *Rock* on which the reunion was built, but she was the rock of my salvation! She'd forgotten I'd ever been called "Rock," but said I was forever at hand, the "rock" of her engagement ring. I let the wire go dead for a moment, until I found breath to wish her a good night, and sweet dreams. I was suddenly very much alone, alone with the sound of the dial tone clicking in my ear.

I fell asleep thinking of her, remembering the Mame, and my time on the Rock. In the deep of the night I suddenly broke up to the surface of consciousness, felt the presence of someone in the dark. I wasn't alone!

Buried in darkness, I listened, and waited, and heard the click, click, click of false teeth!

OF MAD DOGS AND MEN

TIPPING WINGS WITH old squadron mates was flying round my mind when I checked into a Miami hotel for the reunion of my old naval outfit. Highest in memory was my "horse-face" buddy, Eli Dobbins. He had the face only a horse could love, but still figured he got a good deal with himself. His other end was like a horse, too, a stud horse! He was also blessed with the hang of storytelling, could hand out a tale that would hold up a poker game. His cliff-hangers about the ups and downs of mountain kinfolk would keep the whole barracks on edge.

A seabag of memories was unfolding in my mind while I unpacked and changed clothes for the "Welcome Aboard Reception." Gazing out the hotel window I could view Miami Bay and the high-rise skyline of Miami, but I was picturig Guantanamo Bay and the mountains of Cuba skylining the horizon. Our old squadron had been stationed at the *Gitmo* naval base in Cuba, attached permanently to the Fleet

Training Command. It was before Cuba was off limits, and before I found my limits.

I got to the "hospitality room" as soon as I could. It served as our reunion headquarters and was decked-out with memorabilia---squadron pennants and patches, faded photos of planes with folded wings and sailors with cocked hats. The sailors in the photographs looked familiar but not any of the old boys standing around in stuffed sport shirts, not one, not until I sighted Horse-Face Eli sauntering around. I recognized my old buddy's horsey face, thick lips and wide nostrils, high forehead, ears sticking up. The hair he was losing in the Navy was now lost, except for a few dapple-gray strands. Hairline gone, his long face longer, he looked more horsey than ever, but could have been the grandfather of the country boy I used to buddy-up with.

"Eli!" I called out, suspecting he didn't go by "Horse-Face" anymore, "Eli Dobbins!"

"Air Dale!" He burst out with my old squadron call name.

I'd turned a lot of pages in my life story since my character was called "Air Dale!" I told him I was no longer a naval airdale. "I'm just Dale Barker," I said. "You still saddled with the name of Horse-Face?"

"Still fits," he said, nodding his long head.

"A horse name's a tad better than a dog name," I acknowledged with a grin

"Been a coon's age since we ran around together," he spoke up, looking me over with his big horse eyes.

As we shook hands I tried to shake out more recollections of him. I remembered every time he opened his mouth the Old South came out. He made two syllables out of one syllable words, stretched other words way out, took a long time to get every word out. His countrified way of talk used to tickle me.

We picked right up where we left off, all those years ago, and looked for a bar, all the while checking each other out for clues to the kids we used to be.

"What the cornbread hell you been up to?" he drawled as soon as we found the "horseshoe" bar in the hotel and he said it would "fit". We settled down at the bar and got our drinks set up before I could answer.

"Been up to making a living," I said, " now down in retirement. Still can't forget those homespun yarns you strung around the barracks."

"They be cobwebs in my old attic," he said, striking at his head with one hand.

I reminded him of the ghosts and gals he used in his stories. His ghosts hung out in the lowlands, like the fog, and his barefoot gals all ran around with big hearts and bosoms!

"Reckon them ghosts cleared out, and barefoot gals got shoes, and uppity."

"What about Big Flo, the *Nighting-Gal?*" I was proud of my memory that could come up with one of his stories. Who could forget the "Nighting-Gal?" As I remembered Big Flo, the Nighting-Gal, she was a contortionist, worked nights in a carnival, made like a songbird when she nestled-up to him. She was the only gal, he used to say, who could take him on, his "joy stick" being so "humongous."

"Story of Big Flo, my nighting-gal, was stepped-up a mite," he remembered, stretching out his words, and sipping slowly at his bourbon, and thoughts. "She were no secret agent with the cover-up of a circus contortionist, like I made out. She were nothing but a carnival worker, but she sure took me on a merry-go-round!"

The ash at the end of his cigarette was dangling, about to drop off in his whiskey, and the suspense was taking my breath away, but I managed to tell him I'd given up smoking. I remembered how he used to bum cigarettes all the time in the Navy, didn't want him to try again.

"Smoking won't give up on me," he said with the cigarette in his mouth and the ash still growing longer, "but these old coffin nails ain't hammered me in no pine box, not yet!" He shook his head like a horse. "I sure seen a lot of life go up in smoke." He took a final drag on his stub of a cigarette and squashed it out, lit another and kept it in hand as we toasted our old squadron. We got around to distilling our lives since the Navy into a few words, and drinks.

After the Navy, Horse-Face Eli got hitched-up to the railroad, and a wife, kept tracks on the level, and himself, pulled a family load all the way to the end of the line, and retirement. He kept drinking and pouring it on about how he played his cards right, got a good deal on a woman, not Big Flo, but a queen-sized gal. He drew a full house of kiddies and "won the pot" when it came to grand babies.

I summed myself up by holding up my two clean hands, both sides, said I went to college on the "G.I. Bill," studied chemistry, went from the lab to the office and out to retirement. "It all passed in the flick of a bunsen burner," I remembered saying. A good wife was in the cards for me, too, I said, and a pair of kids who "took the pot."

We discovered we were both widowers, at loose ends, the way we were as sailors. We'd hurried through our life stories and whiskies, didn't want the drinks to end.

"Navy was a dog's life," I said, "especially for this here Air Dale. We got our keep in the Navy, but sure got tethered to a mighty short leash."

"Well I'll be doggone if that don't put me in mind of a dog story for you," Horse-Face Eli said, "tale of old man Mordecai Smythe, chained-up like a hound dog, he were."

"You *fixing* to tell of it?" I asked.   I remembered the way he'd say he was "fixing" to hit the showers, or the chow line, but never "fixing" to repair an aircraft. When he was "fixing" to tell a story, men gave him a hearing, bunched together in a corner of the barracks. His best stories came out the nights before inspections when we sat around putting a spit shine on our inspection shoes. There was a Cuban bootblack in the barracks but he didn't have enough spit for a Wing

Inspection! I remember all hands polishing shoes and stories at the same time, never missing a lick at either, but Horse-Face Eli out-shined us all, in shoes and stories.

"Fixing to tell about old man Mordecai," he started again, after a smoky pause. With a whiskey-moistened tongue he started to spit it out. "Back when I were a pup," he said, "no man without six or more coon dogs were in style. Not much farming, just hunting and fishing in summer, trapping in winter. Mordecai were really in style, with eight or nine hound dogs, and he done give 'em a good run every time the moon be up, and the coons be out. One black-hearted night he got his old bones up to quiet them dogs, they was a-fussing something fierce. Old Blue, pick of the pack, took a bite out of Mordecai and then let out for the wild. Got to be a legend, Mordecai's old hound dog did, but it be another story."

"This old Air Dale would like to sniff it out," I said, motioning at the same time for the bartender to set us up again. I still had a thirst, but had gone off the scent of Mordecai.

"They still talk about Old Blue, back in the hills," Horse-Face Eli backtracked, starting another cigarette, and story. "Folks claim they see that dog on moonshine nights, hear dog moans on nights the moon don't shine. Poor critter got snarled-up in the brier-brush, couldn't get hide or hair out. No man alive could wiggle within no fifty yards of the old hound dog, the brush be so snarly and prickly, and the quicksand in the hollows could suck a man down to Hades.

That coon hound was a-howling and a-suffering something terrible bad, but there weren't no way to put the critter out of his miseries. Every dead-shot in the county got his sights on old Blue, missed every time, and the old dog still be there, plain as day on moonshine nights. A body can hear Old Blue moaning when the moon don't shine. Folks say he's a ghost dog, won't never die."

"Seems like everybody in your neck of the woods had a shot at some fool supernatural thing or two," I remembered. "You always had your sights on some ghost story. Got a bead on another?"

"Running low on ghosts," he said, "the old folks back to home still see spirits, but don't trust 'em any more. They be like strangers. Old folks back to home be rattling round big houses full of empty rooms. Young folks be gone, gone like the old days. Old days be the ghosts of nowadays."

"Old days like to come back," I said, smiling, "like this here reunion. Old days look better after they get really old."

"Never got the old dog bite story out my mouth," Horse-Face Eli said. He sat straight up and squared his shoulders for the next round. "Old Mordecai didn't pay that dog bite no never-mind til he got to feeling poorly and got to foaming at the mouth. One time he took a swipe at his old lady, felt a heap sorry for a-doing it. A spell later the madness took him most every day. He figured he be cursed for one of his sin-trespasses, til it dawned on him, plain as day, he got the rabid sickness off Old Blue, ought to get hisself put out of his miseries before he harmed a body. Got the neighbor folks to fussing about his troubles at prayer meeting. They get the word to stake him out at the end of a chain, leave him alone to give up the ghost. Following the word they got they led Mordecai to the old Padgett Place, abandoned since the dust days of them nineteen hundred and thirties. Some folks said the place were spooked. That scared the young folks off, but it were meant, most likely, to scare off them Revenuers!"

Horse-Face Eli caught another breath of smoke and let it out with, "well, the good old boys took Mordecai to the Padgett Place, hooked trace chains round his ankle bones. Mordecai told the boys not to fret none, just leave him be so he could meet-up with his Maker. Folks figured there be no call to let him suffer no more than need be, so they fetched him victuals, and a jug of moonshine. They be mighty careful to stay past the end of his chain. Next night they heared him howl like a dog, and night after night after night. One day they come round and find he kicked the traces, he did, and were on the loose!"

"Did he turn up as a ghost?" I wondered out loud.

"This be a mad dog story, not a ghost story," Horse-Face Eli said. "Folks ransack them hills. Not a shaggy hair of Mad Dog Mordecai do they find, not for a long spell! You know where he be? Right back on his own front stoop! Gone home, he did, fell down slobbering, carried on something fierce, spooked the hens right off the roost."

"Did he give up the ghost?"

Horse-Face Eli paid me no attention, kept to his story. "Posse of country boys strong-armed Old Mad Dog Mordecai back to the Padgett Place, chained him up real good, cooked him a mess of beans and fatback, told the old cuss to eat hardy, it be his last supper. His chow was spiked with enough arsenic to drop a plow horse. Posse cleared out for the night, put a pine coffin box together, showed up next daybreak to fetch Mordecai's mortal leftovers. That critter were still a-breathing! Some folks say they saw a female angel at the end of his chain.' He paused to look me in the eye. "I be a-thinking it be his guardian angel. We all got to be guarded, sometimes from ourselves. We all got a good side and a bad side, don't fly on just one wing."

"Don't leave me up in the air," I said, swallowing off my drink "Did Mad Dog Mordecai end up like Old Blue, howling on nights the moon don't shine?"

"I was fixing to get my story back on track," Horse-Face Eli said, tight-lipped, a cigarette and ash dangling from his mouth. "Folks let Mad Dog Mordecai be, left him straining at the end of his chain, left him to take a mighty long sleep. His old lady kept him company, laid by him at the good end of his chain. The critter woke up a sight later, said he be dry as a *tank in a hot spell*, and finished off a pint of corn-squeezings. For a long spell after that he never come down with no more fits, so his chains got hacked off, and Mordecai got back to business, a-hunting and fishing, and he never got taken down again. Folks swore it were a miracle he come back to life from the dead. I say it were the arsenic that slew the mad dog in him, passed over the man, like the avenging angel."

"You trying to tell me poison can kill rabies?"

"That be the lesson to my story. Good can come out of bad."

"What good came out of our bad times in the Navy?"

"I reckon you could say we got ourselves chained-up in the Navy for some good cause." Horse-Face Eli said, smoothing the top of his bald head with the flat of a hand. "It be a Humpty-Dumpty world, all split up, East and West, North and South in Korea! What if nobody stood the watch? It be a mad-dog world out there, dog eat dog!"

CROSSING THE LINE

"ONCE UPON A *line*," I began telling my story of crossing the Equator, "*Neptunus Rex* came roaring and crashing out of the sea, a dripping spear in hand! Can't say I actually saw the old boy erupting out of the water, but can swear to his fearsome presence on deck." I stopped to catch a breath and check my audience, a former naval officer and his wife. They invited me to join them for breakfast in the hotel where our naval air squadron was holding its first reunion. Ordering a *crab* omelet I joked about being an old crustacean myself, a *Shellback*, and had to explain to the wife that a *Shellback* was a sailor who'd crossed the Equator. At the same time I noticed, over the top of my coffee cup, a prominent crease dividing the wife's neck like the Equator. She'd looked up from under the wide brim of an enormous hat that set her off from all the women in the restaurant, and wanted to know about the "rites of passage," and the "mysteries of the Deep." That's what got my story started.

"I draw the line at *Neptunis Rex*," her husband spoke up, "that's a figment of the imagination."

"The Equator's a figment of the imagination," I ventured to tell my old officer, hardly able to believe I was sitting at the same table, on the same level, with the pilot of the plane I used to grease and oil. "Do you believe in the Equator?"

"You shot me out of the air with that one," he said with a shrug, and picked up his coffee cup with both hands.

I was remembering him as Lieutenant *Crash* Gordon, a flashy young pilot with bright shiny hair. He'd lost his hair, and shine, and the steadiness of his hand.

"Did all my time in our land-based squadron at Guantanamo Bay, " the old lieutenant kept talking, "never served on a carrier, like you, but crashed off one of those *bird farms* in flight training. Almost didn't get my wings. Let's hear about crossing the line. Carry on!"

"Before crossing," I started my story again, "I was a *Pollywog* with a pretty low regard for *Neptunus Rex* myself. I put him down in the company of Davy Jones' Locker."

"*Neptunus Rex* was the god of the deep, turned the sea against Homer's Ulysses," my old officer said with authority, "way back in the legendary Trojan War!"

"He turned up for me in the legendary Korean War," I insisted, "on the zero parallel, when the war in Korea was ending on the 38th, where it began."

"Maybe sea duty put water on your brain," the old lieutenant said with a gulp of coffee, "and *Neptunis Rex* came out of it!"

"*Neptunus Rex* was a joke to me, too," I began again, "and far from thought when my ship was three thousand miles from the Equator. After weeks of battle stations and drills the joke was getting closer, and less funny. I even started looking for the monster in the wide open sea that came up and down with the sun, day after day. The Equator was drawing nigh, and putting all us shipmates on *edge*!"

I bent forward to be heard over the clatter of plates and silverware in the diningroom. "Days were drifting like the sea, and daylight kept getting brighter and brighter. Not a bird stirred the air, not a fin cut the polished surface of the blue sea, not until we faced the imaginary line! Then the sea wrinkled into a thousand grins."

"What's it like on the other side?"

"The stars are different," I said to the wife, remembering myself under a different night sky. "Never thought there was anything but a mishmash of stars up there, except for the Big Dipper. Not so. They form a pattern in our minds, but we don't realize it until it goes away. When the Big Dipper dipped into the sea and went under, a different starry sky came up, and I could see something like a dagger coming out of the dark horizon. It was the Southern Cross, and it rose up over an unfamiliar night sky."

"Think our lives are fixed in the stars?" the wife asked when I paused between words for a sip of coffee. The brim of her hat swept round her head like a sail, overshadowed most of her face, except for the equator around the neck.

"The stars are fixed in our minds," I granted, looking down at the breakfast plate that had just been put before me. I dropped my story for a moment to pick up a taste of omelet, and smack my lips.

"Your story's going down very well," the wife said, chewing her words, motioning for me to go on.

"As the ship bore down on the Line," I started again, "the compass went into a spin! *Pollywogs* on deck duty were ordered to sweep the horizon with brooms and look for the side of the world, if not the end of it!"

"Did they sweep up *Neptunus Rex*?" the wife asked, buttering toast for her husband. He was thanking her for the help.

"Not a crumb of him," I said, "but all *Pollywogs* were so scared they tried to take over the ship! *We* actually took the helm, tied-up the captain, held command until the sea opened all its mouths and spit up *Neptunus Rex*, and his monstrous retinue. These very eyes of mine bear witness to that hoary sea creature and his sea-weeded, green-toothed, rusty-scaled cohorts."

"*Shellbacks* in disguise," my old officer tried to scuttle the story.

"They beat my butt to a royal purple," I continued. "Why would shipmates flog shipmates?"

"Inhumanity to humanity is the story of the world," the old officer said.

"Maybe *Shellbacks* haven't crossed the line between the good and the bad," the good wife surmised with a swish of her head and hat.

"All I know is that my ship had crossed the line of reality," I carried on, "broke with the world I knew, went dead in the waters of the *District of Equatorius*, the *Vale of Atlanticus*, the *Domain of Neptunus Rex*, 0-00-00!"

"All those zeros make me dizzy," the wife gasped. "Can you imagine nothingness?" She turned her whole head and hat in my direction, looked up for an answer.

"I can tell you what it feels like to be nothing," I said. "I was a nobody. Powerless! I got hauled before the *Royal Court of the Raging Main*. My summons had me charged with making love to a *Mermaid*!"

I didn't mention it, but was remembering I hadn't made love at all back then, was uninitiated. It used to worry the hell out of me! I thought I was unseaworthy, out of joint with every member of the ship's company. I was going around the world without knowing what made the world go round.

"I sure was innocent," I got back to my story, "but had to take my lumps anyway, with all the other *Pollywogs*. Fire hoses soaked us to the skin, made every whack of a shillelagh sting all the more. We took a shellacking all along a gauntlet of sea monsters, got beaten with canvas slings loaded with wet rice. We even got a bruising when we had to crawl through the *Garbage Shoot* full of egg shells and coffee grounds, but our backsides were getting hardened into *Shellbacks*! It all ended at the *Drowning Pool.* Dunked under the surface scum of garbage and sailor spit, we were baptized for the life on the other side."

"Crossing the Equator was a pain in the *arse*," the officer's wife thought from under her hat. "I salute you, Mr. *Shellback*!"

"I'm Mr. *Blue Nose*, too," I said, "crossed the Arctic Circle on one of those NATO war games, *Operation Mariner.* No initiation crossing that one."

"There are lines we have to fight our way across," my old officer spoke up when I'd stopped for a bite to eat. "Life's like a football game!" A trembling napkin wiped the words from his mouth. I suspected he had some kind of palsy, maybe Parkinson's.

"And there are lines we shouldn't cross," his wife said, aiming her hat-framed face at me. "I have to keep my man in line."

"The co-pilot of my life thinks we have to navigate by invisible lines of universal morals," my old officer let me know, "but we can't avoid crossing the last line!" He brought up "Tennyson's poem, *Crossing the Bar*," and explained that seamen cross a sandbar when sailing out of port, and there's a bar we all cross in going out to the eternal sea. He closed his eyes, as if in prayer, asking that "there be no moaning of the bar, when I put out to sea."

"Your old officer crossed the line from Navy pilot to English professor," the wife told me, as if to excuse her husband's flight of literary fancy.

"This reunion's taking me back over the line," my old officer was saying, "flying me back to old times."

"Think I passed the line of no return," I said, already sorry I'd come to the reunion, leaving my wife behind, and sorry not to see some vaguely remembered buddies who hadn't shown up.

"We've crossed over to the far side of our lives," the wife said, "can't get back under the old stars."

"Crossed too many time lines?" the old officer shrugged with a cup of coffee shaking in his hands.

"Got lines in my face to prove that," the wife thought. "Time to freshen-up in our room."

"Have to get lined up pretty soon for the next squadron session," my officer said, struggling to get up. "Old age is a hard line to cross," he groaned. He bent down to reach for the check, insisted on treating me. I could leave the tip, he called back over a shoulder.

I was left to finish my crab omelet and digest my thoughts about "crossing of the Bar." Another kind of *bar* crossed my mind, a bar on the Cuban side of the naval base at Guantanamo Bay, a bar with girls on tap. That's where I crossed another line, got initiated into what makes the world go round.

A CUP OF REMEMBRANCE

SNUG IN A bright blue blazer and white slacks, Adam Turner stood tall and gray amid old squadron mates at the horseshoe bar of a Miami hotel. Downing drinks with them, he suddenly came up with the thought of leaving something of himself behind, long before he left most of his life behind. An able-bodied seaman, very able-bodied, he'd made love on the Cuban side of Guantanamo Bay! He really might have left something of himself behind, a kid, a middle-aged adult by now. What might have happened to that life? The radio at the bar was blaring out an old song, "Memories."

The men around the bar were celebrating their naval air squadron's first reunion. "Tork!" The old squadron mates were remembering Adam Turner as "Tork," a name he left behind with his naval past.

"Tork!" It revved-up the recollection of days revolving round the Cuban sun and the American naval air station at Guantanamo Bay. "Tork!" It cranked-up the memory of his first go-around with a woman. He remembered her making the sign of the cross as she undid herself in the back room of a Cuban bar. Reams of long black hair unraveled in his memory, along with bare flashes of untanned skin. Her slender stalk of a body appeared with unexpected curves. Standing at attention, her breasts were stiff and firm, soft and yielding when at ease in bed. She cried out the name of the Creator, at the moment of creation! He really could have left a kid behind!

"Here's to the flyboys we used to be," someone at the bar raised a toast to their high flying days, but Adam Turner never thought of himself as a "flyboy." Only his memory could fly, but it winged him back to the salt water Navy, the heavy cruiser, USS MACON, his first billet in the Navy. His life went from port to port aboard ship, but went nowhere when he got orders for the utility squadron based permanently at Guantanamo Bay. He lived in isolation at *Gitmo*! No pilot, or airman, he wasn't one of the "flyboys!" They had their own view of the world, could look down on it, put it beneath them. He was grounded, buried in the boredom of the personnel office by day and the barracks by night. A second class yeoman, he was only armed with an upright typewriter that shot off memos and official documents. A first class virgin, he thought he was outranked by all the men in the barracks, had to make the "grade" before he was one of them. He passed the test in Cuba, before it was cut off from the American base, before the "pill" made contraception a way of life. He really could have left a life behind!

Childless in America, married and unmarried twice, the man called Tork liked the thought of creating a life, but not a life imprisoned in a dictatorship just beyond the Florida Keys, behind the "Bamboo Curtain" of Fidel Castro! Shiny eyes sparkled in the ice cubes of his raised glass. The name of "Laura" crackled in his mind. He tried to put her down, get focused on his old squadron mates. The flyboys used to be a body of one, all one in the squadron, but they'd come back together in separate, unfamiliar shapes. Their naval youths were hidden in worn-out bodies and bright tropical outfits.

"Here's to the flyboys who didn't make the reunion," another toast went up.

Tork raised his glass again, thinking none of the old flyboys who'd checked into the Miami hotel a few hours earlier, with wives and suitcases and golf clubs, had the look of flyboys, but they were high-flying at the bar. Their old squadron was in the Training Command, never flew in combat, but the boys were glorifying its memory as though it saved the free world! After a few more drinks the boredom and lonely isolation of Guantanamo Bay came up in the belches. Men remembered being trapped in a stagnant backwater between alligator swamps and Cuban dives. Someone raised a toast to their "utility" squadron as a "futility squadron!"

Someone asked why they all came so far to stir up "chickenshit memories?"

"Came to Miami for the sun and surf!"

"Wanted to see what became of all you bums!"

"Used to live for the afterlife," another old boy shouted above the others, "the life after the Navy, but looking back, I never had it so good!"

Someone raised his glass to the women on the other side of the bay, and the rum and coke, and "cha-cha-cha!"

The old squadron talk whirling around the bar whipped a backwash of naval air memories at Tork, but the roar of planes warming up on the hangar deck below his office sputtered back into the talk of old squadron mates. The smell of aircraft fumes was really cigarette and cigar smoke. He brushed it away, remembering how he passed his weight in cigarette smoke every day in the Navy, measured his days by the pack. He'd given up smoking a long time ago, but sometimes, he thought, a cigarette's all a man has to hang onto!

Nothing seems to last, Tork thought, except the past, and he couldn't brush that away. His Cuban girl sparkled in the ice cubes again, swirled around in his head. He didn't want to remember leaving her behind, laying her away with his uniforms, but he knew she didn't fit his life, after his naval life was over. Was it a sin to shake off a woman who used her body to make a living? Laura sold herself to him, at first.

It seemed he was still the son of a preacher, he thought to himself, after a lifetime. He remembered being really laced-up tight in uniform, had to learn to drink and smoke and swear, but couldn't go "overboard," not until he landed in Cuba. Prostitution was not against the law in Cuba. The American Navy couldn't do anything about it, only provide order for its men with a Shore Patrol and sanitary protection with a "Pro-Station." He'd been afraid of catching immorality, and the clap, but became more afraid of being "out of it." He finally got "into it," but only with one woman. She was a barfly for flyboys, but a "pretend wife" to him. She was in the business of pretending. Was she pretending when she said she never loved any man, except him? Was she pregnant? Could he have left a kid behind?

Maybe the past doesn't last after all! Memory changes! Navy monotony was now coming back to mind as the carefree time of his life. His "pretend" wife was coming back as the real love of his life. He wanted to get away.

"Sorry," he said, backing into someone behind him. He came eye to eye with a man who looked too old to be sporting a squadron souvenir cap. He wore it cocked sideways, and wore his shirt cracked open to a grizzled patch of scrawny hairs.

"No sweat," the old boy said, balancing himself with a drink in one hand, a cigarette in the other. "Ain't you the company yeoman?"

"Adam Turner! Mechs called me Tork." He couldn't remember the old boy with the square jaw and cap askew, standing unsteady on two feet, one foot at a time. The old boy touched the bill of his cap, as if in salute, kept his balance, introduced himself as "Popeye, First Class Boatswain's Mate, Pops Popovitch." He squinted to look "Tork" over. "Personnel Office turned round you," he remembered. "And your official name was A. Turner, like the torque of a prop!"

"You sure got your memory cap screwed on," Tork said, unable to place "Popeye" in his own memory. "Hope you don't remember me screwing-up your service record?"

"You got a good record in my memory book," Popeye said, steadying himself, and his glass. "You pencil-pushers sure had it made in the service, no sweat."

Tork used to get a belly-full of talk like that. Anyone working with his head instead of his hands didn't work-up any respect in the squadron. A yeoman was a no-man, doing the clerical work a woman could do!

"Nobody thought you were a pencil pushing pussy," Popeye was saying, as though reading Tork's mind.

"But a typewriter didn't strike a blow against the Commies, or put a plane in the air," Tork granted. "We yeomen only kept the books."

"Had us by the short hairs," Popeye snorted, "all our scores and promotions, leaves and service records."

"Only held your paper lives," Tork said, reminding himself he needed to put his own life on paper, leave something of himself behind before it was too late.

"You're still looking trim in the water," Popeye strained his eyes again, trying to get a better look at Tork. "You get yourself a soft life after the Navy, too!"

"High school teaching, riding herd on teenagers. Call that soft?"

"I was a thirty year Navy man, had deck apes rattling my cage every day of that time!"

"You ran the barracks!" Tork finally remembered Pops *Popeye* Popovitch, the boatswain's mate in charge of the barracks. He was no flyboy either, kept the barracks "taut" and "shipshape."

"Piped you aboard," Popeye said. "Got you a good bunk."

Tork remembered how much the boatswain's mate used to look like the comic strip character. He walked like Popeye, talked with a corncob pipe in his mouth whenever the smoking lamp was lit. He was an old Navy man, always bragged about getting shot out of the water at Pearl Harbor, seeing the "Nips" coming in low, grins on their faces, the rising sun plastered on their wings like "big ripe tomatoes." He "danced" to their thirty caliber bullets, seemed stuck in "slow motion." Tork thought the old boy still had the forearms of a Popeye sticking out of the short sleeves of his sport shirt.

The two men shook hands.

"You got me squared away in the barracks," Tork said, still looking back.

"You were off a cruiser," Popeye said, "needed help to get your land legs."

"And you were a cruiser man, too, a stranger on land, like me."

"I knew the lay of the land by the time you came aboard," Popeye raised his voice over the noise around the bar, "and the "good *lays* off-base."

"You set me straight about Cuban women," Tork said, raising his glass to him

"Cuban women were all *hot-blooded*," Popeye said, "but there be two kinds, one you can put the sweat on, and the other kind you can't."

"But all Cuban women are out to *give*," Tork remembered some of Popeye's old advice. "American women are out to *take*! If you got yourself a Cuban woman you got yourself a real woman!"

"No sweat!" Popeye said. "Cuban woman cooks and waits on her man, lives for her man, worships every inch of her man."

"But don't cheat on her," Tork said.

"You remember my story 'bout the dumb swab stepping out on his *mamacita*?"

"When she caught up with his dumb ass," Tork remembered, "she had a razor blade under her tongue, really kissed him off!"

"Good to remember our *she* days and *sea* days," Popeye said, swaying from side to side, "but them old cruiser days won't wash over our bows no more. This here air squadron reunion can't even give me a whiff of salt air."

"Maybe you need to get closer to the bar," Tork said. "Taking what's left of me and my drink off to my room."

He gave his space at the bar to Popeye, and carried off the thoughts of his own Cuban woman, remembering how she "lived" for him the way Popeye's did. She helped him live through his enlistment, gave him a lift, like a stiff drink, every time he took liberty across the bay, and she was still going to his head.

It all started in his head, "getting it on" with Laura. It started with his thought that a sailor needs a woman. It's not in the *Bluejackets' Manual*, but it's written in the Good Book. Trouble with the Navy, it didn't have women in the ranks overseas, and it didn't have love anywhere. A man needs love. And a sailor needs to be a man. Manhood got calculated by the number of hash-marks of women "laid!" He remembered squadron mates taking off across the bay whenever their "dip sticks got dry."

He remembered leaving his virgin shore one Saturday with the determination to come back a different man. He wouldn't break any law in Cuba. Prostitution was legal. He wouldn't break a moral law if he redeemed himself with "a kind of marriage," legal or not. The "crud" he was afraid of catching could be cured at the Pro-Sation!

He found himself in the "District" of Caimanera, at *Gladys' Bar*, better known as the *Glad Ass*. The *Glad Ass* had a clean bill of health, never got hassled by the Shore Patrol. It had live music, a screened-in dance floor, a bar, and bedrooms in back.

He remembered sizing up the women at the bar like suits on the rack. The woman called Laura suited him. She had a sad look, even though she was wearing a smile. Not like the others, she hung back, eyes down. She sheltered a white jasmine in the cup of her hand, as though shielding it from the world. He thought she was a slender stem of a flower needing shielding herself. She was like a cut flower, out of place, not long to last.

She let herself go for three American dollars, and fifty cents for the room. He fumbled out of his whites, shucked everything off except socks and dog tags. It made him uneasy, looking up at the crucifix over the bed, and the withered palm fronds that might have celebrated a Good Friday. Laura crossed herself, let down her hair, unfastened straps, turned her loosened parts away from him, slid all body parts under a sheet. His dog tags clinked for a little while, and Laura screamed at the end. She pulled a hand from between her thighs, showed him a palm of slime, thought he'd be proud of how much had come out of him.

Adam Turner was shaking at that as he got into his hotel room, happy to be alone. But his memories of Laura followed him in. His "pretend marriage" hadn't redeemed him. Two people in love added up to one in marriage, back home, but marriage to a barfly in Cuba wouldn't have added up to anything. In retrospect, his marriages to American women didn't add up to anything either.

He looked himself over in the mirror as he stripped down to his shorts for bed. He was still able-bodied, but the mirror didn't show his age inside. He knew he'd left his youth behind. Had he left another life behind?

Life was a story, one happening after another, but he thought he wrote the play about Laura. He got the curtain up with the act of faithfulness. No other women of Caimanera for him, not ever!   Maybe he was taking Popeye's advice about not cheating on a Cuban woman, but he found a sense of innocence in faithfulness. Whenever he was at the *Glad Ass*, he waited for Laura. No jealousy or scorn was in the role he played.   He only wanted to know how he stacked-up in bed with other men?   She only wanted to know why "North Americans are so cold!"

There were other acts of love, the act of giving. He gave her trinkets from the Navy Exchange, perfumes and jewelry, flowers made of paper and silk.   Between acts of love they had their own table at the *Glad Ass*, and "*simpatica*" talks in sync with the mambo.

Laura had long ago picked up the swing of American lingo, spoke with an Afro-Cuban beat. Her voice sang, her talk was music to his ears. He said it was her English that kept them in tune.   She said he made music in her heart.

They started taking meals together at a bistro near the *Glad Ass*, bits and pieces of bread and cheese. While they ate, she'd spoon feed him Spanish.   She liked the flavor of English but wanted him to have a taste of her tongue. Spanish is a smiling language, she said.   She smiled with her words, even though her eyes spoke sadness. Her life, she told him, had no value, except in American dollars. Life was a bother, something to be hurried through, "like your enlistment," she said.

Her birthday came up in one of the acts of love, and he celebrated it with her at the Hotel Oasis, only good place in Caimanera, good enough for officers. The birthday dinner was served on the terrace, at a table with linen and silver, beside the sparkling of Guantanamo Bay, under a moon that was full for her birthday. Laura smiled through words that said she felt "a thousand years old," but she admitted to"twenty-four." She wasn't too much older than he was, but twenty-four seemed very old, back then. He gave her a ring with her birth stone, a garnet, and she kept it on her finger, kept touching it to her lips every time they met.

She started giving herself to him, not a "centavo" would she take for herself, only fifty cents for the room. She accepted his gifts from the Commissary, chocolates, soaps, and cigarettes. Sometimes she had to take "autobus trips," for a "*poco*" time, and carry a roll of American dollar to someone in the "far" country. Tork wanted to know if she had a husband, or child. She only smiled and said she was "blessed, unclaimed."

Not married, either one of them, she told him it would be no sin to "cohabit." She took him into her life and "casa" every time he got overnight or weekend passes. Her two rooms were on the edge of the bay, in a house on stilts, a room for sleeping and a room for cooking and living. There was running water under the house, seawater running in and out with the tides, bringing in the scent of salt and fish, taking out the waste of time.

Maybe she considered herself married to him, just as he pretended to be married to her? She'd told him many Cubans couldn't afford church or legal fees for legal unions, made their own vows, lived outside the law of the land and Church.

Laura honored him like a husband, even as she made a living with her body at the *Glad Ass*. Work at the *Glad Ass* was not a public sin. It was a "living," like any other business. Some husbands even brought their wives to work in the bars when they were properly seeded and beyond the impregnation of American sailors.

Tork found himself passing into the Cuban life, accepted and accepting, but his enlistment was passing away, too, and "civilian" life came to be just a turn of the calendar page. He wanted to get on with his life, finish college, find a real wife. It was time to drop the curtain on his made-up play He thought Laura's life would go on, same as always. She expected nothing out of life. If there was a new life in her, a child, she never let on about it.

She only had a few words to say about herself, didn't think there was a future for her, or Cuba. Revolutions are always in the Cuban air like "cane-dust," but nothing comes of them except bomb scares in the cinemas and boys running off to the mountains. There would be an election but it would be fixed. There was no hope in Cuba, she said, except in Jesus, and the lottery.

Laura knew Tork's time was almost up, didn't know his orders were already cut when he came to her for the last time. He was scheduled to ship out in three more days, get discharged at the Brooklyn Navy Yard and get on with his life. He didn't want to give her the last word. He knew she wouldn't kiss him off with a razor, but she might have a sharp word, or a cry. He'd never seen her cry, only look sad.

It was time for the last scene in his play of "pretend marriage," the last supper. They ate in her upper room in the house on stilts, over the water, with the sound of the tide going out. He remembered the bread, and the wine, and her last words. Laura wanted him to know there are two kinds of lovers – those who take and those who give, but only one kind of love. Love, she told him, is "*sacrificio!*" She crossed herself.

She wanted him to know there are two kinds of people-- those who hire and those who hire-out. A body has to make a living. "For bread of life," she said, putting down a piece of bread, "my body is broken." She raised her glass to him. "A cup of blessing," she said, "drink, in remembrance of me."

TRAIL OF THE CUBAN BUTTERFLY

SHE'D NO LONGER be a thing of beauty, but a joy to see again, that Cuban woman who gave me "home loving" away from home! I'd been a sailor killing time at the dead end of Cuba, far away from the shooting in Korea. Now I was almost out of time, past my prime, celebrating my old naval air squadron at a reunion in Miami. My Cuban *mamacita* was a spirit of the past, a phantom vision that came to haunt me in my cups at the bar of a Miami hotel. All my squadron mates were bringing up spirits of the past, times we'd out flown, couldn't get back to. We couldn't get back to Cuba, either! It had fallen under Castro. It came to me that Miami was engulfed with Cuban exiles, my *mamacita* might be one of them. I began harboring thoughts of trying to track her down. She could be around the corner from my hotel, a refugee in "Little Havana."

I couldn't quite remember her name, only that I called her my "Cuban Butterfly." I'd been in mind of Puccini's

Madama Buterfly, the opera that really got to me in a study of music appreciation. Puccini's Butterfly and my Butterfly were the temporary and disposable wives of American sailors. Puccini's Butterfly was a Geisha in the port of Nagasaki. My Butterfly was a barfly on the Cuban side of Guantanamo Bay.

Butterflies were in my mind, and a flutter in my belly at the thought of finding the Cuban Butterfly. I was drinking at the bar with old squadron mates, but I could hardly remember them, or myself strutting my stuff in a skintight uniform. My mind was overflowing with a Cuban girl.

I was feeling a drink too many when I returned to my hotel room, my memory taking off like a plane, the past laying out below me. I seemed to be looking down at the past rushing away like a diminishing and contracting landscape, flattening out, running together, disappearing in the distance, and under the clouds. I snapped on the light, tried to get my naval past in perspective.

I didn't want to ship-over in the Navy. I set my course for college, high school teaching, and taught my life away. I taught history, but let my own history get away from me. My Cuban Butterfly was only a footnote in the pastimes of my past. The important times of my history were the marriages and divorces. I was now flying solo into the point of no return, wondering if I'd dumped the love of my life?

I stretched body and mind out on the bed, tried to uncover the memories of my "Cuban Butterfly." I remembered spotting her in the smoky background of a Cuban bar. Amid music and dancing, she was quiet and alone, clasping a white jasmine in her hand! I thought she was a flower herself, a blossom of a face, a body slender as a stem.

She came to bend over me at my table, asked if I wanted a "cockball?" She must have mixed up cocktail and highball. We had a drink together.

She asked if I wanted a "creation." She must have mixed up creation and recreation. I took the flower to bed. She's still pressed in my memory, even though I threw her away. Had I thrown the love of my life away?

■■■ ■■■ ■■■

Next day I made inquiries at the hotel desk about Cuban exiles, learned of the Cuban Emergency Refugee Center. To locate my Cuban Butterfly I needed a little bio-data, and a spell of good fortune. Backtracking in mind I could barely find a footprint to track her down. How do you follow the trail of a Butterfly?

It came back to me, her name."Laura!" She had a string of other names, but "Cruz" seemed to be dominant. I remembered bragging on base about "taking a *Cruz*" on the other side of Guantanamo Bay.

Place of birth? No idea. I think she told me she was raised in the cane fields. I remember a few times she took half-day bus trips to the country. She assured me she had no husband, no child, only poor relations to care for. I'd say she was born in Oriente Province, in the fields near Caimanera.

Time of birth? January! I remember taking her to dinner on a birthday. She said she was a "Janus" person, in between the past and future. I thought she had no future, only a "past." I bought her a ring with the garnet, her birth sone, and she said it was the best "present" she ever had. She would live in the "present" with me on her finger for ever. Her year of birth was 1930, I guessed. The birthday we celebrated together was in the last year of my enlistment, 1954, and when I wined and dined her she said she was twenty-four, but felt a "thousand years" old. Twenty-four seemed awfully old to me, back then when I was twenty.

The night of her twenty-fourth birthday we took dinner and champagne on the terrace of the Oasis hotel, the only decent hotel on the Cuban side of Guantanamo Bay. The champagne was the only sparkling wine she'd ever put to her lips. It seemed to make her sad. I think she was afraid of happiness, afraid it wouldn't last.

My memory hasn't lasted. I surely learned more about her than I remember. We had many talks in a mix of English and Spanish. Maybe we only skimmed our surfaces. We mostly knew each other by touch, and my fingers had lost their memory.

■■■ ■■■ ■■■

I bailed out of reunion meetings, set my course for the "Freedom Tower," the Refugee Center, on Biscayne Boulevard. It would be a long walk, I was told by the hotel doorman, a safe walk, in daytime, but a cab was recommended. My legs were still sound, and I wanted to feel Miami under my feet again. The reunion was actually in the same hotel I came to when the squadron made recreation flights to Miami. The hotel had been renamed and remodeled. The surrounding neighborhood was now more shaded by high rise buildings than royal palms. I didn't know my way through the canyons of banks and office buildings, so I hailed a cab.

The driver was Cuban, and young, too young to know my hotel had been called the *Mandrake*. He didn't know the neighborhood used to be known as "Dallas Park." He called it "Bayside." He didn't know the old Miami at all, didn't know the old or new Cuba at all. He told me his people got out of Cuba before he was born, but Cuba was in his blood. His blood rose in sympathy for an American sailor who'd been stationed in Cuba. He offered to take me to the Refugee Center by way of "Little Havana." Along the way he pointed out a cigar shop where women still rolled tobacco by hand. He waved at all the "coffee windows" and multi-colored stucco and plaster storefronts with signs printed in Spanish. It was like a drive through my memory of Cuba. I even started feeling uneasy. Danger always seemed under the surface in Cuba, even under the brightness of flowers and merriment of music. There had been discontent and danger under the surface of Cuba, and it must have burst out when Castro rose up to overthrow the old Cuba.

The cab driver pointed ahead to the high Spanish bell tower that marked the Refugee Center. He said it was the heart of the exiled Cuban world. "This is it," he said, stopping long enough to let me out, wish me luck, drive off with a salute, and *"adios."*

■■■ ■■■ ■■■

There was hesitation among Cuban staff members when it came to letting me have names and addresses. I never said anything about the "profession" of the woman I was seeking, but gained their sympathy by mentioning my love for Cuba when I was stationed at Guantanamo Bay, before Castro. "Before Castro," and "after Castro" marked the dividing line of history for so many of the staff workers.

I started hearing about parents or grandparents who worked on the naval base at Guantanamo Bay, before Castro. At every stop in my quest for Laura Cruz, I got introduced as an "Americano" who was in "Cuba, before Castro!" I thought of myself as an ancient of the "B.C." era.

The Castro revolution was so far in the past that most "Cubans" didn't have a firsthand recollection of Cuba at all. It was a state of mind, and Havana was the capital of their thoughts. I could tell them about my five day leave when I bussed from Santiago to Havana on a super highway. My Havana hotel had gold faucets, but didn't always turn on water. The old Cuban government was corrupt, older Cubans let me know. Water officials had to be bribed.

I poured out recollections of Havana's tree-shaded boulevards along the ocean side, the watercolor sunsets over Moro castle, the lighted luxury liners steaming in from the States at dusk. Havana was a playground of rum and coca-cola, casinos and cockfights. Havana was as dazzling as Guantanamo Bay was drowsy and dingy. Cuban exiles told me Batista didn't bother with the eastern end. He only took its sugar to "sweeten" Havana.

All the while I was becoming acquainted with officials, I was getting referred to other offices, one after another. At last I was directed to the Archives, a tomb of dead files in a muffled chamber, all closed up like a sepulcher, silent, deserted, except for a woman in white. I found her at a desk near the elevator.

"Whom are you seeking?" she spoke in perfect English. Her dark eyes were framed in glasses, dazzling eyes well worth the framing! My sight was going dim, but hadn't lost its glint for pretty women. I noticed the arch of her plucked and thin eyebrows, saw her as a white light in the shadows of a vaulted room. She was all white, white-streaked hair, white milky complexion, white linen suit. There was a silver comb in her hair. There was a white jasmine tucked behind an ear!

"I'm trying to find my lost fiancee, Laura Cruz, of Oriente Province," I said as fast as I could, trying to spit it out before getting referred to another office. In my previous interviews

I'd never called Laura a fiancee. I must have thought the woman in white would only respond to a case of love.

I rattled off all my clues, made up the story of trying to get Navy authorization for marring her. There were so many papers and affidavits and chains of command to go up, I told the Archivist, that even as a yeoman I had a hard time with it, got my discharge before the paper work went all the way up he chain of command. Back in the States I lost contact, I fabricated some more, and the Cuban revolution finally slammed the door shut! That was my story. I thought it was pretty reasonable. "Here I am in Miami," I wound up, "for a Navy reunion, giving my long lost hopes a last chance."

"It's a sad story," the woman in white offered, but I thought at first she said a *bad* story.

"Any hope?" I asked as soon as I realized she was in sympathy with me.

"Not much to go on," the woman in white thought, looking up at me. Her eyes were magnified through the wire-rimmed glasses. Penetrating, dark eyes, sad.

"Not even a glass slipper did she leave behind," I said, trying to smile.

'It's a fairytale," the Archivist returned my smile. "It ought to have a happy ending. Let me set the computers on it." She made a phone call, busied herself with papers. "Women change their names in marriage," she mentioned without looking up. "Some refugees change their identities, especially the *boatlift* people, and *rafters*."

"I hate to think of her adrift in that lonely, empty sea," I said, thinking she wouldn't have gotten out any other way.

"I was a fortunate one, got out when airplanes were still allowed to come to the States," the woman in white explained, "but all ways *out* are good." She was paging through a directory.

"I guess we're all looking for something," I offered, thinking I should give her a line on myself. "I'm just a retired history teacher, a Cornhusker from Nebraska, America's breadbasket, and *heart*land."

Making small talk, I was appraising her white hair and creamy looks, trying to estimate her age. If I'd gotten Laura pregnant, an idea that entered my head, the lady in white could be my middle-aged daughter! "Laura was very pretty," I said, coming up with a new angle. "I'd be able to recognize her picture."

"No photo file," the Archivist shrugged, looking up, "but we Cuban women are all pretty!" She slipped off her glasses. Her eyes were penetrating, and twinkling, but deeply sad.

"All very pretty," I agreed.

"And we love our Cuba and love the lovers of Cuba." She stood up, all the way up to my chin, and I felt a squeeze in the hand she extended to me. "I'm another Laura," she introduced herself, "Laura Martinez-Jones, hyphenated in marriage."

"A. Turner," I introduced myself. "Initial's for Adam."

"Adam, the initial man," she said, with another twinkle in her eyes She took back her hand, slipped back down in her chair to check another source.

"Adam never seemed to fit," I wanted to keep talking. I didn't tell her I got called "A-*damn* Turner" at muster.

"No, Adam would not fit," she agreed. "You Americans don't know what it's like to be cast out of paradise."

"Maybe not," I said, "but we're all immigrants at birth."

She gave me a thoughtful look, said she'd have to "cast" Adam out for awhile. "Please check back in about an hour," she waved me off. "I'll work on this, take a late lunch."

■■■ ■■■ ■■■

When I came back, after leafing through journals in the reading room, I got the word there was no word. I was told there might be a clue at *Centro*, a Catholic welfare agency, or I could wait for another computer check after she lunched.

"I've taken so much of your time," I interrupted my new Laura. "Could I make it up to you, buy your lunch? I haven't eaten, either."

She nodded, stood up, suggested good "Cuban cuisine" around the corner, at a "bistro-chic hole-in-the wall." She bent over to sling a purse over her shoulder, a white purse at the end of a long white strap. We hurried out, talked along the way. She walked fast, talked fast, and finally spoke of herself, and the Cuban Revolution. Her family was well-born, her birthright lost in the Communist "takeaway." Her

Catholic school life was lost, too, and she was drafted into "volunteer" work, mostly in the cane fields. She waited in lines for food, got fed the socialist line, day after day. Her father wished his own life away, wished a new life for his family in the States. He wore out and died before the family had a chance to escape. The mother and two daughters managed airplane tickets, got out of Cuba with only one suitcase, some photographs and a few mementoes.

All the while she was talking about her times in Cuba, under Castro, I was thinking about my times in Cuba, before Castro. I said I'd been an exile in Cuba, cut off from home and country. I told her we both had been exiles, in reverse, and she nodded a little.

I was more interested in her age, judging she was too old to be my daughter, but not too young for a man my age! When we sat down to eat, I mentioned that I never picked up a taste for Cuban food, said I'd seen too many animal carcasses hanging out to dry in the sun, pieces of meat bleeding red on the hook and breeding flies. She nodded again, looked down at the menu, suggested something she called a *palomilla* steak. She said I could get it well done, without flies.

My new Laura had a flair with words, and fork. As we ate, and talked, I began thinking the quest for my Cuban Butterfly was only a romantic fantasy, almost childish. I started feeling ashamed, ashamed of the way I treated my Cuban Butterfly, long ago, ashamed of the half-truths I was handing the new Laura.

"Do you think life's a quest for something?" I asked, always trying to find meaning in life and history.

"We don't always know what we're looking for," she thought, swallowing. "Seems to me you are a lucky one. You know what you're looking for, some kind of Holy Grail."

"Think I should stop looking for something in the past, look forward?"

"No passport for the past," she said, "or the future." Her eyes were wide with sadness. She changed the subject, recommended the flan on the dessert menu. "It has the flavor of Cuba."

"Would you go back to your Cuba, if you could?" I wanted to know, "look for something back there?"

"Back to Cuba after Castro's gone?" She slanted her head, looked at me askance. "Cuba will never be the same. It's too late for me. There's nothing back there to look for."

■■■ ■■■ ■■■

Back at her office, after lunch, nothing turned up on the Laura of the past, but I was getting interested in the Laura of the present. We arranged to meet again, and again, between her work and my reunion timetable. One time we attended St. Michael's Catholic Church in Little Havana, a congregation of leading Cuban exiles. She pointed out judges, officials, doctors, lawyers of Cuba, "everyday people" in the States. I didn't see anyone who could pass for the old Laura. I could only see the ghost of my Laura, wouldn't know what she looked like, after all this time.

I kept on the lookout a few days more, didn't even have a vapor trail to follow. My new Laura showed me around the old and the new Miami. I saw more of it with her than on the scheduled reunion tours. I saw more of her than my old shipmates. We started opening up to each other, like different books on the same shelf. We started comparing and contrasting our life stories.

Her father was a water engineer in Cuba. He sometimes got assignments at the American naval base. I told her about water getting shut off, throwing the base on water hours and men on skimpy Navy showers. Sailors thought the old dictator, Batista, was trying to get more money. Laura thought there really were engineering problems.

My father was in water, too, I told her, "Holy Water." He was a Methodist minister, saved others, but I let her know he couldn't save me. "I'm still looking for salvation," I said, "still sinning in Adam."

We compared childhoods. School years were our bench marks. I was in public grade school when the attack on Pearl Harbor put an end to my childhood. Much younger than me, World War II was vague to her. Her childhood was ended in grade school when Castro came to power. Before Castro, she remembered flowers and parties, school and church. She .remembered a visit to the American naval base at Guantanamo Bay. It was Christmas time and Santa Claus came down in a Navy helicopter, passed out presents to base dependents and visitors. After Castro, there was no more Santa Claus in Cuba.

She was living the events in Cuba that were current events in my history classes. She was in target range when the Soviet Union and the United States faced off with atomic missiles in 1962. She was praying for life when my students begged out of homework. It was the beginning of a world that might not have a tomorrow, for anyone. The past was all we could count on.

My new Laura had no past to count on, but loved history. She gave me her history of escape from Cuba, when airlines were still connecting Havana to Miami. In Miami, she was struggling for survival in a foreign country, pooling money and food and space with other Cuban exiles. At that time I was struggling with indifferent students, trying to bring the past to them in a meaningful way.

I was teaching school and she was getting schooled. I was getting divorced and she was getting married. I got married again and she got two children. I lost another wife. She lost her husband, gained a degree in library science. I went into retirement and she got her children on their own. Our lives had both come down to my naval reunion.

I postponed my scheduled departure for Nebraska, stayed on at the hotel after my reunion broke up, waited in vain for replies to newspaper adds. I even took to the Cuban Research

Institute at Florida's International University for help and study, but had lost the trail of my Cuban Butterfly.

I was left with the thoughts of a butterfly as a resurrected caterpillar, my old Laura in the dirt of Caimanera, my new Laura on the wing in Miami. Could my own life be resurrected?

THE FLIGHT FANTASTIC

A ONCE-UPON-A-TIME SAILOR, Mark Truett, was opening the book on the Navy he'd closed a long time ago. Flying to Miami for his naval air squadron's first reunion he figured on turning back the pages to a storied past full of fabled adventures and salty characters. He remembered being known as "True" in the Navy, but could hardly remember his "true" naval past He barely remembered squeezing into whites, adjusting his parts, walking with bowlegged sea legs. He'd outgrown Navy life, and the tight uniform, and needed to reset his clock to Navy time, back to Korean wartime. It struck him, all of a sudden, there were times his wife shouldn't get into. Airborne with his wife, he was flying her into his past.

Dropping out of clouds, memories flying, he caught sight of Miami revolving under the commercial airliner's wing like a sparkling carrousel. Miami was coming up in his window, revolving in mind with remembered rounds of revelry. His squadron's Catalina Flying Boat used to make "whiskey runs" to Miami from its base at Guantanamo Bay, Cuba. The big, lumbering aircraft would be loaded with duty-free Cuban rum in the bomb-bay and liberty-thirsty sailors in the after-station. Back then, the four hundred and eighty-one air miles to Miami from Guantanamo Bay was a long haul in a prop-driven PBY. Now it was a long haul in memory.

In the summer of his high school graduation, North Korea kicked off a war at the 38th Parallel, made a run for the end zone of South Korea. It got him a call from his draft board and a date for a physical that brought him face to face with faces and bodies never seen before, or after. He avoided the Army by enlisting in the Navy, didn't want to see who he'd have to shoot at. What trick of memory pulled that little decision out of the hat? The magic of memory took him to Boot Camp, stripped him of clothes and identity, stamped him with a number, and sent him off on an aircraft carrier. No portholes, no air conditioning, only air blowers, but below decks he never had to see the enemy, not even in Korean waters. He only fought dirt and rust, chipped paint, scraped his way from deck ape to grease monkey, from seaman to airman, and all the way up to second class aviation machinist's mate. Before the hands of the Navy clock rolled around to discharge time, he was assigned shore duty in a naval air squadron based on the far end of Cuba, at Guantnamo Bay. It was that old squadron holding its reunion down below in Miami.

The commercial airliner was smoother than the squadron's old Catalina Flying Boat, he thought, flying back in time to the trembling old Flying Boat on its way to Miami. Whenever Lieutenant "Dutch" Decker was on the stick, True got to sit up front in the cockpit, check out the controls and maps and radio frequencies. The pilot held the plane on the beam of a Miami radio station, took her in on the strains of Benny Goodman's swing. He hoped "Dutch" would be at the reunion

A sudden stroke of memory, like the wave of a magician's wand, turned him from the happy anticipation of reunion to the dread of revelation. The magic wand of memory transformed him from a lowly enlisted man into a prince! He was conjuring up himself in a Cadillac convertible with a bevy of college beauty queens. Memory plays tricks. He must be having a flight of fancy, a magic carpet ride to a make-believe land. A young sailor would sell his soul for the story True was remembering as true, but it wasn't worth an old sailor's soul-mate. His soul mate was silhouetted in the aisle seat. She was smiling, couldn't have been reading his mind.

Christy Truett was as shapely as ever. Her profile still turned his head the way it did when he first got a look at her in a college class, after his naval service was over. She'd kept her hair white-blond, all these years, but swept-up instead of letting it hang loose. She'd weathered the years without wear, even went through the change of life like a change of clothes. She was still flying high.

True remembered how intently he memorized her looks, and his books, in college. He graduated with a marriage license and an engineering degree. Life took off after that, flew by. It was hard to realize his campus bobbysoxer had broken the time barrier of sixty-five! He still thought of her as a blue-eyed doll with pink cheeks and dimpled knees under short skirts. She'd kept herself up, all these years, with a lift and a tuck and a tint.

He turned away, afraid she might see the college beauty queens flying around in the misty clouds of his mind. They were clutching their hair in a speeding Cadillac convertible. Some other lusty sailors made the car scene, along with sandy beaches flashing between clumps of mangoes and golden shower trees. In the flash of an eye there was the flash of flesh along a beach, and the touch of slippery bodies dipping in and out of splashing surf. He couldn't get a good picture of the bubbly girls, only a shimmer of skin and suntan lotion, and an ankle bracelet. He couldn't get a good focus on himself, either, couldn't remember the way he looked in his Navy issue swimsuit, a "nut hugger." He could only recognize one of the frolicking sailors in the sea-shine of a flashback. It was "Slick" flickering in and out of a vision. He was a half forgotten buddy who always walked around in a Texas two-step or a Cuban mambo. He was fast of foot, and lip, might be at the reunion, might let the fairytale weekend out of the bag.

His buddy, Slick, was always in a state of motion, jiggling long limbs and dog tags, practicing the cha-cha-cha even when standing in line for chow. Slick was a dancing fool, a wheeler and dealer, but a good mechanic to work alongside. They were in the same crew, sweated together under the Cuban sun at McCalla Field. They played poker in the line shack when the workload was down. They scoffed-up beers at the enlisted men's club at night, dived and swam in the naval air station swimming pool on weekends. They tooled around in Cuba and in Miami whenever they made the list for one of those recreation flights. Slick was a real liberty hound, had a good nose for keeping on the scent, tracking down women. He really was slick with women and words and schemes.

Slick's memory fell away when the aircraft settled into its landing pattern. True took hold of Christy's hand. He knew she studied every movement of a plane, worried about every change of motion. He knew she thought flying was for the birds, only agreed to fly south with him to enjoy the Florida beaches and get the "skinny" on him as a sailor. She prided herself on reading him like a book, but couldn't get a good read on his Navy chapter. She could make a pants-suit out of an old uniform, but couldn't make anything out of the sailor who'd been in it.

"God, it's good to be down to earth," Christy said, opening her eyes, laying them gently on her husband as the plane touched down, bumped along the runway.

"You're never down to earth?" True smiled, patting her hand. "You always have your head in the clouds with Socrates and those old philosophers you dug up in college."

"That was in my past," she said, "now we're in your past."

The suggestion of his past brought True back to the magical weekend in Miami he didn't want his wife to find out about. Christy put her husband on guard when she asked if the "good times would start to roll" as soon as he got back in the ranks?

"You think it was all fun and games in the Navy?" He shook his head at her. "Enlisted men were shuffled together like cards in a deck, got no space or privacy."

"And no loneliness," Christy said. "That's a fair deal!"

"When you're stacked in a pack of men you can't sort yourself out," True complained, trying to shuffle Slick out of his head. "You can't find yourself," but he kept finding Slick in his memory of life in the barracks. Slick was always hanging loose in a wrap-around towel. Tall and skinny, unfinished, it seemed, in build, he was broad and boney above the waist, narrow and straight below. He'd jiggling around the barracks in shower clogs and dog tags, take mambo steps, back and forth. He said he was born with "mambo feet," and "the Latin beat," and had a mind that could keep up with the feet. His mind was usually taking steps to sidestep naval regulations, or get round some girl. It was Slick who cast the spell for that magical weekend in Miami!

He came up with the idea of two or three men letting their pay ride the books for a couple of months and salt away enough "bread" for a great "staff of life" in Miami. Tailor-made civies on base would give them the "look," and a rented convertible the "way," to make out in Miami like Arabian princes. Slick got True to fantasize about it when they gassed-up planes by day and sucked-up beers by night. In adjoining bunks they talked about it at night when sea breezes seeped through the louvered windows in the barracks and salted down the sweaty air with a touch of the ocean, and bougainvillea and jasmine.

The scent of the sea and jasmine was in the Miami air as True and Christy stepped outside the airport terminal. True sucked in a breath of memory as he whistled for a cab. It was a ten or twenty minute ride to their hotel, depending on traffic, the cab driver assured them. Christy settled in the back seat with True but sank down in her own thoughts. True had his own thoughts, still trying to unknot all the strands of his fairytale weekend in Miami. He remembered a third sailor in on the Miami caper. A third man had to be cut in the deal to make the pot big enough. No face or name came to mind. He recalled three sailors landing in Miami, transformed into princes of the Arabian Nights! The Mandrake Hotel was their palace, the rented convertible their magic carpet!

True was mesmerized by the bright crystal ball of memory all the time the skyline of Miami was sparkling in the windshield of the taxicab. Downtown Miami streets started filling the cab windows with colorful store fronts, dark alleys, signs in Spanish. Downtown Miami seemed like the Cuba he was remembering. It was all flickering by, a moving picture of the Cuba he used to fly to Miami to get away from. He knew Miami was home to Cuban refugees, the exiles from Castro's revolution, but he didn't know so much of Cuba had come across the water.

"Little Havana" went out of the picture. The cab windows were framing scenes of massive marble and concrete buildings, polished glass and granite, bank and office structures, all sculptured under a spiral of overhead highways. The cab slowed, the window pictures flickering by. The flickering snapped to a stop, a canopied hotel entrance in focus.

The headquarters for his Navy reunion was in the same hotel the squadron reserved for "whiskey runs" out of Cuba, but the old hotel's park-like setting was reduced to clumps of caged-up palms. The hotel itself only struck a slightly familiar pose. It had a new name, new decor, new look.

"The clock turns everything around," True said, paying off the cab driver, hoisting a suitcase in each hand. "Time and change go round together." His mind was turning round with thoughts of aging buildings and aging bodies. Buildings can be restored, renovated, renewed for living.

The hotel entrance was barely familiar, but it led to memories of weekend liberties when he took leave of Navy discipline. Inside, the pillars and columns looked familiar and the vaulted lobby was a pleasure dome of marbled recollections.

Clumps of men were standing around, men of his vintage, but bottled in unfamiliar shapes. They were in used-up bodies, not the bodies of young men waiting in line for draft board physicals, or service number labels, but they were wisecracking and swapping stories like the boys he remembered in the Navy. He expected the hotel would soon be all "booked-up" with "sea stories."

"Recognize any bald heads?" Christy asked when she looked around the marble lobby.

"Not a shiny head!" True said, looking for Slick in the huddles of old boys. Most men in the lobby had lost their hair. He wondered if Slick hung on to the hair he was often combing? True was proud of his own hair, would only admit to a touch of gray. He thought he still looked at the world with the same face he "faced-off" with at naval inspections. His face was firm, unlined, set on hold.

"Not a single familiar mug?" Christy asked, "no drinking buddy?"

"I can't even tell the officers from the men," True mentioned, glancing around. Everyone seemed to look alike in their rising hairlines, drooping midriffs, and Florida sports attire.

"What's the difference between an officer and a man?"

"Officers have the good life, and the gold braid," True said, still looking around. "Enlisted men have the good bodies, and bell-bottoms."

"That's fair enough."

"Nothing's fair in the military," True frowned, "but age makes us equal, at last."

"Are all the hotel rooms equal?"

"All fit for an officer," he said, and admitted that this hotel was his *first*!

"You lost your hotel virginity here?" Christy contrived to flutter her eyelashes. "Is this where you became a hotel *man*?"

"You can't imagine the difference between taps and reveille in a barracks and in a hotel room by yourself," True said, looking around, not listening to Christy. "There's nothing like your own room, with a door, and a key, and a bathroom to yourself!"

"You were in a room all by yourself?"

"A sailor couldn't run a girl past the house detective, not in those days, if that's what you're getting at, my dear!"

"Think you'll have trouble getting me in?"

"Times have changed."

"This check-in line doesn't change, doesn't seem to move."

"Just like the Navy," True said, giving her a piece of the past. "Navy life was in a line, a line for drill and muster, a waiting line for chow, pay, and *short arm* inspections!"

"Did you ever get out of line with that *short arm* of yours?"

"Kept it in line."

"You're throwing me a line."

"We had lifelines on ships to keep us from going overboard," True kept joking. "I never went overboard for any *she* when at sea."

"Life seems like a line," Christy thought, sobering up, "a line for growing up in, and a line for growing old in. We're always in line, waiting for something to change."

"Hang on," True said, steadying her arm. "You're going overboard."

"Thanks for giving me a hand, sailor!"

When the line came to an end they found a desk clerk with the dark good looks of a Cuban. He dealt True a registration card, and a smile.

"Years ago," True said to the clerk, as he looked down at the card he was filling out, "this hotel was called the *Mandrake*."

"Mandrake, the comic strip Magician," a voice piped up from behind. "The Mandrake Hotel performed a great escape trick for every jack man of us in the ranks!"

"And made our money disappear," True remembered, turning round to look over the top of a bald head, and down at a squat figure, round and solid. There was something familiar about the face.

"Wish *Mandrake* could make our youths reappear," the old boy said, looking up at True.

True asked him if he'd come for the naval air squadron reunion.

"Got me a Navy brand to prove it." The squat heavy-set man lifted the sleeve of his guayabera shirt, revealed a Navy tattoo fading on the bulge of his arm. "It's a drunken souvenir. Could get myself out of the Navy, couldn't get the Navy out of my skin."

"Tattoo's a duck," Christy thought.

"Our squadron was called the Mallards," True spoke for the tattooed sailor.

"The Ruptured duck,"the tattooed sailor preferred to call it.

"And now you're all flocking back together," Christy managed to get out before making room for the tattooed man at the desk. The Truetts stood a few steps away, waited for him to register.

"Can't place you," True said when the old boy with the tattoo came over to join them.

"Mario Mirabelli," he introduced himself, "grease monkey in the service, going ape in retirement."

"Mark Truett, another grease monkey," True introduced himself, holding out his hand, "did squadron time under Old Man O'Meara."

"Me, too. We're old squadron mates." The shorter man looked up with recognition beaming in his round face. "Remember *Moon*? You surely have me lined up in your memory muster book, somewhere?"

"Moon Mirabelli!" True remembered, at last. "You put on some weight."

"I was just a half Moon back then."

"This pretty lady," True introduced Christy, "is the wife of my life."

"You got yourself a good man," Moon half-saluted Christy with his tattooed arm. "I got me a good wife, but she pulled the grandmother watch, had to stand duty back home."

"Left my grand-babies behind," Christy said, "to get a grand view of their grandfather's past. It's good to meet a real tattooed sailor. True never got a tattoo. Was he a *True* sailor?"

"True blue he was! Sometimes we called him *True-man*, in honor of our President Truman."

"Was my man always true and good?" Christy asked.

"Does the moon shine?"

"Want to know how this old boy came up with Moon for a name?" True asked his wife. "He mooned Miami from the bottom hatch of our PBY. Cracked everybody up!"

"Old Chief Riley put me up to it," Moon was quick to explain. "He held the hatch open, said I didn't have a hair on my ass if I didn't give it a shot."

"Moon over Miami," Christy hummed an old familiar tune. "That puts a whole new shine on Kate Smith's signature song."

"And I'm still hung up with that name," Moon said, "like my tattoo. It stuck to me even after I got my butt out of service."

"Sorry to butt out," True smiled at Moon, "but we got to stow our gear, freshen up."

"There's a squadron reception getting underway in the Cabana Club," Moon mentioned, looking at his watch, "with beer and pizza and lots of old times. How about falling-in, about an hour from now?"

"We'll be present and accounted for," Christy promised, starting to follow her husband and looking back. "It'll be my first naval encounter."

"Your old man and me had us a great naval encounter, long time ago right here in Miami," Moon said, over his shoulder, "a real blast with blond bombshells."

■■■　■■■　■■■

True remembered the hotel "Cabana Club" when he saw it again. All these years after the squadron used the hotel for its recreation flights, it still had a palm-thatched decor, seascape murals, fishnets and blocks and tackles hanging on the walls. The room was reserved for the squadron's "Welcome Aboard" party.

Christy had let her hair drift down to the shoulders, slipped herself into a navy blue skirt and a roomy jumper with True's petty officer stripes on the sleeve. She wanted to look "shipshape."

The two of them stepped into the sound of a live combo, saw couples dancing in the shadows of flickering torches.

Other naval couples were beached way off on the other side of the room, at round cocktail tables.

"*Perfidia*," Christy named the song in the air. She hummed the tune, swung on True's arm as they crossed the dance floor, headed for the background of thatched huts and cocktail tables.

"*Perfidia* means treachery in Spanish," True said, lifting his wife's hand, letting her twirl under his arm as they walked past a few dancers.

"Any *perfidia* between my sailor man and a Cuban *muchacha*?"

"Didn't get very far with my Spanish, or *muchachas*!"

"Too bad Cuba's out of bounds," Christy said, pointing to an empty table. "If the reunion could have been there, some old girl might remember you."

"Cuba was the lowlife of my hitch in the Navy," True said. "Recreation flights to Miami were the only highlights." He helped Christy into a chair. "You know, this is the first time I've been back to Miami, after all these years."

"Back in your fountain of youth!"

"And the fountain's going dry," True said, bowing off to the cash bar. When he got back with a sherry for Christy and a whiskey for himself he found Moon Mirabelli at the table.

"The Moon is down!" Christy proclaimed to her husband. "He thought I looked seaworthy in your revamped dress blues."

"She's trim in the water," Moon said, saluting True with his glass.

"Moon's going to let me in on your naval love life," Christy spoke up, making room for her husband at the table. "Want to see you the way you really were, not the way you dressed yourself up in your tailor-made version."

"She wants the naked truth," Moon cracked a smile at True.

True was starting to see Moon in a different light. He really was in the Miami fairytale, another one of the frogs turned into princes.

"Now that you're at attention," Christy turned to Moon. "It's *about face* time. Look back, tell me what you see of my sailor."

"He was just a sailor, like all the others in the ranks," Moon said. "We were in uniform, all cut out of the same cloth."

"Is that all the material on him you've got?"

"Looking back is only good if you had a good past," Moon said, turning away.

"Is there a dark side to the Moon," Christy wondered, "and a false side to True?"

"Looking back turned Lot's wife into a pillar of salt," True interrupted, hoping a scriptural reference would be good for the last word on the subject.

"I'm married to an old salt," Christy laughed, "might as well turn into one!"

"Your old salt's pretty dry," True said, raising his almost empty glass. "What about you, Moon? What you drinking?"

"Hard water," Moon said, flicking his glass with a finger, "nothing stronger, not anymore."

"That's a new Moon," True thought, turning to Christy. "The old Moon was always glowing with moonshine."

"I used to drink myself into the land of the happy trance," Moon explained to Christy. "Happy trance land's not the same country anymore."

"I'm going to miss you for a drinking buddy?" True saluted him with what was left in his whiskey. He was about to take off for the bar again.

"Wait a minute and you'll have Slick to booze it up with," Moon said, returning the salute. "I ran into our old buddy in the elevator. The woman *he said was his wife* looked like a Playboy bunny, too young to be one of the college beauty queens we picked up on our storybook weekend."

"I'd like a read on that storybook weekend," Christy said. "Is that when you had a naval *blast with blond bombshells*?"

"No big deal," True hastened to clarify, "just a little playing around."

"We got lucky that weekend," Moon said, "drew three of a kind, all queens."

"We were losers, except for Slick," True insisted.

"Who's Slick?" Christy asked.

"An old squadron mate," Moon explained before True could answer, "a grease monkey who struck it rich. He let me know he has his own Cadillac agency in South Florida, and I could see he had a top of the line wife on his arm, and a gold ring on his pinkie."

"I never heard a word about Slick," Christy said. "Was he as slick as his name?"

"Didn't True ever tell you about the magical weekend Slick dreamed up? We all got turned into princes."

"You really can change a frog into prince?"

"Kiss me and see," True tried to smile through the kissing pucker of his lips.

She kissed him, said he really was a prince.

"How 'bout working some of that magic on me?" Moon asked

"You're already a prince, but I'll turn you into a king for a little memo on that magic weekend."

"It was just the magic of money," Moon said. "We bought ourselves royalty."

"Slick dreamed up the play production,"True got in a word, "gave us the roles of millionaire college boys."

"We picked up girls claiming to be college beauty queens," Moon elaborated. "Slick got the pick of the royal litter. True and me got the leftovers."

"Mr. Truett," Christy pouted at her husband, "I thought I was your first and only college girl?"

"I'm not sure they were college girls," True said, wondering if Christy was only pretending to pout. "We just took their word for it."

"Not even sure they were really beauty queens," Moon added, "but they looked like they had the credentials."

Christy closed her eyes in thought, sipped at her sherry.

True wondered what was going on in her mind? Women keep things private, he thought, tucked-up inside, like their private parts. "It was no big deal," he finally had to speak up.

"Didn't you come up with three queens? Isn't that a pretty big deal?"

"Slick's the one who hit the jackpot," Moon covered for Slick. "He picked the long-stemmed American beauty for himself. I got the sorority stepsister. True got a darling."

"Thought I was the only darling in your life," Christy pouted at her husband again.

"Darling was her last name," True explained, thinking Christy was really amused, laughing inside.

"Yeah, Kitty Darling was her name," Moon verified.

"Give me the darling story line," Christy said, tasting her sherry again, "from top to *bottom*."

"Story never got to the bottom," True said, "hardly got started."

"Start with the start."

"We ran into these girls in a Miami diner," Moon picked up on the story. "Place was like a railroad diner, stools alongside a counter, tables lined up beside a wall with painted windows and scenes of the West, mountains and stuff. We thought we'd really made the scene, gone up in the world!"

"We stayed on the track, never got out of line," True assured his wife.

"They wouldn't have given us poor swabs the time of day if we didn't look like big time dudes," Moon said, "fancy duds and a convertible parked outside."

"Picked up hamburgers, too." True kept the story going, "and had my *first* onion rings!"

"We passed ourselves off as college boys from out of town," Moon kept the story going. "Collars turned up in back, hair swept back to a duck's ass, we really played the role."

"Duck-ass mallards," True said, trying to laugh, "decoyed them into a jukebox dance, or two. Slick was fast with his feet, and mouth, and fast with nickels in the jukebox. That's all there was to the story, just a blue-plate lunch and a spin around the diner on a jukebox platter or two."

"And a little spin in the Cadillac convertible," Moon had to add.

"Slick made all the moves," True said. "Me and Moon just followed along."

"What did you do with the darling one?" Christy asked, "the Kitty Darling."

"Her name wasn't Darling, after all. She made it up, didn't want to level with me at first, thought a girl on the first date needs put on a lot of *make-up*."

"How much better did you get to know her?"

"I don't even remember her real name."

"My girl called herself Mary Hall," Moon cut in. "I told her a lot of college buildings must be named after her!"

"Your girl giggled a lot," True remembered.

"She was ticklish!"

"How did a bunch of swabs think they could pass for college men?"

"We talked football, and parties. None of your Philosophy 101 stuff."

"What did you make up about yourselves?"

"I may have told Kitty I was the second string quarterback at Illinois," True said, after he thought a moment, "may have carried on about my old man being up to his navel in oil, stuff like that, pretty dumb line, huh?"

"I can't believe you'd make up a line at all."

"It was the talks with a college girl that talked me into college." True said, "and that's how I met you, my dear."

"Did you pass a lot of lies off on me?"

"We were just play acting," Moon came to True's rescue. "I think those college girls were giving us a line, too. Slick's girl called herself Cindi, like Cinderella. She talked about going to a ball, said our Cadillac convertible would do for a carriage, but she needed six footmen."

"Slick said he was a six-foot man," True remembered, trying to grin.

"We played along with the Cinderella girls," Moon finished, "and really did have a ball driving them around, but it was just once upon a single time!"

"You took those girls for a *ride*!"

"They gave us a guidebook tour of Miami," True explained. "Just sightseeing along Ocean Drive. I only remember an eyeful of frosted cake houses and hotels like grounded ships, things like that."

"Ended up at a waterfront restaurant," Moon said, "a Viking ship for a bar, great sea food, great sea view!"

"We shot our wad by midnight, and the girls ran out on us at the stroke of twelve," True said, striking the table with a hand, "and they didn't leave a single glass slipper behind."

"Some fairytale!"

"That's all there was to our enchanting tale of *The Miami Nights*."

"More than one night? Another time? A thousand and one nights?"

"There was a long time between recreation flights," True insisted. "Slick might have made another night of it? He kept in touch with *his* beauty queen, got her address and launched a fleet of letters from a post office box in Cuba. He didn't want her to know he was in the Navy. I think he let on about being in Cuba to run his old man's sugar plantation."

"I think I see the author of *The Miami Nights* right now," Moon said, recognizing Slick jiggling toward their table in his loose and casual gait. He still had his black hair, True noticed, wet from a swim or shower. He was weaving between tables, managing a tall glass in one hand. He raised the glass at them. True and Moon jumped up. They all slapped each other around.

"You're keeping in Slick shape," True said, sitting back down, pointing Slick to a chair.

"I work out!" Slick said, pulling up a chair, "and who's the beauty queen with you?"

"She says she's the mother of my children," True said, turning from Slick to his wife. "This is Slick, the old buddy you've been hearing about. His real name's Lyon, but he's Slick to us."

"I'm really the Lyon King," Slick introduced himself, "no lyin'."

"I've been getting the word on your magic night of transfiguration," Christy said.

"What kind of night was that?" Slick asked, not waiting for an answer. "This is a night for turning us all into dancing fools. How 'bout it, Mrs. True, you up to a light fantastic round the dance floor?"

"He's a dancing machine," True warned, "really gets his motor revved-up!"

"No dancing fool no more," Slick contradicted, "got out of the groove."

"Time marches on," Moon said, "and we all get out of step after awhile."

"This old music's twisting my propeller," Slick got excited. "How 'bout an old fashioned spin, Mrs. T?"

"Sorry I didn't wear my dancing shoes," Christy begged off.

"I'll put that down as a rain check, not a cold foot."

Slick sat down, kicked one leg over the other, jiggled a foot, mentioned his "swell hotel suite with a top of the line view." He added that the lower part of Miami, at street level, "was bare ass ugly, not what it used to be."

"None of us are what we used to be, at any level," Moon said.

"Wait till you get a level look at my wife," Slick said. "When the Lyon queen comes down, let's all hunt us up some action."

"You looking for a good time?" True turned to his wife.

"Not on your life, Big Boy," she said, pouting. "I'm not one of those good time girls you meet in fancy diners."

"We sure had us some good times in the Navy," Slick remembered, rattling the ice around in his glass.

"Why did we lose track of each other?" True asked, really wondering.

"We're in a machine world of interchangeable parts," Slick thought, rattling his ice some more. "We keep fitting into new times and places, connecting, disconnecting all the time."

"Your Navy buddies tell me you connected pretty well with some beauty queens on one of your squadron flights to Miami."

"Oh, yeah, the beauty queen connection," Slick remembered, "the time we rolled a payroll into a Cinderella ball."

"When you played loose with the truth!"

"What in hell's wrong about pretending to be better than you are?" Slick asked, uncrossing his legs, stamping a foot down.

"Not good to palm yourself off as somebody you aren't."

"Maybe those girls palmed themselves off on us," Slick thought. "Maybe they took us for a ride!"

"Mr. Lyon, what's your version of the Cinderella story?"

"You think your man left a piece of tail out of the fairytale?"

"Not if he told the truth."

"Maybe we don't want the truth, not all the time."

"People can't live together without truth, and trust!"

"Not so," Slick said, shaking his glass of ice cubes. "People want fairytale lives and happy endings. It's not always written that way. Me and my Cindi girl might have lived happily ever after. Truth is, she loved me for the lies I told, hated me for the truth!"

THE FEMALE CONTRABAND

"WOULD YOU BELIEVE I smuggled a woman aboard a man-of-war, way back in my seagoing days?" I thought that would pipe old shipmates aboard my sea story! We were celebrating our naval air squadron's first reunion at a hotel bar in Miami by swigging drinks and swapping stories. The barroom seemed to be drifting slowly in circles, like a ship swinging at anchor, and some of the old boys were on the brink of going under.

"Was your ship flying the red flag to signal taking on explosives?" The question came from an old squadron mate I remembered as Harry Seaman, an unforgettable name for a sailor. There was derision in his voice. "Every seagoing sailor knows," he went on, "it would be easier to get a warship in a bottle than a bottle of booze in a warship, and no way could you bottle-up a female in a ship!"

Like me, Harry Seaman served at sea before landing a billet in our land based squadron at Guantanamo Bay. Sailors among us who'd never gone to sea respected his seaworthiness. Harry Seaman had been salty enough in our air squadron to pick up "Sea Dog" for a call name.

"New Navy's got women on ships," one of the old squadron mates challenged Sea Dog, "and a ship's a *she*, ain't she?"

"She-shaped she ain't, but bears us like a mother," another old sailor speculated, "and gives us our *berth*." He saluted his smile with a glass of whiskey to his lips.

"Ship was no mother to me," Harry Seaman talked back. "Most of you boys never had sea duty. It's a bitch compared to shore duty at Gitmo."

"The word for ship is female in the Latin," our former yeoman broke in, "same as a vessel or container or womb." He never missed a chance to teach, had come to the reunion as a retired high school teacher.

"You want a lesson on ships?" I asked, "or a story on spiriting a full-bodied Italian vintage aboard a ship?" I was wondering why I always had trouble holding an audience. I'd made a living, since the Navy, as an actor on daytime radio and television, spoke well, but only the words I was given.

"Your story won't float for a sailor or fly for an airman," Sea Dog said.

"Uncork that Italian vintage," another old boy at my table tuned me in, "try it out on us."

"My ship never got to Korea," I got started, "got assigned to the Sixth Fleet for a six month tour in the Med. It got to be holiday time, Christmas-New Years, and we tied-up at the pier in Genoa, just a gangway from the merriest liberty in the Med. Ship sank into holiday routine, and that's the setting for my female contraband story."

"Carry her aboard in a seabag, over the shoulder?"

"Stacked her in Navy blues and walked her up the gangway in the dark of the New Year. Officer of the Deck was waving drunks aboard."

"They say the uniform makes the man," someone said. "That proves it."

"Proves an idiot or a bullshitter can pass for a sailor," thought the old pilot we used to know as "Dutch." His Nordic good looks had been worn down through the years and every hair on his head had been polished off. "It's no easy trick to put a plane down on a carrier," he kept up, "but no man can land a woman on carrier, and no tailhook could hold her down, except in your dreams."

"It's a sailor's dream all right!"

"Keeping her hooked down would be harder than landing her," another man at my table considered. "How in hell did you figure on hiding a woman on a ship where no man's ass is private?"

"Just thinking about a female racked-up next to me in the bowels of a ship," another one of us said, "gets me hot, even from my sunset point of view!" He had to light a cigarette, his hand shaking.

"Wish we had women aboard ship in our day," another old sailor was heard from.

"It was a man's world when we were in the Navy," Sea Dog remembered dreamily. "A man's world out of the Navy, too!"

"Times sure have changed, men, and women set the clock for equal time. It happened on our watch!"

"Free Love came with the change," someone thought, getting off his bar stool and turning himself around, "but I missed out, got married too soon! Young men these days can get it without marriage strings attached."

"Women are free as men!"

"Too much freedom nowadays," the old pilot, Dutch, thought, striking his Annapolis ring on the table for emphasis. "Like the Cole Porter song, *anything goes.*"

"World's like a ship," Sea Dog suggested, "keeps moving on, dropping anchor at new ports, different ways of life keep coming up."

"It's a good deal that men and women are on an even keel," our former yeoman said. "We're all in the *same boat!*"

"Ship's a *she*, but not a *boat*," Sea Dog piped up.

"You swobs want the sex of a ship or the sex on a ship?" I asked.

"Give it to us straight," Sea Dog shrugged. "We're drunk enough to swallow anything."

"Me and my buddy, Enzo, were cruising joints along the Genoa waterfront," I got started again, "and ran across a trim little craft willing to tie up alongside. Between my Italian and her English I got her hooked on seeing the world through a

Navy porthole! Hardest part of smuggling her aboard was getting her down all the ladders to our division compartment. She was loose as a rag doll and we only had the red night lights to see by."

"You really were nuts," someone interrupted, "or just had a lot of balls!"

"Life was a ball to me," I said, "seemed like I was a cat with the world on a string."

"Time's put us out of action," Sea Dog interrupted, "put us in mothballs, like old ships."

"I been feeling like a creaky old ship," someone spoke up in a cloud of smoke, "and been taking *leaks* at night, all night long." I recognized him, all six feet six of him, our parachute rigger. Carrying a chair in one hand, a drink in the other, he came from the shadows and crashed at our table. He might have shrunk a mite, or my memory had, but he was still enormous. His hair and trim little beard had gone mostly gray, but the long hairs sticking out his sleeves were jet black. Curious, I thought, traces of gray age and black youth in the same body!

"Dropping in without a parachute," the parachute rigger we'd called Big Six said, getting himself comfortable in the chair, still head and shoulders over the rest of us, "heard there were some stories going around at this end of the bar."

"Marino the Mech's trying to pass off a fishy sea story on us," Dutch spoke for me. "He tells of smuggling a waterfront woman on a seagoing ship in the Med."

"How's a sea story jive with a naval air squadron's reunion?" Big Six asked, stroking the point of his beard. "Our stories should hang in the air."

"Any man of us try to smuggle a woman in our naval air barracks at Guantanamo Bay?"

"Weren't some of you married, living in civilian housing?" Big Six took charge again. None of us around the table or bar answered him in the affirmative.

"The married men must be dead by now," Big Six thought. "I got me the tale of a Navy nurse at the base hospital that will get your wheels off the ground."

"Let Marino ship us out on his orgy sea story first," Dutch spoke up for me.

"Don't expect a gang bang," I warned my listeners, tuning up for my story.

"Maybe you couldn't make out," Dutch interrupted instead of Big Six, "even with a whore in the same bunk?"

"Making-out doesn't come easy in a fish bowl," I managed to speak up to an old officer. "Enlisted men didn't have private staterooms like some of you pilots. No man wants fifty witnesses to his hump in the sack."

"Racked-up with a woman sure would get a man's ass in a sling," Big Six spoke up, "and get the book thrown at him."

"That's the way I read it," Dutch said. "Soon as word got out, a court-martial would be the last word!"

"Let the old boy get on with it," somebody protested, "I feel the climax coming on."

"It was going to be harder to get the woman off the ship than on," I started again, prompting Big Six to say a good man could get any woman *off*!

"Before getting her off," a man on a bar stool looked my way, "what was your come-on for talking the Italian broad aboard?"

"She was liquored up, like me and my buddy," I got going again, "but with a name like Carmine Marino I always had a way with Italian women, always got the *paisano* treatment."

"She was in the hometown of Columbus," our yeoman-teacher reminded us, "ready to discover America!"

"Wanted to live off the Navy," Dutch contradicted. "She was one of those women who follow the fleet. Bet she thought her business would really take off on an aircraft carrier!"

"Well, she was a woman with her hand out," I granted, "but times were hard for her country just out of World War II, with bombed-out buildings still hanging around the waterfront."

"I'll go along with the old girl on the lookout for American aid," Sea Dog granted, "but how in Hades did you happen to have an extra uniform on liberty with you? You plan this caper cold sober, ahead of time?"

"No way," I said. "The idea just popped out of a bottle, like the New Year," and I started the story again. "Me and Enzo were moored in a waterfront bar next to a flea-bag hotel that rented rooms by the hour. One of the sailors at the bar had a good-looker lined up, wanted to rent a room for the whole night, and then some. That's the time I thought of a good use for his liberty card, and the uniform he wanted out of!"

"You let a buddy go AWOL?"

"No buddy. He was from another division. Hell, it was New Year's," I reminded everyone. "We were smashed, must have wagered his woman worth a Captain's Mast, maybe a summary court."

"So you gave yourself the detail of getting the female undressed and into dress blues," Big Six summed up. "That was better duty than rigging up an airman for a parachute jump."

"Don't get your wheels in a spin," I started up again. "Me and Enzo just stuffed her, dress and all, into the uniform, rolled up the sleeves and pants, stowed all her hair under the white hat, steered her down to our division compartment, got her laid out in an empty bunk by the peacoat locker. Me and Enzo forgot what we were up to, crashed down in our own bunks, passed out!" I caught my breath and spoke of "a reveille in the morning to write home about, except to mothers and girlfriends." I looked around to see if the old boys were still on course with me.

I started up again. "Reveille at the ass-crack of dawn came up on a holiday routine. Only a few chow hounds hit the deck. There was a scrambling among the racks, a rattling of supporting chains. A few locker doors got banged open, some chatter broke through the clatter. I heard a guy say he'd been dreaming of lying next to a woman! Another voice thanked God he wasn't bunking next to him! Another voice was complaining about a stranger in an inside rack by the peacoat locker, probably a drunk who landed in the wrong compartment. Another voice announced that the stranger was sleeping in dress blues, hat and all, lying on canvas, no mattress. The talk started getting to me. There really was a woman in our compartment! My night-on- the-town came to light as I opened both eyes!"

"You sure came aboard with a great Italian souvenir," a man at the bar thought, raising his glass to me.

"I came out of the rack like a shot," I continued my story, "as fast as the words flew out of my mouth. *Don't touch the kid! He's a buddy from the fourth division, got crocked with me last night in Genoa!* I could see at a glance that my female contraband was wide-eyed awake, uniform askew, neckerchief undone, hair starting to escape from the white hat. I told the guys to stand easy and let me handle it. One of the boys standing flatfooted on the polished steel deck looked over his freckled shoulder and told me to shut my bloodshot eyes before I bled to death."

"Didn't those boys know what a woman looks like?" someone wondered out loud.

"They got the idea soon enough, when a sock came off and painted toenails showed up. One of the kids said this was the best treat since Spanish oranges got procured in Majorca!"

"You ever get to jump the old girl?" the parachute rigger wondered as he sucked noisily at his whiskey.

"Jump without a parachute?" I asked him with a laugh. "We had to think of a safe place to land her first."

"Thinking with your dicks, you were," Dutch said. "Think you could ever get her to pass muster?"

"We just wanted to hide her until we could come up with something."

"Didn't she want to get right down to business, take on the crew?"

"She was jittery as a virgin," I said.

"Who wouldn't be scared of all you bare-assed uglies?"

"We were desperate to find a place to stow the female baggage," I kept up. "Overhead pipes were insulated with asbestos but she might take a fall. Division laundry bag would be a good coverup but men were all day dumping gear in it. We cleared out a space in the peacoat locker, stowed her in there." I had to catch my breath, line up the next move of my story.

"We had to make her look like a sailor," I got on with it, "had plenty of gear for any uniform of the day, but needed to cut her hair. My buddy, Enzo, took off for the barber shop. Freckle-face went for a bedpan in Sick Bay. I picked up some chow for the female and got in the peacoat locker with her before the whole compartment came to life."

"You always got yourself in the good duty section," Big Six interrupted.

"Only had room in the peacoat locker to play around with words," I talked back. "Me and the female were smothered by all the peacoats hanging down, and we were still a little hung over ourselves."

"Did the female have a name?" Big Six wanted to know.

"Francesca," I supplied. "Loved that name, always kept it in the back of my mind for a daughter's name. Got me a Francesca, after the Navy!"

"Francesca's the name of an Italian painter," our yeoman-high school teacher instructed us, "a Renaissance artist, I think, known for his altarpieces."

"My Francesca wouldn't be good at altars," I said.

"My sister-in-law's an Italian war bride," Big Six took over again. "Italian women make good wives, set a man up like a prince." He went on to tell about his older brother in the Italian campaign of World War II. He found his wife-to-be "back of the front," when he was on "rest and recreation." He came back to claim her after the war.

Before I could get back to my story, Big Six wanted to know if Francesca could have come from Tuscany, be related to his sister-in-law. He seemed to think all Italians were related.

I only knew she came from a village liberated by GI's. She got candy bars from American soldiers, and a few words of English.

"My Dogface of a brother might have tossed her a Hershey," Big Six said.

"You think I missed out on a sweet Italian wife?" I asked, sarcasm in my voice.

"We miss out on a lot of life," Big Six said, "if we're not ready for it. I missed out on most of Big Bro's doings in the war, never bothered to ask. Was just a school kid, hated history, didn't care about the history Big Bro was making."

"History's a story school kids are too young to fit in with," our yeoman-teacher thought. "I had to force feed tenth-graders."

"Big Bro fed me on the *Gothic Line,* below Bologna where the sausages come from. He was stuck there in the same foxhole and same underwear for months. He said war is more exhaustion than fear. How 'bout that? His job was cutting through minefields! Now you got to admit that sneaking men through a minefield is a better story than sneaking a woman through an aircraft carrier."

Everyone around the bar nodded up and down, as did the barroom.

"Big Six has it right," I managed to steady myself and break back in, "my female contraband wasn't a land mine. She was a hang-fire! We didn't know when the explosion would come?"

"When did it?""

"Well, our ship pulled out before dawn, dropped anchor in the stream! We had a woman stranded on board, and one of our deck apes stranded on the beach, and a sea way between."

"You should have thought of dumping your hang-fire on the garbage scow," Sea Dog suggested, "and she'd get towed back to land with all the refuse."

"Before we could come up with a getaway plan like that," I said, "our woman got away! We couldn't find her anywhere, checked fore and aft, gave every sailor a second look. That's the end of her, and my story, except for the lover stranded on the beach. He made the next liberty boat, said he was a favorite with the girls at the hotel, got packed off to the fleet landing in leftover sailor duds. No court-martial, only a night in the brig for him, and a lot of restriction."

"You let us down too fast," the parachute rigger complained.

"You think she jumped overboard?"

"Well, I can let you in on a little scuttlebutt," I said. "At chow one day, I got talking with the boatkeeper of the captain's gig. He threw me a line about standing watch in the cockpit one night when a sailor tried to get down the Jacob's ladder."

"Jacob's ladder is a rope ladder," Sea Dog explained to the airmen.

"Well, the sailor on the ladder got messed up in the footings," I continued, "and the boatkeeper said he held out a bow hook to steady the old boy, but he wasn't a boy at all, or a sailor! Boatkeeper said he'd hooked a mermaid with bellbottoms! He gave me a wink and a poke. Some fish! He carried on about the cushions in the gig's cabin, and riding the "mysterious sea creature" all the way back to shore. The coxswain, engineer, and steersman all enjoyed the ride, he added, saying I could believe him or not. I believed him. I guess our female contraband made it back to the beach in style, in the Captain's gig."

"Well, we finally got a little sex out of your story," someone sighed.

"The story wasn't about sex," I said, "it was about beating the system, flying under the radar."

"Wish fulfillment," Big Six insisted, "a story made-up like a bunk that won't pass inspection."

"I may have squared away some of the corners," I admitted, "but there really was a Francesca in Genoa, and I really had a mind to smuggle her aboard."

"You men aren't going to believe this one," our yeoman-teacher came up with a concluding thought, "but think about it. The greatest things in life are in the mind."

THE ANGEL CONNECTION

"CHICO THE FOOT Fool!" The name sounded out in the Miami hotel lounge where my old naval air squadron's reunion had gotten off to a flying start "Chico the Foot Fool!" It came to me as I was passing through the high-vaulted hotel lounge. Drink in hand, I came to a halt, held up amid the potted palms and stuffed chairs, took a gulp of whisky, and memory. Chico was the name sailors hung on the Cuban shoeshine boy who worked our barracks at Guantanamo Bay. He was a shoeshine boy without shoes, toes bulging out of canvas sneakers, big feet.

"Chico the Foot Fool!" His name was really "Angel," a name that didn't fly in a den of airmen. They dubbed him "Chico," added the "Foot Fool"because he polished the empty air with rag and brush, danced the mambo on one foot and then the other, sang off key. He'd mimic and ridicule our officers, crack us up with splintered English. He acted the fool, but was no fool. He only wanted to catch our attention.

He caught my friendship, got me in correspondence with "Madeleine," a convent girl on the Cuban side of Guantanamo Bay. Angel was the messenger who carried our letters back and forth between the naval base and Cuba, carried our love back and forth between two worlds.

"Chico the Foot Fool!" The name was ringing out of a corner in the lounge. Some squadron mates had "fallen in" around the lounge piano. Standing at attention, presenting beer mugs, they seemed about to perform a manual of arms, but toasted our shoeshine boy instead, sang his song. "You are my sunshine, I am your shoeshine, your only shoeshine!"

That song used to announce his arrival in the barracks. One time he didn't show up, must have missed the ferry from Cuba. We finally got word he'd stripped down naked in a public street of Caimanera, folded his clothes, emptied a can of stove-gas over his head, struck a match!

"You are my sunshine, I am your shoeshine, your only shoeshine," and the song hung up in the air, died down. The old sailors at the piano sighted me, hailed me over, wanted me to "come alongside and drop anchor." We'd been savoring salty jargon all day, as if the words would talk us back to our young sailor days.

"Remember the Foot Fool?" the man playing the piano asked, looking up at me with a cigarette dangling at his lip. He was "Woogie" Woods, still known by the "Woogie" laid on him in the Navy. "Woogie" had gone from our squadron runways to radio airwaves, from barrack ballads to Bach and

Bebop on radio's *Boogie with Woogie.* He'd gone up in the world but down in looks. The old boy didn't resemble the aviation mechanic I remembered. His body used to be lean and rangy, clean cut and crew cut, but the old piano player wasn't "regulation" anymore. Grizzled and prickly, half-shaved, he wouldn't pass inspection. His straggly mustache and ponytail would have gotten him a Captain's Mast, and "restriction to base." I wondered what kind of old man would wear his hair in a ponytail as I acknowledged my memory of the "Foot Fool."

Woogie asked if I remembered the "bootblack's last *shine?*"

"There was more to our shoe-shiner than his finish," I said, trying not to think of his flaming image In a flash I remembered when news of him going down in flames blazed around the barracks! There was no official word, only the say-so of Cuban base-workers, but no one questioned the word, or wanted another. Going down in flames was not a pretty picture for airmen. Even I shuddered a little when *lighting* a candle for him at chapel.

"The foot fool was a foot *fuel*," Woogie said, spelling out "fuel," letter by letter to the notes of the shoeshine song.

"Foot Fuel" brought back to mind the wave of wisecracks that swept over the barracks after the initial shock died down! I remembered:

"The shoeshine boy really polished himself off!"

"Foot Fool sure gave himself the hot foot!"

135

A thousand quips were launched in his name, all sailing across the counter in the Personnel Office where I was striking for yeoman.

"Why didn't he kill himself like a normal man?"

"If he wanted to get rid of himself, why didn't he drink himself to death?"

"Why didn't he get himself strangled between a woman's legs?"

I know that the men were trying to release tension, but I didn't know why I remembered their words.

"Why'd the Foot Fool pull a dumb trick like that?" the man at the piano was now asking me in a breath of smoke.

"God knows" was all I could answer. Glancing around the piano I saw the old boys checking me out. They used to look down on me, called me "Roy Boy!" Now they were looking up. I was taller than most, but the men seemed to think I'd become more than a man. I'd gone from military orders to holy orders! They were looking to me as a priest, but the priesthood didn't invest me with higher powers. I had no idea what got into the bootblack's head, why he gave the order for his own execution. What Inquisition of the Mind sentenced him to the stake? One day he was making light of himself, the next day an ash. "God knows," I said, always wondering about that myself. He burned my bridge to Madeleine. No messenger, no messages. I never got another word from my convent girl, couldn't even find her in Cuba, or anyone who admitted knowing her. It was as if she'd never been.

"God knows," I repeated, still wondering myself.

"God knows the Foot Fool went from one fire to another," a man at the far end of the piano sounded out. It was Billie Lighty, the only African-American in our outfit. We'd dubbed him "Black Bill" but considered him "one of us." He still was, but he'd gone from "cool" to "fire and brimstone." When he showed up at the reunion he called himself the "Reverend Lighty," and began selling his religion as "fire insurance!"

I was remembering his gift for hypnotism. He practiced on us, played tricks with our minds. He could put a man out and make him wake up on his own for the midwatch. He could put a man out and make him remember little details of his past. We used to think Black Bill was into "black magic," but he said hypnotism was only suggestion. Now he was suggesting that our shoeshine boy was condemned to Hell's fire.

"You can't hypnotize us into your religion," one of the squadron mates around the piano brought up.

"Why's it a hell-fire sin to kill yourself?" the grizzly piano player wanted to know, plunking at a single piano key. He mouthed his words with the cigarette stuck loosely to his lower lip.

"It's in the Good Book!"

"Our Chico snuffed himself out in the prime of flaming youth," Woogie talked back, cigarette in mouth, "didn't have to take a drag on the butt-end of life!"

Woogie didn't have to remind us we were getting down to the last pack in our lifetime of breaths! The slim bodies that used to man our squadron were now sagging out of shape.

"Not much fire in my engine room, but I keep cleaning my pipes," one of the men on the other side of the piano said.

"My butt ain't ready for the ashtray," another man spoke up.

Woogie started playing *Smoke Gets in Your Eyes*, squinted through his own smoke as he played and crooned "when a lovely flame dies, smoke gets in your eyes."

My own eyes started burning with the pain of my Cuban love that got away. My Madeleine seemed to have gone up in smoke, like the shoeshine boy.

Woogie kept the old song going, his ponytail keeping time like a metronome.

My thoughts of Madeleine kept running back and forth with the music.

"This hoary piece has more age on it than me," Woogie said, striking a final note, "but music never gets old and feeble." He adjusted himself at the piano. "Music never loses its tone or heart beat." He looked at me, asked why God didn't make us like music, sound in mind and body all our lives?

"Aging is God's way of mellowing us," I suspected, thinking about the new-found comradery with my old shipmates. The men used to snarl and snap at each other in the barracks, growl like caged animals, curse the Navy and everyone in it. Now they seemed congenial, connected.

"Now hear this," Black Bill sounded off from the far side of the piano. "You want to know why we age and die? It's the sin of Adam! Are you boys ready for the big Inspection in the Sky? Judgment Day?"

"Shoeshine my soul past God," Woogie started to sing, drowning out the man who was putting our minds on edge. "Shoeshine my soul past God," he sang again, "shine-up my feet of clay, buff dirty deeds away." His fingers remembered most of the music he'd written for our shoeshine sessions for Captain's inspection. Our fate was in the Captain's hands.

"That old piece of ragtime was for shining shoes," Woogie reminded us, "the times we worked for hours on a spit shine. Our shoeshine boy could work up a good shine, but not good enough for inspections. He could work up a good shine, but not good English. He thought my song called for shining the bottoms of our shoes," and he spelled the word, "sole."

"Listen up!" Black Bill raised his voice over the laughter going around the piano. "Spit and polish won't shine us past the Lord Almighty!"

"We're all spit," I said, "and dust."

"Down to the ash," Woogie said, dusting off his cigarette with one hand, playing *Smoke gets in your eyes*, with the other.

The airmen were starting to take off for other destinations.

■■■ ■■■ ■■■

With what was left of my drink, and memories, I let myself down in a leather chair by the piano, settled into my thoughts of Madeleine. I was barely aware of Woogie still toying at the keyboard or Black Bill letting himself down next to me.

"What got you in the collar?" Black Bill asked.

"I wasn't made for the Navy," I said, "or for the world, always felt out of place, closer to God than men, or women."

"God wants us all together, one people," Black Bill Lighty came back at me, "united as brothers!"

"What got you into religion?" I asked, thinking he still looked young, not a wrinkle in his smooth polished mahogany face.

"I got born again," he said with hardly a movement of his lips, "got to know my Lord Jesus was born lowdown, like me, and got put down, like me, didn't get treated equal, like me."

"Weren't you treated equal in the Navy?" I asked Integration was new in the Navy when the Korean War started, but got accepted like everything else when the civilian was stamped out of us in boot camp. I remembered Black Bill drawing attention to race, saying his "kind" got born in the dark, my "kind" in the light, but day and night made the world go round.

"Were any of us treated equal in the Navy?" Woogie interrupted, still reaching for tunes with his fingers. "We were enlisted men, for God's sake, as lowdown as a man gets."

"Not as low as a man's feet," I said, tapping my foot, "or as low as the bootblack."

"The bootblack wasn't as low as me," Black Bill spoke up. "You white boys weren't born enlisted men, with no way up, or out."

"What brought the lowly bootblack up for a toast?" I asked, trying to change the subject.

"We had enough thirst to toast everybody," Woogie answered, starting to run a musical scale up and down the keyboard. "We got around to everybody from top down, top brass to the shoeshine boy. Couldn't forget to toast the kid who made toast of himself?"

"What made a pretty white boy do a fool thing like that?" Black Bill wondered.

"Maybe he got bewitched, bothered, and bewildered," Woogie suggested with a Rogers and Hart tune at his fingertips, "or maybe some Cuban voodoo did something to him," and he picked at a Cole Porter melody.

"Who knows what made him kill himself?" I broke in. "We never knew much about the Cuban side of our shoeshine boy, only knew the side he showed us."

"The kid sure was light-skinned for a Cuban," Black Bill remembered.

"He claimed his keel was laid down by an American sailor," I mentioned, picturing the shoeshine boy blonde by nature, bronzed by sun, dazzling gold in memory. I used to think he was a better catch for Madeleine than myself.

"What really made that white boy put a match to his pretty white body?" Black Bill kept wondering, rolling his eyes up to Woogie's cigarette smoke curling toward the high ceiling.

"He didn't like the hand he was dealt,"Woogie answered, "cashed in his chips."

"Why take himself out in *fire?*" I asked, still uncomfortable at the thought

"God knows that, too," Woogie came back at me, picking out a new melody.

"Maybe I can do a hot number on him, and a hot mamma who probably made him flame out."

"If you're going to polish off another song about the bootblack," I said, "let's get his name right. He was Angel, not Chico!"

"No Angel to me," Black Bill shook his head. "No Angel prances around the barracks like some organ grinder's monkey and looks for handouts."

"You Evangelicals don't take a shine to angels," I kept smiling. "Maybe Angel didn't take a shine to you?"

"Re-buffed by the shoeshine boy," Woogie leaped to another lyric. He put both hands together to produce a solemn chord.

"No more foot foolin' around," Black Bill said. "Give him a rest."

"How about my *Gitmo Indigo?*" Woogie asked. He began stringing notes together that mixed New Orleans blues and Cuban rhythms. "Far out," he gasped, striking sounds of dissonance.

"Puts me in tune with the universe," I mused, beginning to ride the waves of *Gitmo Indigo* into blank space.

"The universe is out of tune with us," Woogie talked back. "Universe doesn't care about you, or me. *Gitmo Indigo's* about caring, and loving, getting cut off from home love, disconnected, marooned on the island *Gitmo*."

"Getting connected," Black Bill leaped to thought, "that's what the Gospel wants." He began tapping his foot to Woogie's music. "It's got that Cuban beat, the sound and silence, sound and silence."

"That's the separation I'm talking about," Woogie smiled, "sound separated from sound." He bent over the keyboard, ponytail keeping time, back and forth. "Our Padre wouldn't know about the beat of separation. Padre wouldn't know about wanting to be with a gal back home so bad it hurts. Padre wouldn't even know what it's like to be separated from God." Woogie's face was going vacant, his ponytail going limp, his liveliness draining down to fingertips.

"Maybe I do know about being cut off from love!" I spoke up, trying to get in tune with my old squadron mates.

"You priests got to be cut off from love," Black Bill insisted.

"When I was one of you sailors," I surprised myself with my own words, "I'd have given my soul for the body of a Cuban girl!"

Woogie's hands went up from the piano! "Que passa, Padre?"

"I was cut off from the love of a convent girl in Guantanamo City!"

"Give us the word," Black Bill gasped. He bent forward, cocked an ear in my direction.

"Love is beyond words," I said, even as I realized my love had only been made in words.

Woogie shook his head, turned a glass ashtray upside down, held it up. "Let me look in my crystal ball" he said, "I see a crack in Paradise, a couple of bare butts crushed together." He returned his crystal ball to an ashtray on the piano.

"You saw the ashes of love," I said, smiling at his play of psychic. "I only knew the girl through letters and I made ashes of them before taking vows."

"She was only a paper doll," Woogie sang out, another melody at his fingertips.

"Didn't the word ever become flesh?" Black Bill wondered, settling back in his easy chair and crossing his legs.

"You want to hear a priest's Confession?" I asked. I seemed to be hearing my own confession, bringing up thoughts of Madeleine, and her letters. In one letter she said she loved me the way she loved God, from a distance. Another time she wrote that her letters were prayers to me. I was her lord on earth. Her letters gave me wings, made me think of the Scriptures as God's love letters to us!

"Paper doesn't make love," Woogie said, hovering over the piano keys, picking at *Gitmo Indigo*. His search for notes was like my quest for fragments of Madeleine's letters.

I came up with her school girl question. Why was English loaded with so many things in ships, like friends in ships, relations in ships? Were we in a court*ship*?

"How'd you ever get lined up with a nice Cuban girl?" Woogie interrupted my thoughts.

"There were nice girls in Cuba," Black Bill spoke up before I could put my story together. "You had to get out of the *District* in Caimanera. I found me some good girls of the colored persuasion, but the only way round them was with a wedding ring."

"I would have married her," I said to Black Bill. "Angel got me the name of a convent school girl," I said to Woogie. "She wanted to practice her schoolbook English on an American sailor."

"And you wanted to learn about women," Woogie thought as he watched his fingers look for more notes of *Gitmo Indigo*.

"Now it comes back to me, you and your love letters," Black Bill gave a kick to his crossed leg. "Got me a whiff of a perfumed writing paper that got whipped around the barracks, got me the taste of some juicy quotes."

I'd almost forgotten my torment in the barracks when one of my letters got ripped off. Getting private letters and thoughts thrown around the barracks was only part of my grief in the Navy. I remembered getting ridiculed for looking young and acting young and not knowing anything about women.

Madeleine's letters had begun to open the book on women for me, even though she was as foreign to love as myself. She'd never been with a boy without a chaperone. She only knew about schoolwork and copybooks, and her letters told the story of a life she planned to dedicate to the Church, or to some good man.

Both our life stories, it seemed, had been written by others. Her life was censored and edited by others, kept bound between the covers of a convent. My story was written by others, too, foster parents, teachers, naval officers.

"You can't make love with words," Woogie was talking straight through my reveries.

"How do you make love?" I asked, not wanting an answer.

"Love's not something we share with priests," Woogie said, hands starting to fly up and down the keyboard, ponytail flying round his back. *Gitmo Indigo* seemed to be coming to an end.

"Love is much deeper than the skin," I let him know, thinking of the "skin games" sailors talked about. I didn't know Madeleine the way sailors knew girls, but I knew her deep down, many skins deep. She dropped veil after veil, letter by letter, stripped herself down to the heart.

"I'm betting you never knew a woman skin deep," Woogie said, letting his voice penetrate the music pounding out of his hands.

"Are you looking in your crystal ball again?"

"I'm looking in my memory book, don't recollect you taking liberty over there in the fleshpots of Cuba."

"Your memory skipped a page," I said. "I hit the beach in Caimanera one time, got convoyed with all the other sailors to one of those *bars*." I confessed in a whisper that I thought I was in a USO and that Cuban girls were much more friendly than American. I got a laugh out of that, and laughed at myself, but the bar I remembered was nothing to laugh about. It was Hell. I still think Hell is a pleasure dome where the condemned have to pursue their favorite vice, like sex, for ever and ever.

"The boys in those bars wanted to lose themselves," Woogie said, still laughing at me, "just wanted to be one of the boys!"

"I lost myself over there," Black Bill had a word on the matter, "but got born again, and found myself, and got married."

"I wanted to get married to my Cuban girl," I said, "even made out the legal papers. Lieutenant Gordon didn't want to sign, but sent my request up the line with a disapproval."

"Wasn't that *Crash* Gordon?" Black Bill remembered. "Who could forget Crash Gordon?"

"He figured my Cuban girl was only looking for a free ride to the States," I said, nodding, "and a meal ticket."

"You sure would have a different life," Black Bill figured, "if your papers went through, and you were under a wife's orders, instead of Holy Orders!"

"I can't imagine that," I thought. "But I'd never have known God without knowing love."

"Why didn't you marry her, after you got out of the Navy?"

"I lost track of her, after my messenger burned himself out."

"Your Angel put the flame in your heart, then blew it out," Black Bill thought.

"I went looking for her," I found myself saying, "did the best I could with *poco* Spanish and clues. Madeleine wrote about feelings, not names and places."

"She should have let you have a *dear John*!" Woogie was looking over his shoulder at me as he talked and played out his *Gitmo Indigo*.

"A common sailor was too common for uppity folks in Cuba," Black Bill offered his opinion. "Any American sailor would be a catch for most Cubans, but not for the high and uppity. Cubans lived by a color line, too. White folks called me a *smoked Yankee*. Black gals a shade lighter than me wouldn't give me a second look."

"Bet her people shipped her out," Woogie said over his shoulder, "lay down a smokescreen so you couldn't find her."

"She came from landed aristocracy," I said, "the *latifundios*."

"A Romeo and Juliet story of forbidden love," Woogie was saying and trying to find music to go with it.

I was no Romeo, I thought to myself. More like Dante, I loved from afar. Once upon a time I wrote Madeleine about Dante's *Divine Comedy*, told her she was my "Beatrice," only to be loved at a distance, untouched, the unattainable ideal, like the Madonna! Her letter in reply thought our love was "divine," but not a comedy.

"You were star-crossed lovers," Woogie was saying, and finding the "love theme" from Tchaikovsky's *Romeo and Juliet Suite*.

"Her people married her off, or got her to a nunnery," Black Bill pronounced when Woogie's music died down. "All Cuban female-gals were put down as low as blacks. Women had no say about who they had to marry-up with."

"She got married off to someone of her class," Woogie thought, "or maybe got caught up in one of those revolutions over there. Our shoeshine boy might have lit himself off in protest!"

"That Chico fool wouldn't turn himself into a political sacrifice," Black Bill thought. "He was more into sin than politics. On weekends he peddled raw oysters to sailors living it up in the brothels, might have even peddled himself. Foot Fool would only be good for a burnt-sin offering."

"The word of God wasn't a lamp unto his feet," I admitted, "but he had religion, only thought the Church was too *politico*, and on the wrong side."

"Sorry, Padre," Black Bill said, "but your Church in Cuba *was* on the wrong side, backing up the Batista dictatorship."

"Batista was against Communism, must have had a little good in him!"

"All everyday folks were against Batista," Black Bill kept sputtering. "He may have been black like me, but sure wasn't my kind."

"Didn't Batista cut off our water a time or two?" Woogie tried to remember.

"He did that. Now Castro's got all of Cuba cut off," I had my say.

"I'd sure like to get back to that old Gitmo for a look-see," Black Bill reminisced, "get a little more of that Cuban sunshine and cha-cha-cha!"

We started fishing up *Gitmo* memories, caught things we did in the hangar, barracks, swimming pool. We reminded ourselves of the bowling league, and our baseball team. How could we have been bored? All except me remembered drinking at the club, poker in the barracks, and the price of a gallon of rum—one dollar! We all remembered counting the cost of things and the days we had left on our enlistments.

"Lucky we weren't there for the Missile Crisis," Woogie brought up, "that awful time our world came close to blowing up!" He started banging out some marching music.

"Atomic bombs would have made our world go up in smoke, like our shoeshine boy." Black Bill looked at me as he talked. "Too bad your Cuban love affair went up in smoke!"

Woogie's music marched us off in step with each other.

"Ever think your girl might be one of the Cuban exiles over here in Miami?" Woogie asked me, letting his music and ponytail slow down.

"I've made inquiries."

"What would you do if you found her?" Woogie asked, whipping his head around in my direction.

"It wouldn't change my life," I thought.

"She'd be old by now," Black Bill calculated, "all dried up like that Old Testament wineskin hanging in the smoke."

"She wouldn't be dried up to me," I said. "She's like music, always the same."

"Did you ever lay eyes on her?"

"One time, at the basilica in Guantanamo City," I said as my mind was looking back. "Angel set it up, a secret tryst in a side chapel named for her family." I stopped talking, looked for her in the shadows of my mind, shaded and veiled as I remembered, a moving picture in filmy sashes and scarves and shawl. A veil kept me from seeing very much of her. I wanted to part the veil some more, but she said a girl should keep a boy guessing!

She'd kept me guessing a lot of years.

"Did you put the moves on her?" Woogie wanted to know, sneaking a smile at me from over his shoulder.

"In Church? We only talked of marriage, and pretty soon Angel had to get her right back to the convent."

"Angel would be dried up by now," Black Bill was still thinking of the Biblical wineskin, "if he hadn't burned himself up."

"Time turns all things to ashes," I said, thinking of Madeleine's stack of letters getting burned up before I took vows and died to the world. The letters were a funeral pyre in my mind, but only the paper went up in smoke.

"Life's just one cigarette after another," Woogie was saying as he took the last puff on his cigarette.

"God be a consuming fire," Black Bill said, "Hebrews 13:29."

Woogie crushed out his cigarette in the crystal ashtray. "Time to fold our wings," he said, looking around. "We're the last of the airmen still up!"

"We sure took ourselves off on a long flight back." Black Bill thought as he stretched up to his feet "But we be leaving Roy Boy's mysteries up in the air."

"Ah, sweet mysteries of life," Woogie sang as he turned his back, and ponytail, on us.

"Life's an unfinished story," Black Bill said to me as he waved off, "to be continued tomorrow."

"Every unfinished story's a mystery," I said to myself, heading in my own separate direction. I'd never forget the mystery of Angel's death and Madeleine's disappearance. It's the unfinished stories that stick in memory!

MOON'S MADELEINE

SHOULD I TELL him the truth about Madeleine? She was the Cuban convent girl who got his balls in an uproar, left him hanging! He racked-out next to me in the barracks at Guantanamo Bay, probably still wonders what happened to that convent girl!

I'd just run into him in the Miami hotel where our old naval air squadron was homing in on a wing-ding of a reunion, our first get-together since the Korean War. The moment my eyes met his I could see in him a younger version. Memory guided my eyes back to his unfinished face of youth. His wet plaster shine of boyhood still showed through the hardened cast of his features, but I could see him bunking next to me in the sweaty naval barracks, still picture him stretched out in his skivvies, toes twitching, hands holding up a letter from that Cuban convent girl. I remembered her name, Madeleine. I couldn't remember his.

"Moon Mirabelli!" He remembered my name.

We clasped hands, and memories. I still couldn't shake his name out, just the image of him sacked-out next to me. We didn't work together, or hang out together, but he was in my face at reveille and taps, day after day, all those many days ago. Sometimes I'd hear his voice in the night, at prayers, murmuring the name of "Madeleine."

"Roy *Boy*," I said, his name popping out of my mouth. It came to me even though I could see he wasn't a boy anymore. Not much of the boy I remembered was showing through his face and white-streaked sideburns. I had my sights on a tall, well set-up figure of a man, snugly packaged in navy blue slacks and white turtle neck sweater, a silver cross at half mast between the lapels of his sport jacket.

"Roy *Boy*," I repeated. "You grew up!"

"It's about time," he said. "Life is a matter of time."

He hadn't been on the same time line as the rest of us in the squadron. Back then, he looked too young to be a sailor, and he never thought like the rest of us, never thought about women. He was as clueless about women as he was beardless. That's why I got him in correspondence with Madeleine, a convent girl on the other side of Guantanamo Bay. He only knew his half of the story. Should I tell him the other half?

It started out as a game to pass the time away. "Chico," the Cuban botblack who worked for shines in our barracks, let me know about a convent girl who was studying English and wanting to correspond with an American sailor. I figured a cloistered girl, on the Cuban side of Guantanamo Bay, was learning book English and book life, wouldn't know the difference between a man and a boy. The two of them were set up for each other.

Chico ran letters back and forth across Guantanamo Bay, got the letters in and out of Roy Boy's hands, in an out of the convent. I remember Chico's real name was "Angel," a good name for a messenger.

All along, Chico and I sneaked open his letters, got our laughs before licking them shut again. I volunteered to help Roy Boy spice his letters up with a pinch or two of passion. Chico worked on his English though the letters. I guess I was having fun, making fun of the kid. Reading thoughts hot off his mind, I was getting into a head that held no knowledge of women, or love, except love of God. I used to feel a little ashamed at reading his letters and mind.

Using Roy boy's letters for Chico's English lessons, I was getting into the Cuban boy's head, too, but it seems I never got myself into the dark corners of his mind. One day, he torched himself on a public street in Caimanera, made a flaming spectacle of himself! His light went out forever. No more Chico to put a shine on my shoes, or a shine on my face. Our fun with Roy Boy was over, and there were no more love letters delivered to the lovesick kid in the next bunk. I gave him a hand in search of the girl in Cuba. We got liberty together and found a cab driver in Caimanera who spoke English. We got driven all over Caimanera and Guantanamo City, skipped Santiago. I thought it would have been beyond Chico's reach. We checked all kinds of convent schools, no one admitting knowledge of Madeleine. She had disappeared!

A high born Cuban, she was probably hidden away when her correspondence with an American sailor was discovered. I warned Roy Boy not to try the police. They were corrupt, probably in the pay of Madeleine's family.

There was more to the story. Should I tell him the truth about Madeleine? He was telling me how good it was to see me, how good it was to remember the old times. I was hard pressed to remember any good times. I remembered hard work in the two-story hangar, open at both ends to catch a little breeze It was full of dead air, noise, and boredom. I was in a ground crew, keeping my hands busy and greasy. I had my own coffee cup in the line shack, my bunk in the barracks, not much else. I had a girl back home, not much else. I remember Navy time running so slowly. Every day was a rerun of the day before, same old flashback, over and over. Days ended where they began, in the white frame barracks, upper starboard compartment, lower bunk. That's where I opened my eyes at daybreak and closed them at night, where I eyeballed Roy Boy in the next bunk. Those days were as empty and rough as the coral and fossil shells that crunched under foot as I trudged back and forth between the barracks and the hangar.

"We were carefree in those days, " Roy Boy was coming through my wandering thoughts, "free as the breezes off the sea."

"Free, you figure our Navy days were free?"

"Carefree. No decisions, no worries. Our lives were planned and cared for."

"Yeah, but I wanted to plan my own life," I said. I was getting hypnotized by Roy Boy's silver cross swinging back and forth on his chest, like a pendulum, swinging my mind back and forth between past and present.

"We had a home, good food," Roy Boy kept on, "safe and sound, and a good place to lay our heads every night."

"We were bottom bunk buddies!" I reminded him, "only got a look at the bottom half of shipmates going back and forth to the showers, the ugly half."

"You sure are a pretty sight,"Roy Boy said, "top and bottom, but you turned into a *full* Moon! Still carry that name around?"

"It got hung on me," I said, "not because of my shape you know." I supposed he remembered my reputation for "mooning" Miami from the bay hatch of our flying boat, the PBY! That reminded me that this reunion was the first time I'd made it back in Miami since squadron "whiskey runs"out of Cuba, so long ago. I was thinking of doing the town again.

"A round moon was better than the skinny kid I used to be," he was saying. "This old boy couldn't cast a shadow."

I pictured him as a long-legged kid running around base in Navy khaki shorts the airmen called "whistle britches." I smiled at what I thought was my "short" memory. I recalled the Navy regulation that tropical shorts couldn't be worn any higher than two inches above the knee! I guessed there were only man's legs to whistle at Guantanamo Bay. I kept my stubby legs in dungarees, or bellbottoms.

"There wasn't much to me in those days," Roy Boy was remembering, not needing to remind me. I used to look at him as my mirror opposite. I was fire hydrant short and stocky, tattooed, tough-skinned. He was tall and skinny, tender and soft. I worked on the line, kept planes up. He worked in the office, kept paper records up. I was a man.

"Not much to me on the inside, either, back then," Roy Boy kept talking, almost to himself.

"We were at the shallow end of the pool, just getting in the swim of life," I reminded him, but thought to myself that he was way out of his depth in a sea of men, a real "square rigger!"

■■■ ■■■ ■■■

We'd run into each other at the doorway of the hotel's "Cabana Club" where the squadron's reception was warming up amid the artificial palms and flickering oil-lit torches. In the midst of men I didn't yet recognize, except for Roy Boy, I kept searching for a familiar face. My eyes were full of unfamiliar sailors who'd gotten heavy at the waterline. Some of them were cruising around the dance floor with their wives. Bangers and hitters were somewhere on piano, drum, and guitar. I led Roy Boy around the dance floor to the cash bar on the far side of the palm-thatched Cabana Club.

"*It's been a long, long time*," I said, naming the tune in the air, and Roy Boy agreed with the long time.

We got settled at the bar. I went for a ginger ale, with a twist, told Roy Boy my drinking days were on "the other side of the Moon."

"No more moonshine?" He asked with a smile. "That used to be the light of the world for you, if I remember right."

"Scuttled my liver," I said, "but here's cheers to you and the reunion,"and I raised my glass of ginger ale. "Down the hatch,"I said with a sip. I wasn't looking back anymore, only looking around the Cabana Club for some old drinking buddy.

"I'll bless our tongues," Roy Boy said, crossing himself before tasting his scotch. He drank almost down to the bottom of his glass, down to his deepest memories. He came up with the name of Madeleine, the girl "who plied me with letters, gave me a lifetime hangover."

"Madeleine?" I was afraid he'd ask about her. I rolled the name around on my tongue, with the ginger ale, as if to find the taste of her memory. "Madeleine's a French pastry," I said, moistening my lips again, "and a sweet name for a girl. Gave it to my first daughter, call her Maddy." I'd decided not to tell him the other half of his story.

"You can't have forgotten my Cuban Madeleine, the girl who got me high on love? You helped me with some of my letters."

"Think I remember you on a binge of letter writing," I admitted, "and a Cuban shoeshine boy slipping the letters back and forth across the Bay."

"The shoeshine boy went up in flames!"

I couldn't deny memory of that. "Ashes to ashes," I said, toasting him with my glass again. "Seems like your love turned to ashes, too."

"Love doesn't die," he said, swallowing his words back down with another scotch.

"You kept Madeleine's memory bottled-up inside, all these years?"

"Like fine spirits! Are you surprised that a priest keeps a girl's spirit on tap?"

"A priest!" I gasped, choking on my ginger ale "You, a priest?"

"I thought everybody knew," Roy Boy apologized. "I'm on the program for the banquet and memorial service. I'm a priest here in the Miami Archdiocese."

"Well, I'll be damned," I said, "and reckon I will be, but I'm putting you on report for being out of uniform! No dog collar, no black cassock." I was now feeling out of uniform myself, all exposed, sins hanging out. I hadn't been to confession in half a lifetime, wondered if it showed?

"I'm allowed a little liberty," the priest said, smiling, "and a civilian clothes pass."

"Can't figure you for a priest!" I knew he was full of faith, made of different stuff, but not cut out for the cloth.

"It was easy to take off the military uniform, put on the armor of God," he said, nodding over his drink. "I took off the old self, put on the new."

"Are you here in your old Roy Boy self, or do I have to call you *Father*?"

"I'm here in the old self, the Roy that Madeleine said meant *king* in her language."

"You always were above everybody," I said, thinking he'd been set apart, separate from others. Men stood clear of him. "In our Navy days, we lived a common life," I continued, trying to be friendly, "but you were always uncommon."

"Shipmates gave me a wide berth," he said.

"You were different," I explained, rolling my glass of ginger ale in my palms, "kept yourself in line, lived up to regulations, and your morals!"

"I guess I was avoided, like a conscience."

"You made our consciences hurt," I agreed, "but we took our anger out on you instead of ourselves. We were really mad at the Navy, mad about getting called up for a war nobody called a war. We were lucky we weren't getting shot at, but angered at the boredom, and inconvenience of it all."

"I never resented the Navy," he said, "only some of the men in it."

"Maybe you were a born priest."

"Not a born sailor, that's for sure," he smiled. "I didn't even know how to go with the tide, or goof-off."

That reminded me of my hand in trying to break him into Navy life, initiate him into the ranks of men. I went along with those who'd steal some of his gear and get him put on report for "gear adrift" at inspections. I even handed him false scuttlebutt, told him our war in Korea was going to break out in Indochina and extend his enlistment. Once, I put him on a mailing list, got him snowed with junk mail. Maybe I felt sorry for the kid? He never got a letter from home.

"You always had a good word for me," he said.

I wondered why our memories were different?

"Well, we were bottom bunk buddies, shared a common view," I laughed. Inside, I couldn't remember a good word I ever had for him. He was beneath me. I did a man's job in the grease pits, he shuffled papers in the personnel office. He kept to himself, never got bent out of shape in bars, never got laid in a Cuban brothel. Maybe I disliked him because I envied his clean yeoman hands, and clean life?

"You always had a good word for me," he said again, "good words to put in my letters to Madeleine."

"I was good at hooking girls with words," I remembered, "had a string of girls back home jumping on the end of my line, but couldn't hold 'em." I was too short and bulky to land any of those fish in the sea, not until I found a girl who liked words. My wife hadn't come to the reunion with me, stayed back home to help out with the grand kids.

"You sure jump-started my love life."

I could hardly believe I was hearing that from a priest. "Guess I was a good *tool* man," I laughed, "mechanic, that is."

We laughed together, but I wasn't laughing inside. I was sorry for ever getting him started with Madeleine, all those years ago. After the Navy, I put that story on the shelf. Should I tell him I'd opened his letters, read his mind? I remembered his letter of explanation to Madeleine's question about the meaning of "*making* a woman." It was common "sailor talk," but he thought only God could "make" a woman!

Chico and me read Madeleine's letters, too. She wrote about being "only a schoolgirl yet," wanting to study love with him. I wished I could have gotten a letter like that.

Once she wrote that he was her "secret love," like the American song on the radio "Hit Parade," and said it wasn't easy to get her secret love past the Sisters. In one of her letters she said she wanted to be joined to the body of Jesus, but to his body as well! She wrote things that would give any of us bluejackets a case of blue balls!

One time she sent him a black and white snapshot. She looked like a pretty American girl in floppy sweater and skirt. He asked about the color of her eyes, and she claimed her eyes were deep blue. I told him to write that she had "sea eyes," the color of the sea, the eyes a sailor would want to be *in*! I guess I did give him a good word or two. She wrote back that everyone could "sea" with eyes, but she could "sea" him with her heart.

Getting a look at those letters was like a shot at someone's cards in a poker game. It gave me the upper hand. One of her letters was a real "winner." She typed it, said she was learning the "touch" system in her typewriting class. She could touch the right keys without looking, and see him without looking. That's one of the letters he offered to show me. I told him to say her typewriter held the *keys* to his heart. I guess I did give him a lot of good words.

I remember his letters kept begging for a meeting. He wanted to see her, face to face. She wrote that it wasn't possible, until the end of her "cloistered" life. She was trapped in a convent with girls in blue uniforms, the way he was trapped in the Navy with boys in white uniforms. She prayed for the night they'd be pressed together, the way his letters were pressed under her pillow.

I got my kicks out of letters like that, and the shoeshine boy said he was improving his English at every reading. Chico was hoping to end up in America, instead of the ferry boat going back and forth to Cuba. I hated to think of the way he ended.

"Madeleine's letters saved me," the priest said while I was wondering why no one saved Chico.

"Those were hellish times," I said to the priest, "in that caged life we had on a lonely naval base. We all thought we served our time in Hell, would go straight to heaven when we died."

"*Gitmo* should have been Heaven on Earth," the priest thought. "We had everything we needed, a home, medical care, recreation, chapel, and heavenly weather. We had it all, and a well regulated, ordered life."

"Well *ordered*," I agreed.

"Why wasn't everybody happy?"

"Life's more than three slops and a flop a day."

"More than bread alone," the priest agreed, "but we were part of something bigger than ourselves. We belonged to a community!"

"But no unity in our comm*unity*," I threw back.

"And no communion in our community," he mused.

"We had care, but no loving care," I summed up.

"I grew up in foster care homes," he said, "found a home in the Navy, but no love until you got me in communion with Madeleine."

■■■ ■■■ ■■■

I'd decided not to tell him the truth about Madeleine! I tried to change the subject.

"My old lady couldn't make the reunion," I said, "had to take the grandmother watch." I was about to reach for my wallet and pull out snapshots, but Roy Boy looked away, got to mumbling something about Madeleine, and God. I decided to get him focused on God instead of my grandchildren.

"This old Moon is coming round to religion," I said, catching his attention.

"I think you always had a head for religion," he cast a look at me. "If memory serves, I caught you at your beads sometimes, and at chapel, and some weekend sessions at the Chaplain's Corner on base."

"I was raised Catholic, couldn't get out of the habit," I said, "but I always wondered why there was so much bad in a good God's Creation?"

"Why not wonder why there's so much good?"

"What makes you put your money on God?" I asked "What makes you bet on something you can't see?"

"Poker players bet against things they couldn't see. Airmen bet their lives on something they couldn't see, the air beneath their wings."

I liked his point, but said I hated flying, never had faith in it.

"Flying takes faith," he granted

"How do you get faith?"

"Are you asking me to put on my new self, the armor of God?'

"Your old self had faith. I heard you praying, lots of nights, back in the barracks."

"I don't remember when I didn't have faith, when I didn't think God was watching me."

"I wouldn't like that," I thought, "not some of the times."

"Not if you lived the way God intended."

"Did God make us up, plot all the things that would happen to us?"

"God's the author."

"Why so many sad stories?"

"Life's a mystery story," he squeezed at his glass as he seemed to be looking within. "We haven't gotten to the end. God keeps us waiting. In the end, Madeleine's mystery story will be solved."

"You ought to forget her," I said. "Memory can't change the past, and memory doesn't always get the past right anyway."

"There's redemption in remembrance," he said, holding up his glass with both hands, like a chalice.

"You only had her words to remember."

"One time we got off the written page," he was saying, putting down the cup and raising the silver cross to his lips. "One time," he said, as if in prayer, "we came face to face in her family's chapel at the basilica in Guantanamo City."

"Think it's coming back to me," I remembered. "You fussed a lot about the way you looked, got a good spit shine up on your shoes, put on your inspection whites."

"She appeared as a shadow in lace and veil, in a hallowed space, and we touched, and breathed the same air."

"Without a chaperone a Cuban girl doesn't know how to say no," I remindered. "Did you make a move?"

"In Church? God was our chaperone. She wanted to hug me. I asked her to marry me first. As soon as I got back to base I got the paperwork started, all the official forms for permission to marry a foreign national."

"I knew it wouldn't work," I said, remembering how I couldn't stop him. He worked in the personnel office, knew all the regulations, but I knew it wouldn't work out!

"Our marriage wasn't in God's plan," he agreed with me, taking a last sip.

"You think God's got a flight plan for us?" I asked. "Seems like we just get catapulted into life, get left to hang glide?"

My old shipmate wasn't listening. He was mouthing Madeleine's name, and asking himself why she got spirited away.

"Maybe she *was* a spirit," I said, picking up on his mumbled words. "She left no footprints, like a spirit. You should leave her behind, give her spirit a rest."

"Leave her where? Where you think she is, after all this time?"

"Maybe she got tired of dedicating letters to you and dedicated herself to God, got herself to a nunnery?"

"I'd like to believe that, but sometimes I think her family disowned her, put her in the streets, let her end up in one of those Cuban bars."

"'God wouldn't write her off like that," I said, getting close to telling him the other half of the story.

"Her letters weren't the Holy Word," he said. "She wasn't my religion, not my God, but she was my way to God, the love way!"

"So, maybe there never was a Madeleine," I said. "Maybe you made her up, made her up the way you wanted her to be? Maybe she's just a fiction of your imagination!"

I knew she was the fiction of *my* imagination, a creation of my boredom! I was his Madeleine, the love of his life!

DAUGHTER OF THE SQUADRON

I CAME A long way to get a look at my first love, the first look since I was a swabby in the Navy, a reluctant volunteer when the war in Korea tore a hunk out of my life. The first look I had of my first love was in a naval air squadron hung up at Guantanamo Bay, way out in the faraway Caribbean. I was an airman apprentice striking for machinist's mate, and a journeyman third baseman swinging for hits on the squadron's baseball team, the "Flyers." The best hit I made was with that girl at the base dependents' school. A Navy brat, she was the daughter of my commanding officer, the "daughter of the squadron." It was me, a lowly airman she took up with, and it was the Old Man of the squadron who shot me down.

A love that's lost stays up in the clouds. I'd just come a long way to bring that love down to earth. The beloved of my memory was scheduled to speak for her father, our commanding officer, at our squadron's first reunion. I'd get to see how well she'd weathered the course of life.

Winged recollections of a flighty girl, feisty and frolicsome, came flying back, wing to wing with the starched sailor in whites I used to be. Memory was touching me down on the runway beside the sparkling blue of Guantanamo Bay, running me into my naval past and the love of a flighty girl. She was a sleek little craft, giddy as she went, playful from curls and headband to bobbysocks and white bucks. She teased me, poked fun at me, jabbed me in the ribs! She would pinch-up her mouth, twitch it like a rabbit, hop up and down like a rabbit. "*Bunny* Claire," I dubbed her. To everyone else she was "Claire of Naval Air, daughter of the squadron." She was Bunny Claire to me.

Porcelain smooth and doll-faced, she was one part child and two parts woman in a tight sweater. In-between child and woman, she was in-between me and my commanding officer! I wasn't good enough for the daughter of the squadron. As soon as he got wind that his daughter was going overboard for a common sailor, he got my orders cut, and all but my heart shipped out. Before I could get my bearings I was on a baby carrier headed for the war between North and South Korea. Like Korea, I was divided, cut off from my first love.

It's said that a sailor's first ship is like his first love, unforgettable, but my first ship took me away from my first love. Old memories whirled round me like a tropical depression, sucked me down to the lowest level of my life, that empty time I was stranded at sea, cut off from land and love, unable to get word to Bunny Claire. My letters came back, stamped *return to sender.* Even after I was out of the Navy, there was no way to get through to a naval officer's daughter who was no longer at the Guantanamo Bay dependents' school, and there was no Internet to help me track her out of thin air.

After all these years, my squadron's reunion is going to bring us back together. I was about to see what she'd done with her life! She used to talk about getting into nursing or teaching, or *marriage.* It seems that was all a girl could do back then. She talked about going to college, joked about majoring in "boys." It was her favorite and weakest subject. She only had two boys in her senior class at the naval base school, and "the Old Man" kept her away from sailors, away from the hangar and inspections and squadron parties. She only got liberty for chapel services, outdoor movies, horseback riding, and baseball games. Baseball's how I hit it off with her. Good hands at third base got me on the squadron's baseball team, and that's how I caught her eye.

Now, all these years later, I'd be catching her eye again. There was more of me to catch. I'd taken on ballast, like all the shipmates waiting with me for the hotel banquet hall to open up. We were looking ahead to the reunion banquet and program, but I was mostly looking back, looking over my shoulder for traces of Bunny Claire. Back came the time I pulled duty as the Old Man's driver, chauffeured him around, got to see where he was billeted, way out on the far side of the base, out by the sea cliffs, in a frame bungalow on piles, under a canopy of palm trees.

It was common knowledge our Old Man was the father of "Claire of Naval Air," but uncommon for anyone to see her. Our commanding officer looked so good in khaki shorts he was expected to have a good looking daughter, but I found her a sight better than anyone imagined. When I drove the Old Man home for the first time, his daughter came jumping off the porch, curls and sweater bouncing. She knew me, had seen me play third base. Right off the bat she knew my batting average, squared herself off and imitated my stance at the plate, said I needed to get closer, take a shorter swing. She kept a score card on all the "Flyers," knew my weight, height, age, and where I was born, Brooklyn! She let me know she followed "dem Brooklyn bums" on the Armed Forces Radio.

She'd struck me out with glances that caught the corners of my eye. After seeing her at home, I started seeing her from home plate when I looked up at the stands. She would be waving at me. She began to meet me after the games, game after game. One time she asked me to join her at the riding stables, next to the Marine barracks. A Brooklyn boy, I'd never mounted a horse, never wanted to, but I'd do anything for the Old Man's daughter. I must have held on to that horse as hard as I was now holding on to Bunny Claire's memory. We were happy as colts the time we trotted our horses up and down the hills and looked over the base to the distant blue mountains of Cuba. We thought our horses, and bodies, would carry us on forever.

As I waited for the diningroom doors to open I started warming up pitches, the things I could serve up to her. She might like to be reminded of her rabbit imitations, and her "rabbit" punches. She'd want to remember us winging around the naval air station and the recreation center, the swimming pool where we dipped and dove, the roller skating rink where we glided around and around in the hot Cuban air, and my ball games and the outdoor movies in the cool of the night. I was still working on the right "pitch" when the diningroom doors opened. Squadron mates and wives started moving forward, easing me along with them.

The banquet hall was crystal bright. I'd soon be feasting on Bunny Claire in the flesh instead of the mind. What would the friend of my youth say to me? She might remember things I'd forgotten about myself. I could hardly wait to run around the bases with her again.

Looking for Bunny Claire in the dining hall, I could only find memories of her cheering me at the baseball park, waiting for me after my shower. I'd convoy her around the base for ice cream, movies and popcorn. Saturdays were for horseback riding, or roller skating, or swimming at the air station pool. Sunday mornings were for Divine Services at the Naval Base Chapel. We shared the same prayers, but I wasn't allowed to sit up front with the Old Man's family. I had a religious experience just seeing my girl in her Sunday dress. We got together at the social hour after chapel service, sat together with body parts touching, and I would daydream of sharing the same space with her, in bed at night.

When her old man first got word about the two of us flying around together, he commanded his daughter to ease off, got word to my line chief, and the *Flyers'* manager, to get me to lay off. After that, I had to steal around base with Bunny Claire. I got myself wheels, a run-down motorcycle that had served several tours of duty with other sailors. I picked up Bunny Claire at appointed places, spun her around the edges of the base. She loved the way I leaned into the curves of the road, and into her curves! She loved to hold on to me and scream as the wheels spewed up dirt and gravel. We motored way out to the fenced-off wastelands on the Cuban border, and to the coral cliffs on the seaside. One time the ignition lead broke on my motorcycle, stranded us way out! I daydreamed of being alone on a desert island with her, but finally managed to splice the wires, get us back on the roll.

We sandwiched picnics between Saturday horse-back riding and swimming, hunted for hideouts. One time we scared-up a big horny iguana, scared all three of us! One time during the week, I had time off after a night shift, and Bunny Claire played hooky. We slipped off to the deserted Windmill Beach, at the far end of the naval reservation, out to a shore line stretched beneath the ledge of a cliff. Shyly, we stripped to skivvies, kept our shoes on to get us past the sharp coral in the shallows. Quickly we hid our bodies in the deeper waters, joined schools of darting yellow fish. Bunny Claire was afraid of seeing a moray eel or a sand shark, and mostly afraid I'd see too much of her. She wanted to surprise me on our wedding night. Neither of us ever found out how much we were missing!

I was wishing I'd seen more of Bunny Claire, the more I looked for her in the hotel banquet hall. She wasn't at the head table, not anywhere. I could only see her in the back of my mind, snuggling with me in the dark of outdoor movies. The movies were beside the bay where standing lights of ships riding at anchor were reflected like stars. Ship lights and stars sometimes took our eyes off the moving pictures on the screen. Those flickering memories now seem as far away as stars.

Bunny Claire was to be a star speaker at the banquet, I was thinking, but she was nowhere to be found. I couldn't even find my assigned table, number *fifty-two*. The fifty-second year of the Twentieth Century was the year of my birth in the Navy, the year I cut the cord to my life in Flatbush and began to see the world in the Navy. It was in that fifty-second year I found and lost my love. I finally found table *fifty-two*.

"Jack Zais," I introduced myself to the couple already at the table, spelled my last name because it was pronounced "Sass," and didn't fit well with Jack. The man at the table I didn't recognize, but I envied him for keeping his hair, and shape. The woman beside him had kept a really good shape.

"We're the Truetts," the wife said, smiling. "I'm Christy."

"I'm known as *True*," the husband said, reaching around his wife to shake my hand. He wanted to know if I'd been a pilot?

I must have showed my surprise as I shook my head, and his hand. Pilots were way over me. I'd been an enlisted man, an inferior breed in the Navy, a different species from officers and pilots, lower in rank, apparently lower in tastes and morals, and supposedly uneducated, unreliable. Enlisted men had to be commanded from above, told what to do, and were unworthy of any officer's daughter! "No officer," I said, and asked if he'd worn "gold braid?"

"Only got to be a petty officer," he said, letting go of my hand.

I was about to say something about myself becoming an officer of industry. After the Navy I rose to the top of the emerging computer industry, but I only said, "you can't tell an officer from an enlisted man, out of uniform."

We tried to find a connection in the squadron, but our paths had barely crossed. He came aboard about the time I was shipped out. He remembered the "Old Man" I wanted to forget. We traded anecdotes about the maintenance of World War II crates at *Gitmo* and the jazzy jets on carriers. We touched briefly on the bases we'd rounded after the

Navy. True's wife, Christy, kept looking back and forth like a spectator at a tennis match, finally said she was getting tired of being "out of it."

"All you boys have stardust in your once-upon-a-time stories," she said. "Seems like you all lived happily ever after!"

My first love was like a fairytale, I thought to myself, but it hardly ended happily.

My thoughts of Bunny Claire were interrupted by other couples finding their places at table *fifty-two*. I recognized some faces from earlier squadron meetings, but still couldn't find a face that matched my mental roster of the squadron. I never really got to know anybody in the outfit, not well. We lived close in ranks, but kept our distance, at arms length, as though in marching order, afraid to touch.

Introductions went around the table and we sat down, forgetting all the names as soon as we heard them. We sank into our own thoughts again, felt uneasy, separate and distant.

One of the men on the other side of the table was savoring my name, Jack Zais, scratching at the scrub of his short gray beard, asking if I played for the *Flyers*?

"Played the hot corner, but wasn't so hot," I nodded, feeling good about being remembered.

"You got to remember me, *Tip* Tyler," he spoke up. "I was the only southpaw on the team."

I shook my head, apologized. "Seems I can't remember faces or names, but can't forget the pitch I hit for my only homer. It was off-speed, on the outside corner, high."

"I got a memory like that," Tip Tyler said, "can't forget the angle of my pitches that got hit out of the park."

"Seems like we're all striking out," someone said, "can't connect with each other anymore."

I was thinking retirement had taken me of the game. I could hardly remember myself as a sleek sailor, or slick third-baseman. The hand I was reaching out for a glass of water didn't even look like my hand. The fingers were knotty. The skin didn't fit like it used to, didn't suit me. I thought the top of my head must look like a rubbed-up baseball.

"Memory throws curves," I said, shaking my head in disbelief. "Can't remember a teammate, but can't forget that pitch I hit, high on the outside corner."

"I always went for the *highballs*," Tip Tyler said, saluting me with a smile and the cocktail he'd brought to the table, "and can't remember a thing after hitting a few highballs."

"Tippy pitched two no-hitters," his wife intervened, smiling at everyone around the table. "He no-hit the Leathernecks and Seabees, in a row, an Inter-Command League record!"

"I didn't remember we had a baseball team," one of the men at the table spoke up, shaking open his napkin.

"We were too busy keeping planes up," another man thought.

"I was flying planes while you ball players were flying out!"

"This old boy didn't have time for games?"

"All our squadron ever did was play games," Tip was tired of the talk going around. He was squirming around in his chair, adjusting his parts. "We only played games," he repeated, "war games to train the fleet."

"Bet my new shoes that baseball kept morale flying high," Tip's wife came to bat for him.

"You got a good bet going,"one of the wives got into the table talk. "My old sailor couldn't get through a day of retirement without baseball and football on the tube."

"Life's a lot like a baseball game," I thought, "we have to rub-up our skills, play by the rules, compete, take our chances."

"Everybody's a hitter or a pitcher," Tip followed up on my line of thought. "We're all trying to outguess each other, anticipate the other's move."

"It's more like football," somebody thought. "We have to give and take ground, play against time. The clock's always ticking on us."

Christy Truett reminded us the time was running out for the commanding officer's daughter to appear at the head table. It was something I'd been thinking about, looking up all the time. I'd been getting the sinking feeling my old love might not turn up! She had no way of knowing I'd be here at the reunion in Miami.

"Scuttlebutt has it the Old Man's daughter's widowed, or divorced," Christy Truett said, looking my way. Her eyes were sparkling like the wine in her glass. She really had kept a good shape.

"She's available, I guess, if you're not married," her husband said, giving me a knowing look. He obviously made a mental note I was alone, unattached at the reunion, wearing no ring.

"I went for a hitch in marriage," I volunteered, returning the smiles of the Truetts, "but got a hardship discharge, never signed up again."

I was still embarrassed about not lasting long in the married ranks, less than a four year hitch in the Navy. Even before falling into marriage I'd fallen out of step with love, couldn't get back in the swing of it, not after Bunny Claire. I never felt comfortable with any other girl, never got the same feeling! Something was missing in me, like a missing body part.

"You have to try again, break the Soul Barrier," True suggested.

"My ex-wife was too trying," I said, turning away, "and not soulful!"

My voice was lost in the clicking of glasses at the head table, and a call to order. Dutch Decker, our president, greeted us through a microphone, announced that our commanding officer's daughter was held up by a delayed flight. "She'll be hitting the deck," he said in his gritty voice, "before we finish drawing our rations."

Our president, Dutch Decker, was a pilot and Navy career man, had retired a full commander, but he didn't stir any recollection in me. I only saw a man who'd lost more hair than myself. Without hair his prominent features seemed carved out of a single block of headstone. I was still trying to place him in memory when he waved a priest up to the podium, introduced him as "Father Roy." He asked us to remember "Roy Boy, a yeoman in the personnel office."

I couldn't recognize or remember Roy Boy either. I wondered if I'd be able to recognize Bunny Claire when she showed up?

"Father Roy has come up in the world," our president said, "come up from record keeping to soul keeping. I've asked the Father to get our mess started with a blessing."

"Our Heavenly Father," the priest began, bowing his head.

As I looked down, my thoughts of fathers came up. Bunny Claire's father exiled me. My own father dropped out of my life in the Depression, left my mother and me and two brothers to fend for ourselves. I wanted to believe in a good father, wanted to be a good father myself, never got the chance.

"Our Heavenly Father has set a special place for airmen in the sky," our priest was saying. "We're logged in His Book of Remembrance."

I started paging through my own book of remembrance. Why had the Heavenly Father written Bunny Claire out of it? Could she be written back in?

"The Heavenly Father works through us," the priest was saying, as we raised our heads after his "Amen." The priest asked us to look around, see God in our neighbors, look for God in our own histories. "This reunion is historic," he said before we could look within. "Our squadron was decommissioned, dead, and now raised up again."

I wondered how God worked through naval air power, or through my life? I wondered why God took Bunny Claire out of my life, but I'd go back to church if I got her back again!

I was hardly aware that the priest had returned to his chair, and salad dressing was going around my table. The main course turned up, grilled salmon. Someone said salmon was appropriate for a reunion. "Salmon go back upstream to their beginnings."

One of the old boys at the table laughed and thought he was too old to remember what the salmon goes upstream for. As we were eating, one of the wives said she was sick of fish, and sick of anything that comes out of the sea, except for her sailor husband!

I was sick of fish, too, remembered being sick unto death at sea. It happened to me off the coast of Korea, a burst appendix, and no facilities on a baby flattop to handle it. Japan was too far away for urgent treatment. It looked like I might end up with the fish! Bunny Claire saved my life, came to me in Sick Bay, begged me to fight for life! I did, came out of the fever, and danger. Corpsmen laughed at my story of Bunny Claire, said she was more temperature than temporal. They did admit there was a degree of miracle in my recovery.

It was now a miracle I'd be seeing Bunny Claire, after all these years. I was hardly aware that dishes were getting taken from the table, that Dutch Decker was talking again. He said it was time for the program to "lift off."

"Now hear this," he said, getting the banquet hall to quiet down. "Listen up! Our Call Sign was the *Mallards*. We weren't eagles of war, only sitting ducks for the fleet to practice shooting at, but we carried our weight in the Cold War!" He paused to look around. "Now we belong to the Ages, *the old ages* that is, but there's one of us who seems ageless, our Old Man's daughter, Claire O'Meara!"

"Attention on deck!" she smiled as she moved into the limelight. I could hardly believe my eyes as she glowed in a beam of light.

Everyone in the banquet hall shuffled to his or her feet. My mind must have reached the clouds. I'd missed her landing at the head table, must have been flying around in my past. Now I saw her, standing at the podium, radiant in the spotlight. My muscles tensed, as though straining at the deck of a rolling ship!

"At ease," she spoke into the microphone, her voice vibrating all the way through my body, echoing in my memory. "All hands, at ease!" She shot off a smile that pitted dimples in both cheeks. It was the same smile she used to aim at me when she wanted to get me excited. She'd say, "down boy," and make a face like a rabbit. "Down boys," she was now smiling at her audience.

Her audience fumbled back down noisily, looked up at Bunny Claire as she sparkled in the light of chandeliers. She was turning sideways to Dutch Decker, thanking him for the introduction. Swinging back round to the audience she said no one probably remembered our bald-headed master of ceremonies as a Norse god! "When he got his first duty assignment in our squadron," she said, "his Aryan looks earned him the name of *Dutch*. He was the *Flying Dutchman* to the squadron, the flying dreamboat to me."

I was thinking he looked more like an old tug boat. I still couldn't remember him as a squadron pilot in my day, but remembered Bunny Claire better than ever.

"Your Old Man would have given his wings to be here tonight," Bunny Claire settled into her talk. "He lived to fly, and command. I'm not sure he lived to be a father, but he never had to command my love. Most of his fathering was from overseas, from a distance, like God's! Your base at Guantanamo Bay was my heaven on earth, first time I could settle down with my father. I thought the *VU* designation for your utility squadron stood for *Vacation Unit*. I had the vacation of my life down there in the everlasting summer of Cuba."

She paused for a sip of water, seemed sculptured in blue, statuesque. "Wouldn't it be lovely," she began again "if we could have our next reunion in Cuba? It's been cut off for so long. I loved the Cubans, loved our Cuban maid. Carmella didn't know much English but taught my feet the language of dance. You have to put your whole body in it, you know," and she raised her arms, gave her body a little twist.

"I couldn't get enough Cuban dance," she resumed, "or enough Cuba. Your Old Man flew me to Havana and casino floor shows, art galleries, and those rum distilleries. I especially remember the big guns of the American battleship *Maine* mounted in a massive monument by the sea. I wonder if Castro left that memory of America in place?"

She caught her breath, looked around. "I was a flighty high school girl when you boys were flying high in Cuba. You were boys in age, but men of war. I've always loved boys. They're so playful, curious, adventurous, puppy-dog cute, and cuddly!"

She got a good hand of applause, and a few hoots and whistles. I didn't remember myself as a playful boy, except for playing baseball, and I was lean and hard, not puppy-dog cute and cuddly! Was she talking about me?

"I had two sons," she said, "puppy dog playful. When I was a girl, your Old Man tried to protect me from the play of sailor boys." She got another round of applause, and whistles.

"Well," she said, "our hot youths are past, and the Cold War, too. I'm a grandmother. Would you believe this old broad once kicked up her heels on Broadway? Your Old Man wanted me to be the wife of an admiral, but I got in step with a hoofer. Your Old Man flew up in a raging storm over that, but got his wheels down on the ground when I gave him two cuddly grandsons. After my marriage ran out of gas, I pumped out a series of children's books, made a storybook living. I was known for rabbit stories, took *Bunny* for my pen name, Bunny Claire. Would you take me for a Playboy *Bunny*, or a Bugs *Bunny*?"

She made a rabbit face, paused again. "You came to this reunion to learn about your Old Man, not his old daughter. Zach O'Meara's been gone now, about ten years, dropped on a handball court, missed out on a hitch or two in some nursing home."

Her voice was fading out in my new digital hearing aid while my mind was working-up something to say to her. I could hardly wait for the program to be over. A wave of laughter shocked me out of my thoughts. Bunny Claire was getting laughs about her father as a midshipman. "Every fleet sailor, even your skipper," she was saying, "hit the Gaiety Theater in that old Navy town of Norfolk. The Gaiety was a shrine for sailors," she clarified for the wives, "a burlesque house where maidens were sacrificed to the goddess of bad dancing. I'm told the Gaiety Goddess had the answer to the riddle of life, but kept all the boys guessing."

She looked around. "Here's the riddle. What, do tell, do pilots and burlesque strippers have in common?" She answered the riddle herself. "Pilots and strippers both use *runways*, and *take off* a lot!" She bowed to the applause, said she couldn't fly any lower.

Dutch Decker, smiling, rose up, raised both arms to hold back the applause. "Can't top that," he said. "She's the top!"

When the roaring and hooting settled down, Dutch announced that our old squadron mate, *Woogie* Woods, would swing us back to the nineteen-fifties with his combo. "Woogie went from airman to airwaves," Dutch told us, "up to stardom in radio and television."

Woogie's combo got us to our feet with *Anchors Aweigh*, got our feet in the mood with an old Glenn Miller tune. Dutch taxied Bunny Claire onto the dance floor, got squadron mates and wives up and scrambling to join them.

I waltzed into the music, charted my course for Bunny Claire. Reaching out, I cut in on the president of our association, looked down at Bunny Claire, searched for words. I could hardly believe I was seeing her again. "Is that really you?"

"I've always thought so," she said, looking up, smiling, "and you are?"

CARNATION FOR A WHITE HAT

THE BODY OF my naval air buddy was never found, that lean body with long brassy-haired arms and a cross-shaped airplane tattooed on a shoulder. He was just getting the hang of a man's body when he lost it, took it down to the bottom of the Caribbean. His body was lost in the flash of a plane crash at sea. I've been losing mine a little at a time, the trim of it, the get-up-and-go of it, all through the years. When some of us old salts got together for our squadron's first reunion, we'd all lost our savor, but my "lost" buddy was salted away in memory, same as ever.

Reassembling in a Miami hotel, my squadron mates came together from all parts of the country. Back in ranks, we lined up the recollections of ourselves in Cuba, at Guantanamo Bay, dressed our lines up for inspection, and sounded off, day after day.

On the last morning, we turned about-face to *re*-member the missing gaps in our ranks. At our memorial service we honored those absent members, most of whom had been shot down by time. Seated with our wives and friends in the hotel assembly hall, row after row, we stood for the passing of the colors and military escort, bowed for a moment of prayer, sat back down to hear the homily of our chaplain. He was a priest who'd come out of our ranks, had been one of us before taking higher orders. I remembered him in the clay of a common sailor, a yeoman striker in the personnel office. He was the clerk who couldn't get my buddy's request to marry a Cuban girl up the chain of command. Now that same man was letting my buddy down again, assigning him to the depths of the Caribbean, lost at sea in a secret mission.

Our chaplain had reminded us that the squadron we were celebrating was born in war, but in the whole life of it, "only Lieutenant Eugene Lazerov and plane captain James Mann died for it, and disappeared in a shroud of mystery."

My buddy wouldn't be remembered as James Mann, I thought to myself. He was known as "Manny." Our chaplain praised him, but couldn't raise his spirit on the wings of a prayer. Not a face I could see around me lighted up with a ray of recognition at the name of "James Mann."

Our chaplain recalled for us the occasion of Manny's disappearance. "Lieutenant Lazerov and plane captain Mann took off in 1954 of the last century, never came back. The hot war in Korea was barely over, but the Cold War carried on, and we got put on alert for a cargo ship carrying guns to

Communists in Guatemala. They were tense times, before the Communists took over Cuba."

The chaplain paused in speech to cross himself, fold his hands in prayer. "Lazerov and Mann gave their lives, but we're all mortal, changing like the clouds, but immortal like the Sky."

Our chaplain ended with an appeal to muster-up our "fallen comrades." He asked those of us who remembered a squadron mate taken "down to death" to come forward, pick up a white carnation and lay down a few words in his memory.

The grim reaper had mowed down a lot of us, I imagined, noting a pile of carnations on the table up front. A carnation seemed appropriate for remembering Navy White Hats. I could picture Manny as a carnation, snug in his white jumper with the broad bib in back, and topped with a white hat riding his crest of yellow hair. I thought of the stem of him in bellbottoms, and the way he breezed around.

All the while I was envisioning Manny, old squadron mates were going up with words of commemoration and coming back with carnations.

It seemed that most of the airmen they were calling back to mind had gone high in the world before crossing over to the next! I was wondering what I could say about an airman barely airborne in life? Was his disappearance in a "shroud of mystery" all that could be said of him? What do you say in memory of someone nobody remembers?

Did anyone remember servicing his plane the time it disappeared so mysteriously? I always wondered what brought it down? Nobody ever knew. All I know for sure was Manny logged-out one night, never logged-in. There was no record of what happened to him and his pilot, only an oil slick in the Windward Passage between Cuba and Haiti. A board of inquiry "found Lazerov and Mann died in the *line* of duty." Our squadron was lined-up and marched into the base chapel for a military memorial. A Navy chaplain said the pilot and plane captain wcrc assigned "a higher duty station."

How should I bring Manny to life in everyone's memory? He'd been washed down at sea, everything he was or might have been was dissolved in the Caribbean. I needed to dredge up something to remind the old squadron mates he had a life, and they were part of it.

I could remind everyone that his feet were always out of step with the Navy, but that wouldn't set him apart. Most of us were not professional sailors, only served in time of war.

Maybe I should wave a white carnation and say Manny loved to fly, keep his nose up, go with the wind, hang free! I could say he loved suspension between worlds, between heaven and earth. He loved to feel the pulse of the engine, the vibrations that kept him up and alive, but his love for flying wouldn't set him apart, either. I most likely was the only airman who hated to go up. I got no thrill out of seventeen hundred horses plowing me through the clouds. I didn't like getting squeezed in the bilge hatch, tied-down in life-vest, harness and chute. I hated the headphones pinching my ears, and the garbled messages I had to make sense of in my head. I hated bouncing around in space while ships below tracked me with in their radar and gun sights. I hated it when the pilot swooped down at masthead level and pulled-out just above the open mouths of the grinning sea! The waves lapped their tongues at me, seemed to hunger for me. Playing with life in the air was no game for me! It made life a gamble, a toss-up.

Manny played the game and lost. I could say he was so young he didn't have much life to lose. I could ask the old boys if there's life after youth?

It should have occurred to me sooner. I could say that Manny's death gave me a new life, a wife! The wife I got through him was next to me, sitting stiffly in black hat and gloves, her handkerchief at the ready. She loved Manny before she loved me She loved him still, liked to think he was missing on a desert island and would come back again! Maybe I shouldn't take up a carnation and say anything about him at all?

I still shuttered at the thought of Manny going down, down, down, wondered what flashed through his mind? I remembered going down in a practice parachute jump, thought I was dropping out of life. The spotter was ahead of me, falling backward, yelling, "see ya below." I was thinking of below, in Hell! Diving head first behind the boots of the instructor I remembered flying right out of sound, out of the roar of plane and wind. I was in slow motion, rolling between green and blue, earth and sky, between worlds, got jerked back to the rush of sound and time, but the earth was a long drop away, and I was shaking, starting to forgive all the guys who owed me money, all the way down. Money seemed unimportant, until I hit dirt, scrambled back to my feet, wanted my money back.

What went through Manny's head when he was going down? Airmen liked to say they could be in the air one second, thinking of home, and in hell the next, or back on base, which was about the same thing as hell. Now it was hell for me to think of something to say about Manny!

I could say he maintained planes on base and a woman off base. That would bring everyone up to attention! The men would like to know he had a life before losing it, but the wives wouldn't go for it, especially my wife. Shacking-up with a woman wouldn't fly at a memorial service, either. I was at another dead end.

Maybe I should put my baseball memories in play. Manny caught me on the Naval Air Station baseball team, the *Flyers*. I was a pitcher, had lots of movement on the ball, tossed two no-hitters, figured I'd fly high in the majors as soon as my enlistment ran out. My arm went and died on me. There should be a memorial service for my arm!

It wasn't *my* arm I should be thinking about. I should bring back the quick snap of Manny's brassy-haired arm, and the way he called a game. I couldn't say much about his hitting. Not known for much of an average he couldn't hit his weight, a scrawny weight at that. He wasn't built like a catcher, but sure had a good arm. Maybe I should say he came to the plate for our squadron's baseball team and "flew out?"

Maybe it would be better to say he only got to first base in life, but didn't have to run past middle age and slide into senility?

Maybe no baseball pitch should groove the strike zone at a memorial service, not even the thought of Manny as the Catcher in the *Sky*!

Time was running out for me to come up with something to say about Manny. Someone had just praised Lieutenant Lazerov, Manny's pilot, and said he left a wife and son. I remember Manny leaving the team after taking up with his Cuban *muchacha*. That Cuban girl, he told me, was his "best catch!"

I knew I shouldn't put his *muchacha* in play at the memorial service, but she'd come to plate in my memory, and I couldn't get her out. Her name? Juliet Romero! Manny liked to call himself "Juliet's Romeo." She was a maid in service at the civilian housing units, commuted back and forth to Cuba. Manny ran into her at a squadron party where she served drinks and washed glasses. He went for her, right off the bat!

Juliet Romero lived on the Cuban side of Guantanamo Bay, on a dirt street in a row of dingy house fronts She shared a living room, kitchen, and patio with two other families, had her own bedroom, and her own kid. Her little girl ran free of diapers or pants, like all the other bare-assed children. Her little girl was fairer than the mother, the offspring of an American officer in one of the housing units she'd served. Manny never bothered to find out about the father! For him the past was yesterday's baseball game, didn't figure in today's box score.

As soon as Manny took up with that Cuban woman he wanted to get married, support mother and child, live off base with them on a family allotment. He got the petition started for marrying a foreign national. Our Personnel Officer didn't want Manny gambling with his future! He seemed to think every young man had a future! Our Personnel Officer thought every body ought to reject a foreign body.

I remembered Manny moving his body and soul into Juliet's life, unsanctioned by the Navy. He lived with her on every liberty and weekend pass. I didn't see much of him in the barracks anymore, but I got invited to some of his chow-times in Cuba, and some rum and coke in the Cuban sunsets.

After Manny flew off and never flew back, I made liberty on the Cuban side of Guantanamo Bay, looked up his woman. Juliet saw me through the bars of her window, opened her door to me and reached out. One hand was clinging to a kicking child. She let the child slide off her hip. I followed the two of them into the living room. No one was in any of the chairs or in the sofa with a few springs coming out. Manny's woman waved me to the best of the chairs, poured me a drink, fanned me with a folded newspaper. I remember her as a Polynesian-looking woman in a Gauguin painting, her figure flattened in a Puritan smock. Her face was shiny brown, laced with ringlets of black hair. She managed to say in English that she knew about the air and sea searches for Manny, the memorial service at the base chapel, and the gun salute that "shot him off to Heaven." She read about him in *The Indian*, the base newspaper she was using to fan me. She was still constructing her thoughts in English when I stood up to leave. She wanted me to hang on. I flipped the wallet out of my waistband and slipped her some folding money, said I owed it to Manny. I only kept enough of my month's pay to get drunk at "Sloppy Joe's," a Cuban dive where American sailors could scuttle their Guantanamo Bay blues.

I never saw Manny's woman again. Now I'm wondering what became of her, and her bare-ass little kid? The mother might be underground, in Communist Cuba. Her little sprite with grins and dimples might be smiling at grandchildren in Communist Cuba.

Manny should be running round with grandchildren, I came back to thoughts of him, and what I could dig up to say. I remembered there was nothing left of him but a seabag stuffed with whites and blues and mattress covers. I wasn't on the inventory board that got his gear sorted out, but he'd requested me as his "escort" in the case of death. There was no casket for me to accompany when I pulled the duty to carry his seabag home, and a flag, and letters of condolences. His hometown was way off in the Texas Panhandle, a couple of long hops on military air transportation.

He was from the "wide open spaces" that he called "God's country," and I thought I was in heaven when his folks put me up in a bedroom all to myself. I had naval authorization to get a hotel room, but Manny's Ma and Pa wouldn't let me go. They kept wanting to hear about their only son. I told them about the hangar where we worked, and the barracks where we hung out, and all the baseball games that Manny caught for me. I'd been cautioned not to say much about his last reconnaissance mission. It was still classified as secret, but I didn't know much about it anyway. I did tell them about our planes scrambling night and day in search of his plane.

Manny had a scrawny kid sister with braids and scabby knees, the "brat" he used to complain about when we talked of "home." He called her "Punk." I started calling her "Punkie," found nothing "bratty" about her. She took to me right off, followed me around like a rookie begging to learn about curve balls and change-ups. She kept setting me up to catch her pitches. I was reminded of my own kid sister, the one who stuck me with the nickname that still sticks, "Tip!" Punkie was now sticking me with "Tippy!"

I couldn't make transportation connections back to *Gitmo* right away, got to extend my escort duty, got to keep rattling around the Mann's big Victorian house. It was gingerbread all around the outside, full of massive furniture all around the inside. The furniture was plain and simple, a little dull, like Manny's folks. I knew how to spray paint our squadron planes, volunteered to liven-up some of their furniture, but Manny's old man said it was "Mission" furniture, had a useful mission, wasn't meant to be pretty. I said something about Manny's service being useful, too. He was a good mechanic, but I think we both were thinking about Manny's last "mission."

His folks weren't ready to let go. They stowed his seabag in a corner of his upstairs bedroom. Not much of the Navy was on display up there except model planes hanging in dogfight suspension from one of the overhead beams. His high school baseball shoes were still lined-up under the bed, and baseball pennants were pinned on all four walls of the room. I don't think his folks really "got it." They never spoke of him in the past tense. I know for sure Manny's "Punk" never got it through her little head he wasn't coming home. She seemed to think he was playing a game, like hide and seek.

His folks were good about feeding me up, and showing me off, all around the town. They never asked about Mann's Cuban woman. Maybe they didn't know. I didn't bring her up. In those days it was shameful to live with a woman outside of marriage. Those days seem to have passed. My daughter's in that kind of set-up! Time shoots down a lot more than airmen.

Never mentioning Juliet, I did ask about "Wilma Jean," the "homespun" girl Manny used to bring up when we sat around the barracks to polish inspection shoes. Manny chewed the rag a lot about Wilma Jean, and his "time of sickness," a winter in bed with weights on his legs. The family doctor thought he'd been growing too fast, had come down with some malady that might cripple him for life! The doctor sure was wrong! Manny got back on his legs, and up and down behind the plate, but had to keep taking pills, on account of that "time of sickness."

It was Wilma Jean's role in Manny's story that stuck with me. She kept him company all that winter he was confined to bed. She came to him every day after school. They were both in the same class, fifth or sixth grade, and she brought him school assignments and stood by to help out. Manny told me about her chestnut hair that flopped in her eyes when she was reading to him. She kept flipping her head like a colt throwing back the nuisance of a mane. Manny loved horses, had a quarter horse of his own pastured in his Texas backyard. I think he really loved Wilma Jean, too.

All those winter days in bed Manny looked for Wilma Jean when school let out. From his upstairs window he'd watch schoolboys trooping by, sloshing through the dirty snow, but they weren't thinking of him. Only Wilma Jean stopped off, all those melting winter afternoons. She was the only highlight in his day. Those were the days before television, and no baseball games were on the radio in wintertime.

Wilma Jean helped him learn to walk again! She held him by the hand, kept him at it, no matter how much it hurt, or how much he was "afeared" of falling. He walked again, and ran, and played baseball. He forgot the "time of sickness." He forgot Wilma Jean as he passed through high school and flirted with a baseball career in semi-pro ball. He ran into her one time, not long before he got his draft notice. She'd gotten herself engaged to a boy she met in junior college, a boy drafted and shipped right off to the war in Korea. He got himself captured, couldn't even get a letter off to her.

Manny used to tell me how his fondness for her changed from a childish warmth to the "hot and hairy," but he didn't make a move on Wilma Jean, didn't want to steal the girl of a poor bastard caught in some North Korean prison camp! Manny said he never spoke to Wilma Jean about love, and never spoke to me of Wilma Jean after he took up with his *mamacita*. He only said there were different kinds of love.

By the time I got to meet Wilma Jean in Manny's hometown, the armistice had put the Korean War behind us. Wilma Jean's soldier had gotten his freedom from the North Koreans, and the Army, but hadn't gotten his imprisonment out of mind. He didn't know what to do with himself, except get lost in booze. Wilma Jean thought it was all over between them, and I dated her right off, took her to a drive-in-movie. I think we put on our own show in the backseat of Manny's beat-up Chevy, but Wilma Jean wanted to know more about what happened to Manny than what was happening on the screen, or with us in the backseat!

I kept a handle on all my Texas friends after I got back to base in Cuba and after I got out of the Navy. I got into professional baseball, worked my way up the minors, made the Texas League before my arm went out. After the arm let me down I took up the G.I. Bill, got me some college, and a good job, and made a "home run" with my Texas girl, married her.

I'd been getting my swings at so many of my own memories that I hadn't hit on anything to say about Manny. I had to take my eye off the past when the daughter of our squadron's commanding officer came up front to take a carnation, offer a tribute to "our Old Man." She was still a good looking woman, only been a school girl when her father was our squadron's "Old Man." She'd caused a sensation at the squadron banquet the previous night when she discovered a long-lost sweetheart, one of my teammates on the *Flyers*. He played third, but was first in the heart of our Old Man's daughter. She was now telling us that carnations were named for the color of flesh, stemming from the Latin root of *caro*, as in carnal. She said something about all of us being carnal, only in bloom for a season, but perennials in soul.

I wished I could come up with something flowery like that to say about Manny, but I could only see him spitting in his glove, scratching at his crotch, flipping off his mask and staggering around home plate with eyes on a ball in the sky.

Words couldn't reach that high, I thought, as I found myself walking up to the plate, trying to pinch hit for Manny.

"This carnation is the carnal remains of James Mann, better known as Manny," I heard myself saying. "He was cut off in the flower of youth!"

"Sailor, rest your oar," I heard our chaplain's refrain as I was walking back to my seat.

"Punkie," I whispered to my wife, passing on the carnation to her, "he's come back in full bloom."

THE LOVETT CURSE

Part I: SEEDS IN THE WIND

A NAVAL AIRMAN came off leave with a civilian girl in tow, rushed her through the squadron hangar, past parked planes and gawking sailors, and topside to the personnel office. "Lord a-mercy," the girl kept gasping, her body in rejection of the banjo strung to her back and the shiny black shoes ankle-strapped to her feet. "Lord-a-mercy!"

"Hooked me a swamp gal for a wife," the airman announced as soon as he popped in the tropical hot personnel office. He leaned over the counter, addressed a yeoman by name, *Tork*. "Need me all them family allowances!"

The yeoman called "Tork" looked up from the typewriter long enough to nod in recognition of the airman he'd mentally kept on file as a nuisance and first class "square." Square of head, square of body, square of mind, he was a solid square all over. The blockhead even wore his white hat squared.

Now he wanted to get squared away with a child bride and set up housekeeping in a run-down town on the Cuban side of Guantanamo Bay!

Not missing a stroke at his typing, Tork hit on the key to the kid at the counter. He was the mech with the "curse!" It wasn't anything like the "curse" women complained of once a month. His curse made women "hot" for him, all the time, but the downside was that he'd never know "love!" He figured *love* must be a sight better than *making* love, or his curse wouldn't be worth the spit of the cult-woman who lay it on him. Squadron mates didn't give him much sympathy, only wanted to know how to get hold of that cult-woman.

"So the man with the love curse got himself a love wife!" Tork said, looking up.

"Swamp gal's gonna un-curse me," the "square" assured Tork, and whipped off his white hat, rolled it up and took a swipe at the dark-haired girl by his side. "This little woman be fixing to blow that curse right outa my hair."

The hair of his head was already getting agitated under the overhead fan. Thick and bushy it was parted in the middle, balancing the halves of his square face. Raven black wings of hair were beginning to lift off the flattop of his head, starting to fly.

"So you want the squadron to keep up a wife for you?" Tork kept thinking and typing as he talked. "My striker, Roy Boy, can give you a hand with the paperwork." The yeoman spoke loud enough to alert a seaman apprentice cramped at a desk by the opened windows. The kid looked up, baby soft in face. He got long legs unwound from a chair, got himself together, stood up, stuck all over to his sweaty whites.

"Not Roy Boy!" the airman groaned, slapping at the counter. "Got me a man-sized job! Hear?"

"Since when you grease monkeys think paperwork's a man-sized job?"

Tork was always resentful of the attitude mechanics held for clerical work. Aviation grease monkeys also looked down on "black shoe" seamen like himself. He was a yeoman off a cruiser and still felt out of water in a naval air squadron.

"Paper work don't put ring-grease on the fingers," the airman said, turning up his blackened palms, "don't break an arm cranking-up a prop! You got it soft and easy."

"Easy enough for the kid to do," Tork said as he kept typing, swinging back the carriage at the sound of the bell.

"Out on the line we don't put no striker on a big engine overhaul," the airman kept protesting. "If my allotments don't get done up right proper, I won't get the extra pay to keep up the little woman. Throw me a line for pity sake!"

The yeoman called Tork flashed another look at the square-heavy airman. His whites were wilting, losing their grip, but his wife was holding on to him so hard he tilted to her side. Women were a treat to see around the air station, but this pretty little woman was really a treat. Round of eyes and mouth and cheeks she was round all over. The banjo strap crossed in front of her was deeply dividing the breasts, very deeply!

Up went Tork's two hands from the typewriter keys, up came his whole body glistening bright with sweat, stringy and sinewy in skivvy shirt and tropical khaki shorts. He twisted his erect body to get the kinks out. "Belay that," he called off Roy Boy. "I'll get the man squared away myself."

The airman at the counter let out a sigh. "You be getting a big invite to home cooking, soon as me and my woman get a home. Hear?"

"First off," Tork said, leaning on the counter across from the airman, "there's no home on base for you and your little woman. You don't pull enough rank to rate dependent housing in Central Bargo."

"Never counted on Navy quarters," the airman shot back. "Rather live it up off base, free and easy. Just write me up all them dependent allowances, ComRats, PerDiem, shit like that."

"No snug harbor in Cuba for you to drop anchor with that American dreamboat," Tork said with a shrug. He eyed the square airman and his round wife. He felt sorry for the round one.

"Gal want to go where I go," the airman spoke up. "She want to be where I be."

"Maybe she didn't count on landing in Hell!" Tork replied.

"Just line me up with them allotments, and mind your rudder! Hear?"

Tork turned away, strode bare-legged across the office to the row of filing cabinets. He looked back to ask for the airman's name.

"Lovett!" the airman shot back. "How the cornbread hell could you forget my handle? Ain't I been cluttering up your office enough?"

"Lake Lovett, and you don't answer to Lake," Tork remembered, having associated "love" with "Lovett" and "Lake" with the Naval Training Station at Great Lakes. He remembered there was no love in Lovett and nothing great about Lake!

"Lovett, Lake," Tork said, pulling a thick service record out of a file drawer. "You carry more cargo than any of the three hundred airmen in this here outfit."

"Been bucking a lot for a hardship discharge," Lovett said, "and my hard-*ship's* coming in some day."

Tork flipped open the service record. "Does your little bride know about that female hardship you put in for a while back?"

"The little woman knows I got the Curse," the airman said, putting hands on is wife's head as though blessing her.

Tork opened up to the hardship discharge petition claiming he got two women pregnant and had to marry one! "You had a pregnant imagination on this one," Tork said, holding up the opened service record

"That should have been good for two hardship discharges!"

"You had no affidavits," Tork noted, flipping a page. He turned up another petition. It claimed a widowed mother, who was "poorly" and unable to keep up the ranch without her son. A check-up showed no evidence his mother was sick, widowed, or had a ranch.

"You sure ran up the paperwork" Tork said, skipping through the pages of applications and petitions, "had yourself a million wrinkles back home to iron out!"

"Would give my left ball to get outa this chicken-shit outfit!"

"You're on the ball this time," Tork said, "a wife will get you off base every night you don't have the duty."

"You be my permanent liberty pass," Lovett said to his wife, mussing her hair. She looked up at him with a round smile, clung to him.

"Miss Liberty!" Tork bowed to the airman's pretty wife. "Miss Liberty!"

The wife lowered her eyes in shyness, eyelashes flicking. She sneaked a look at the yeoman's legs in khaki shorts, thought his legs were better than hers, except for the hair. Her eyes kept adventuring around the office, across the counter to the desks and filing cabinets and bulletin boards, out through the slats of the louvered windows to the high rising slopes around the base. She felt walled-in, imprisoned, but liked to think of herself as "Miss Liberty."

"No more screaming blues in the barracks for me," Lovett was saying, mostly to himself. "This old boy gonna be a brown-bagger, going back and forth between the base and Cuba, as free as the Cuban workers."

Tork was still checking out the wife, didn't think Lovett had gotten her with child. She looked more like a child herself.

"Got me a swamp gal that ain't web-footed," Lovett kept his mouth going. "Tell the man, Little Lukie, tell the man how I put on fins to fish you outa the red water swamp."

A smile began loosening the wife's tight round pout of a mouth. She tried to form words but only a giggle came out, and the tip of a tongue to lick at a bead of sweat. It was sweaty hot in the office, even under the lazy fan wind-milling overhead.

Suddenly, a roaring noise hurt the ears and shook the office. It was an aircraft cranking up on the hangar deck below. Lovett's little wife rushed both hands to her ears.

Tork raised his voice. "I'll write you up a wife," he said, slipping the record under his arm.

"And get me them allotments on the dotted line," Lovett hollered over the sound of the aircraft engine, "and some of them dependent identity cards. Had me a bitch of a time checking the little woman on base! And need one of them brown-bagger passes for the ferryboat to Cuba."

"*Caimanera* won't make good muster for your little American wife," Tork warned, shaking his head. He knew firsthand about the low life across the bay in Cuba, its poverty, its bars and brothels, its swarms of flies and homeless kids bugging sailors for money or shoe shines. The town was spoiling in the sun like a load of dead fish! "She's gonna miss running water and flushing toilets."

"Gal's gonna have all she wants, in me," Lovett said.

"You won't be around a lot of the time. You'll be leaving her hung up in an alien world."

"Alien!" the little wife found her voice, "like space people?" She began struggling to get the banjo back in place again.

"Alien meaning different," Tork tried to explain.

"Alien, like being OUT OF IT," Lovett carried on the explanation. "You soon be IN IT! With your senorita hair and shady looks, you be passing for a gooney right pronto."

"What be a gooney?"

"Gooney's a name we lay on the Cubans," the husband shrugged, never having thought much about it.

"Don't think it means a goon," Tork gave it more thought, "think the gooney bird is like the albatross around your neck. Don't think the name flies well in Cuba."

"Ain't Cuba one of our American states?"

"Cuba's a foreign country," the husband tried to calm his wife down.

"We're the foreigners," Tork said, knowing the wife would be in for the shock of her life as soon as she got across Guantanamo Bay to Caimanera!

"What be a foreign country?"

"A different country," the husband took over the explanation. He shrugged his squarish shoulders, threw up his hands as if in disbelief.

"Were Florida where we laid over last night a foreign country?"

"A foreign country's a place where you don't savvy the lingo," Lovett frowned down at his wife, and exchanged a look of disbelief with the yeoman. "You be getting the swing of foreign ways, and your banjo be picking up the Cuban beat in a snap."

"You're at the U.S. Naval Base, Guantanamo Bay, Cuba," Tork told the airman's wife, "a base the U.S. leased for a coaling station way back in the age of steam, right after the Spanish-American War."

"Too bad the lease ain't run itself out," Lovett commented, shifting his weight from one foot to the other, anxious to get going.

"Well, I knowed I be at a Navy base," the wife said. "My man's a pilot. Guess it don't make me no never mind where I be, long as I be with my man."

"Never let on I was a pilot," Lovett was quick to speak up. "Little gal figures all airmen are pilots and don't know I only be a grease monkey in a ground crew."

"You never told her where she'd have to hang out?" Tork asked.

"We hang out in this here *hangar*?"

Tork could hardly believe his ears, managed to tell the wife she'd be alone across the bay when her airman had to be on duty.

"All that little woman's got to do is warm the nest and wait on me to come home to roost." Lovett had to lower his voice a little when the roaring noise broke off. "Ain't that pretty good duty for a cotton-picking little old gal?"

"What's this about a cotton-picking gal?" a commanding voice broke the noise that started to grind up again. It was the voice of the personnel officer standing in the doorway of his inner office. He stood tall, his body put together like a uniform made to order. The brass on his collar struck sparks out of the sunlight coming through the windows. Everyone blinked at his commanding presence.

"Cotton picking gal, Sir, that's the new wife Airman Lake Lovett picked up."

"The Lady of the *Lake*," the officer sparkled with a smile. A recent college graduate, he liked to throw around a degree of English Literature. "Lady of the Lake's a poem by Sir Walter Scott," he felt bound to explain, and went on to introduce himself to Lake Lovett's lady. "I'm the Personnel Officer, Lieutenant Gordon. You getting settled in all right?"

"Just landed, got most our gear checked at MATS," Lovett spoke for his wife.

"How's the Lady of the Lake taking to Guantanamo Bay?"

"I be liking the palm trees," the girl managed to speak for herself. She tossed back her head, flipped the strand of hair out of her eyes. "But it be so powerful hot!"

"Cools off at night," the Lieutenant promised. He kept smiling at the Lady of the Lake.

"We just flew in," the husband took over. "Had to pay the Little Lady's way on military transport. Can I get reimbursement?"

"Yeoman Turner can look into it," the Lieutenant said, motioning at Tork. He never called his yeoman, *Tork*. "See about it," he told his yeoman, "and put me down for an hour of flying time." He tipped his garrison hat at the lady, let himself out, let in more noise until closing the door.

"Well, let's get on with it," Tork said, raising one arm and a damp armpit. He motioned for Lovett and wife to come around the counter. "Make yourselves to home at my desk."

"Don't take me off leave!" Lovett said as he made his way to the yeoman's desk. "Got me another day on my papers, got to find me a nest in Cuba for my gooney bird."

"You'll be lucky to nest in some bamboo hut on stilts," Tork thought, grinding an official form into the typewriter, lining it up, thinking all the while that Lovett's wife had a well filled-out little form herself.

"Wife and me dropping anchor tonight at the Oasis Hotel in Caimanera," Lovett bragged, knowing it would impress the yeoman. The Oasis Hotel was good enough for officers.

"Keep her out of the "district," Tork warned in a lowered voice, "or your little bird will discover she's sitting on a gold mine."

"Scuttlebutt has it you're panning for some of that gold in Caimanera," Lovett talked back in a louder voice.

"What's the wife's name?" Tork asked, ignoring the question about his love life in Caimanera. He'd long since stopped bragging about it.

"Lukie," the husband said.

"Full name!"

"That's it!"

The wife managed to speak up. "I be Lutie. Maiden name be Curry. Ain't no maiden no more."

"Thought you was Lukie," the husband said. He turned to the yeoman. "Had me a sidekick, name of Luke. Got himself drafted and shot-up in Korea, made me go for the Navy to keep out of ground war."

"Lutie Curry Lovett," the yeoman typed the wife's name, wondering how a man could not know his wife's name. "What's your birthday?" he asked the wife.

"October the very first," she spoke right up, blushing a little. "Year of the bad harvest, Nineteen and Thirty-Seven."

"Sixteen years old!" Tork calculated. "You're too young to be weaned from your mother."

"Old enough to mother-up a batch of kid-brothers and sisters," Lovett spoke for his wife. "Got me the pick of the litter."

The yeoman called out for the time and place of marriage.

"Lost me my independence about the Fourth of July in this good old year of Nineteen and Fifty-Three," the husband spoke up, "in city of Texarkana, on the line, half Texas, half Arkansas, best of both worlds."

"Got to see the marriage license," Tork said.

"Figured you for that chickenshit." Lovett said, starting to dig in his ditty bag. "Got the damned piece of paper stashed somewhere." As he looked for it he kept his mouth in gear. "My little woman's got a drop of Cherokee blood, Indian kin on both sides of the blanket. She be a patch-quilt of a body, pieces of redskin and old settler stock, and be a daughter of the Confederacy, I reckon."

"Don't want to breed her," Tork said, as soon as he got the license handed to him. "How'd you ever win yourself the best of breed?"

"Must be my curse at work!"

"More likely your allotment check, and the ten thousand buck life insurance."

"Got all her allotments and insurance right here," Lovett said, groping between his legs.

"I be blessed," Lutie spoke up. "Got ring on finger, good man in hand,"

"Think you're blessed? Got yourself a man with a curse."

"Don't pay that curse no never mind," Lutie said. "We all got the Curse of Adam!"

"You got the man with a double curse," Tork kept on, not really believing in the Lovett curse. It seemed more like a blessing. He had the bragging rights of being "fucked-out" all the time, only the complaint of "lovelessness."

"No more love curse," Lutie said. "Adam got his Eve. Lovett got his Lutie."

"A man without love is bread without leaven," Lovett said.

Tork thought that was a pretty thought. He wondered if he was bread without leaven? Did he know love? There was a girl back home he wanted to make love to, but she wouldn't have him. He didn't think he had love for the woman he kept in Cuba.

"Jesus takes away our first sin curse," Lutie was saying as Tork's mind wandered in and out of love. "Jesus be love!"

Tork wondered how that "square" could have lined-up the blessing of a girl like that? Maybe he did have that curse? Maybe it was the way he fit the uniform? Squeezed so tight in his whites the outline of circumcision showed through the bulge at his crotch. Maybe girls thought more about bearing a man's children than his company?

"Got you written up," Tork said, leaning back, wheeling his chair around to put a breath of air in motion. "Navy's got you ranked as a married man, got you a brown-bagging pass and a wife to pack you a brown-bag."

222

"Rather be *unranked* and out of this man's Navy," Lovett said, gathering together his papers, "but got these passports to free nights," and he stood, squared his shoulders.

"A married man's not free like a seed in the wind," the yeoman leveled with the airman, eye to eye. "A married man takes on roots."

"No roots in this here Navy," Lovett looked over his shoulder, leading his wife out, "no roots in air, or water."

"That marriage won't stay the course," Tork said to Roy Boy after the airman and his wife were gone. "It's a bad fit. He's square and she's round, and the two of them won't fit Cuba."

▄▄▄ ▄▄▄ ▄▄▄

Tork fit Lovett's service record back in file, but couldn't file away the thought of him, or the little country girl he was going to hang up to dry in Cuba. Across the bay, Caimanera was a waterfront dump where Cubans lived off sailors, and lived poorly. It was a dump where sailors sought their level in the lowest part of town, down by the water, with women who rented out their bodies for three dollars a whack.

He recalled the first time he got a load of Caimanera, the time he assumed the belt and stick of shore patrol. Sailors and marines and mongrel dogs, all in heat, roamed the streets. Dogs sniffed and licked at their private parts. There was the smell of sex in the air. Sailors who'd come on liberty in starched whites were un-starched in a hurry and stumbled between bars to look for their "drunken allies." Marines, stiff as ramrods, lined up on the dusty streets and performed the manual of arms with empty bottles.

Inside the bars there were fights to be broken up. A shore patrolman had to keep sober in a world that was falling-down drunk. When it was time to catch the last of the liberty boats back to base, sailors had to be shooed out of bars and back rooms like roosting chickens. Some of the nesting sailors got away, had to be pulled out of hiding places in stinking outhouses. On the way back to the Fleet Landing there would be sailors dropping out of windows, stepping into pants and shoes as they ran. One sailor showed up at the Fleet Landing out of uniform, completely out, said his uniform got "liberated" in a house of "free love." Wrapped in a bed sheet, drunk as a skunk, he gave a whole new meaning to "three sheets to the wind."

He finally learned to laugh at the Cuban world where sailors escaped regimentation, and themselves, in drink and the mechanics of love, and he learned to escape himself. Over there, prostitutes were no better or worse than any other working women. Rolling in bed with a stranger was no different than rolling cigars or cutting cane. It was a whole different world over there, a world without comforts, or guilt. How would Lovett's little woman make out?

■■■ ■■■ ■■■

The yeoman striker called Roy Boy kept mumbling to himself that Caimanera was no place for an airman to put down his wheels with a wife! Caimanera was bad enough, but the little wife with the banjo on her back had a man with a curse on his head! She couldn't keep in tune with a man who played around. She'd get abandoned, stranded over there, end up in one of those bars, selling herself!

Hunting and pecking at his typewriter, Roy Boy found it hard to believe men and women were carbon copies, in the image of God! He struck a wrong key, was angry that every official form in the Navy had to be typed in triplicate, the naval version of the Trinity! He bent over the tpewriter to "white-out" his mistake on all the carbon copies. As he worked at it, he couldn't wipe out the memory of his one and only liberty on the Cuban side of Guantanamo Bay.

It happened one Saturday when he was new to the squadron, just out of boot camp, excited about seeing the world. In Caimanera he saw too much of it!

A motor whale boat whipped him and a load of sailors across the bay. He jumped ashore and was caught up in a tide of white-capped sailors rushing into a dead sea of bars and debauchery. He got washed up in a bar that served-up women like drinks. There was no other place to go, only other bars. He had to hang on for an eternity, until time for the liberty boat back to base.

He managed to hold off the women, held his ground at a little round table on the far side of the dance floor.

Most of the sailors were strangers to him and left him alone. He made friends with his first bottle of beer, *Hatauey*, the "one-eyed Indian," and kept his eye on sailors and women dancing and drinking and going back and forth to rooms in back. The women seemed to think they were at a regular job, like waitresses. The sailors seemed to think they were doing something natural, like eating.

Getting back to hunting and pecking at his typewriter, Roy Boy suddenly struck up the key to a memory of the ugliest woman he'd ever laid eyes on! He paused between the words he was typing to picture her coming onto him in that bar! Black as the soil of the Mississippi Delta, pregnant as a mountain, he remembered her ugliness, but was thinking of her as the "Good Earth, carrier of life."

She wasn't one of the regular "bar-girls!" She came off the street, made the scene without permission, held the stage like an interloper. Crazy-angry, yelling, sputtering in Spanish and English, she was mad that no man would have her! She went from table to table, tried to pass herself off as a "Cuban souvenir," but no one wanted a souvenir like her. She ended up with him in the corner, squeezed herself next to him, spread her legs, said she'd "do" him for "two-bits," turn his "frown upside down."

He yanked the cross from round his neck, held it up as if to ward off the devil. She was the ugliest woman he'd ever seen, ugly as sin, but he started thinking that sin wouldn't be ugly. Sin had to be tempting, beautiful. He thought she might be an angel in ugly disguise, an angel testing his reverence for God's poor and downtrodden!

He remembered offering his "one-eyed Indian" to her. She put the bottle to the lips of her crooked mouth, sucked it dry. He thought of her carrying the genes of those who'd been sold for rum in slavery time. She was selling herself for less.

She smacked her lips and thanked him in English for the drink, said he was a "good man." It was the first time Roy Boy remembered being called a man.

Trying to think of something to say, he asked how she came by her English. She got it off a "Jamaican gentleman." He "cultivated" her, she said, planted the seed for one of the mouths she had to fill up. She had three other mouths, not counting her own, and another hungry mouth on the way.

No man would have her or keep her, she kept saying, stirring herself up into another rage, a fit that caught the attention of a shore patrolman. Flipping his stick as he made his way across the dance floor he loomed tall over Roy Boy's table. He thought Roy Boy must be drunk. "Kid, you able to see what ugly bitch you got yourself lined up with?"

"I see straight enough," Roy Boy managed to say. "She's a human being, with human feelings."

The shore patrolman twirled the stick at his side, grinned, handed Roy Boy a salute, and left him with his "lady friend." Roy Boy's woman was suddenly becalmed.

"This ugly bag of bones, she not good enough for you," she said to Roy Boy. "You could have that archangel over there, that pretty yellow woman!" She pointed a boney finger. It was still stuck in his memory, the boney finger, and the white palm of her hand that he stuffed with dollar bills. It was not for her body, he told her, it was for her many mouths. She made him take back a dollar, in case he had a "thirst," and left him in peace, but didn't leave his memory.

■■■ ■■■ ■■■

Across the bay, in Cuba, the good earth bore grazing grounds, and little farms, and patches of thatched huts. A railroad track stretched ten miles between the waterfront town of Caimanera and Guantanamo City in the interior. Like the Toonerville Trolly of comic book fame, the rickety train tooted back and forth, about twice a day. It was the same old train on the same old tracks the Spanish laid in the 19th century. Same old steam engine and rolling stock, same old rattle. It still carried passengers and sugar and molasses as slow as ever. It was faster to go back and forth by taxicab.

There was a dirt road between Caimanera and Guantanamo City but it was run down, full of ruts and wandering goats and fluttering chickens. A taxicab could make a better road on its own, follow the contours of least resistance, slash through the brush and scrubby terrain. Cabs ran on demand, unless a rain came up, and the creeks rose up.

Lovett knew all the bumps and grinds of the taxi ride, had hit them on many a freewheeling liberty in Guantanamo City. He remembered the empty countryside bumping by in a blur, spiny branches scratching at the window glass, and cab drivers rolling round with the steering wheel, braking and clutching and pumping their feet. Not one of the wheels ever touched ground at the same time.

"Guantanamo City's a bustling town, like Texarkana," Lovett promised his wife. He got her excited about the market places with fruits and vegetables fresh off the land. Churches and parks were handy, and there was a movie palace! "You can see all the Hollywood picture shows," he talked the place up, "but the flicks got subtitles in Cuban, or got Cuban words coming out of American mouths." Bob Hope, he told her, "don't sound so funny in Cuban talk, but Laurel and Hardy be still a scream!" He promised Lutie more things to do in Guantanamo City.

Caimanera just wasn't panning out. Each day Lutie was left by herself, stashed in a room not much bigger than the bed. Her married life was confined to a bed with a piss-pot under it, a room with a couple of hooks on the walls, a beaded curtain for a door. Left alone most of the day, no one to talk to, Lutie was lonely, and afraid she might not be alone. The portable radio Lovett got from the Navy PX only tuned into foreign sounds, and her banjo sounded hollow, like the emptiness inside her.

Lovett had figured Caimanera would be good enough for a countrified girl, but his countrified girl had gotten "uppity." She figured marriage should be a step up, a step up to paved streets outside, running water inside. She cried and fussed with him when he got back from base, only calmed down when they got into bed.

The little wife had been cranking-up marriage with a man's body she hardly knew, in a country she didn't know at all. Her husband was just beginning to get the idea his wife had a life when he wasn't with her. He was just beginning to call her Lutie instead of Lukie.

"There's better quarters and more action in Gitmo City," Lovett promised his wife, and promised to take her there. This was his first "long weekend" as a married man off base. He'd bought civilian clothes, could strut around in slacks and a t-shirt that sported an alligator print He'd learned that "Caimanera" was "alligator" in Spanish, learned it from one of the Cuban commuters on the ferryboat. He promised an alligator purse for Lutie some day, and alligator shoes, and a better life in Guantanamo City.

It was a bright Saturday morning as Lutie pranced barefooted beside her man, sandals stuck in the straw bag she carried. A sweatband held back her hair and showed off the roundness of her smile and face.

Lovett was on the lookout for a cab, sighted one at the Oasis Hotel. The hotel beside the shimmering bay triggered a different memory for each of them. Lutie remembered dinner on the terrace, under the moon. Lovett remembered the room with a door, and the bill.

While they paused to catch their flights of memory, two large Cuban women, their big-brimmed hats flopping in the wind, slipped past them and into the cab. They were willing to make room for the Lovetts. It was probably the only time they squeezed their legs together, Lovett thought, assuming they were off-duty whores. Prostitutes were well dressed, never accompanied by men.

The cab had room up front for another passenger. An enlisted man slipped in next to the driver as the cab geared up. The women with the big hats started flapping their folding fans, sharing some of the breeze with Lutie. Lovett hoped they wouldn't share their talk, and they didn't. They probably had no English in them. Lovett didn't recognize the sailor in the front seat. He was a third-class electrician's mate, must be based at Gitmo. The fleet sailors wouldn't know about the faraway treats of Guantanamo City. The electrician's mate kept his mouth shut, like the women, but fingered dogtags, like a rosary.

The cab was vintage Cadillac, Lovett judged, probably a prewar 1941 model, a museum piece in the States. It was revved up to make its own road across the countryside. Like a sailor, Lovett smiled to himself, the cab was in search of the best *lay* of the land, wheeling one way and another. The land began to level out, flatten into a plateau clawed by a few dried-out stream beds. The wheels churned-up dust and pebbles that hardly disturbed the vultures roosting in trees along the way. The sulking birds only ruffled monstrous wings and huddled back down inside them. They eyed the passing cab, looked for death.

In the semi-arid landscape all life was fortified and dug-in. Shrubs were armored and saber-sharp. Amid the thorns and spurs of the bush-country a solitary Brahman bull followed the cab with red eyes and snorting nostrils. He seemed strangely fat in such a lean land, Lutie thought to herself, and kept on the lookout for other bulls, all along the way. They stood like sentinels on hillocks.

The world of brush and thatched huts kept rushing away in dust and feathers and scattering chickens. Every now and then the horizon broke through the spears of defiant cactus, and a jagged horizon of mountains looked as remote as the sky.

Lutie held her breath when the Cadillac sloshed into a shallow stream, water gurgling up to the hubcaps, windows popping with globs of mud. Up the bank the wheels spun round, got better footing, got back on track. Guantanamo City began showing up, little by little, ramshackle grass huts at first. The outskirts of town were spread out, sparse and bare. Buzzards circled overhead, signaling all the life and throwaway leftovers ahead.

Concrete houses began piling up alongside the road, houses with pastel paints flaking and peeling. Canvas awnings guarded windows from the sun, bars guarded them from the streets.

The cab geared down for pedestrians, stray dogs and pigs, swerved to a stop in the old town square, in the shade of a stone church with a high bell tower. It was an old church, as ancient looking as Spanish colonial time. Its weathered walls stood over a gasoline filling station like the old power trying to lord it over the new.

The cab emptied and the floppy hats of the Cuban women were in the wind again, like billowing sails carrying them off. The Lovetts, not sure where they were going, got hemmed in by a gang of street urchins. The ragamuffins were begging for handouts, or trying to sell shoe shines. Lovett tossed pennies over their heads, and they scattered in a frenzy of arms and legs.

"Some of them are blue-eyed, like Americans," Lutie said, walking briskly to keep up with her husband.

"They be the leftovers of sailor good times," Lovett said, keeping up his long stride.

"None of your leftovers I reckon."

Lovett only kept walking fast.

"This gonna be too much of a trip for you," Lutie managed to gasp, still trying to keep up. "Think you up to all this hustle back and forth to base every day?"

"Won't seem so long, with a good woman at the end."

"And no pee-pan under the bed," Lutie giggled, keeping up with her man.

"You be the only *necessary* I got to have."

They strung along together, searching for the address a Cuban bootblack in the barracks had given Lovett. They came to a block of pink buildings and a doorway that bore the number Lovett was looking for.   A pot of blooming yellow flowers stood beside the door.

"It be a storybook house," Lutie said, touching the plank door studded with fluted brass.

Lovett's knock got the door to open a crack.

"*Casa* Manrique," a voice sounded as the door opened wider. "*Americanos*," the voice proclaimed loudly, as though the Lovetts betrayed some clue of nationality in their appearance.

"*Arrendatario.*" Lovett said. It was a word he got from the Cuban bootblack to identify himself as a cash renter. "*Quanto*," he asked. That was an indispensable word for a sailor on liberty in Cuba. He thought everything had a price.

"I *savez* the English," said the woman in the doorway, opening the plank door wide enough to show most of herself. Stuffed in a black smock; she was bulky and ungainly in the torso, shapely in the arms and legs.

"I'm a sailor, American," Lovett said, realizing he was not in uniform, "and be in the market for a home to plant myself and wife" He mentioned the name of his "amigo" named Angel, the Cuban bootblack in his barracks. Squaring himself, the alligator on his t-shirt seemed to stretch itself out.

"Angel, ah, *si*," the woman recognized the name. She showed the whole of herself in the doorway. She waved them in with an arm that bore a black band. She called herself

Magdalena Manrique, led them into a hallway, all the while explaining her connection to the "grandiose" American naval base. As a *muchacha* she'd been a maid in the housekeeping service on the American base. She laughed, said she was born in Cuba but "maid in America." She said she gave up work on base when she married a "pharmacist," got two sons by him, one still living with her. She talked as she had them follow her through a narrow passage. The husband was warm in the grave, she kept talking, his relations still under her roof, and she apologized for a "full house," said it would be empty "*manana.*"

The Lovetts kept up with her, looking around as they went. Magdalena pointed out a shrine to her late husband, a shrine with offerings of his favorite food and drink. On and on she led them, past an opened door where the foot of a bed held three pairs of men's stocking feet.

"*Siesta,*" she mentioned in passing. Farther down the hall she showed them the kitchen. The women of the house were at work there. The "colored maid" that Magdalena pointed out was only a little darker than herself.

Finally, Magdalena opened a door to a burst of sunlight, and a spacious patio, enclosed on all sides by walls of the house. It was big enough for a shady mango tree that hung its branches over the four surrounding walls. Potted plants hung from pegs in the patio walls, and a large bird cage hung from the tree. A colorful parrot strutted around inside.

"A tree in the house!" Lutie cried out, delighted.

"It make for the shade," the woman of the house said, "but the chicken, they get the first peck of the mango."

They moved across the courtyard to a red painted door on the far side. Magdalena gave a knock with her plump fist and opened the door, showed the Lovetts a "sitting room" with a leather rocker, a table and lamp, several folding chairs stacked up against a wall. The room was filled with light from the window. Magdalena mentioned a "place to wash and pee not far off."

"*Dormitorio* closed off for now," she said, pointing to an inside door. "Son of house, university man, sleep in room for now, till house guests *vamos*."

"Lord a-mercy, how much?" Lutie wondered, looking around.

Lovett liked the place, too. Sailors crave space.

"Not too *mucho* for the *Americanos*," came a voice from the other side of the bedroom door. The door opened and framed a young man, chest bare, bronzed like gold. He let go of the door and fastened the trousers together at his waist, introduced himself as the "son of the house, Ramon." He went on to explain that he was a student of English at the Havana University, home on "holiday." He motioned for them to join him inside. "Rest eyes in the sleeping chamber," he said, "bed unmade, but make for plenty sleep." He looked Lovett over, asked if he played "the American football."

"Played a good tackle in my year of high school," Lovett was happy to say, surprised that the Cuban knew about football.

"I play football, too," the young Cuban said, "but you Americans call it soccer."

"Talk the business," Magdalena said, "not kick of the ball."

"Never did I look for heaven on earth," Lutie raved, "but this sure be a step up."

"And let there be light," Magdalena said, pulling a string. "We got the electric power."

"Any place to eat?" Lovett wanted to know.

"You get run of kitchen, a shelf in my ice box, any burner you want on gas stove. You get table for your own, out in patio, under mango tree."

"Lord a-mercy," Lutie said again, "how much?"

"American eagles fly high in Cuba," Magdalena said, calculating in her head. "It be low price for you."

"The Yankee dollar is the coin of God's realm," the son of the house spoke up. "*El Presidente Batista* buy the army with the American dollar, get Cuba with army!"

"Ramon *mucho politico*," Magdalena explained, "but Cuba got bad taste in mouth for Batista, and *Batistianos*! God don't speak good of Batista."

"The Mama of the house speaks to God," Ramon said, teeth glistening in the light of his bronzed face, "and God talk back."

"God don't talk good about *el* tyrant," the mother said, "but God don't meddle in Cuba.   We got to make do ourselves."

"*El* tyrant don't go for backtalk," Ramon said, buttoning himself in the shirt he picked up from a chair. "He only dictates, talks down to us."

"My commanding officer's like that," Lovett thought. "Sailors live in dictator-*ships*."

"You make the joke with words," Ramon grinned, "but Batista, he no joke."

"You free enough to bad-mouth him," Lovett noted.

"When I was a-growing up," Lutie broke in, "two half brothers went off to war against dictatorships! Home folks said a body couldn't open a mouth in one of them places. This little gal couldn't figure how anyone ate or brushed teeth." She giggled.

"*Americano* sailors free to *bitch*," Ramon said, "but Cubans go to hoosgow for bad mouthing Batista! Cuba is run from top down, by top, for top," and he fastened the last button of his shirt.

"That's the Navy way, too," Lovett insisted, "run from top down."

"God rule from top down!" the mother said. "Magdalena rule house from top down! Now we talk the business, out by the mango, where we catch the air."

"If we rent-up with her," Lovett whispered to Lutie as they followed Magdalena out the door, "don't leave me alone with her. She got the hots for me." In a loud voice he called after

Magdalena. "Can't talk big bucks. This here sailor only got airman stripes."

"Make sale price for sailor."

They found shade under the mango tree, sat around the patio table, alongside cackling chickens.

"How much time you got for Cuba?" the woman of the house wanted to know.

"My squadron's stuck permanent here," Lovett said, "like fleas on a hog. Reckon I finish my enlistment here, two more years."

"Cubans make you a *paisano* in two whole years," Ramon broke in, flashing a sunny smile, a smile Lutie reflected.

"God tell me to make good nest for Americano love birds," Magdalena said, her hands pressed together as if in prayer. "Ten American eagles, first of the month!"

"You got it," Lovett said, figuring it cost more than two dollars a night at the Oasis Hotel, and you had to eat out. "I got the first month rental on the barrel head," and he flipped out his wallet. "When can we take up quarters?"

"Get your key to *Casa Manrique*," Magdalena said, "*manana*, God's day." She made room for the ten dollar bill in the heart of her bulging black dress.

"We be here tomorrow, suitcase in hand," Lovett said, happy to think of leaving the cramped quarters in Caimanera.

"*Tia Magdalena* make *Casa Manrique* your *Casa*," Magdalena said to the Americans.

"Can we throw parties?" Lovett asked.

"My house your house."

"Sailors party hardy," Lovett warned, wondering if he could find anything like "white lightening" in the land of rum and coca-cola.

"My house your house!"

"Bless your dear heart," Lutie said, looking all around. "Love it here!"

■■■ ■■■ ■■■

The Curse that Lovett thought kept love out of his heart kept jealousy out, too. He never worried about leaving his wife each day in a household that sported a flashy university man. He never worried about showing off his wife to horny, sex-starved sailors. Back on base he was quick to invite some of his crew mates to check out his little woman in Guantanamo City, and chow down on some home cooking.

Three sailors showed up at the *Casa Manrique* on a Saturday afternoon liberty. They were drooping in the heat, like the black neckerchiefs dangling round their necks. One of the sailors carried a guitar case. It seemed to be attached to him, like white jumper and bellbottoms.

Ramon met the sailors at the door and showed them to the Lovett quarters in back.

"Ahoy, good buddies," Lovett hailed his crew mates. Lovett had gotten himself off base the night before and was out of uniform, relaxing in sport shirt, shorts, and floppy slippers. He waved the men into the half light of the sitting room.

Lutie had been hoping to see the yeoman with the curvy legs in khaki shorts. He wasn't one of the sailors. She didn't recognize any of the uniformed men They all looked alike, at first. She hovered barefoot in a corner but managed to speak up, tell the men she got "all gussied up" for them. She said she "sacrificed a maiden chicken" for their coming. Once she started talking she couldn't stop. She went on and on about bartering for the "sacrificial" hen, all by herself in a Cuban market, wringing the old bird's neck, cleaning it good, turning it on a spit over hot coals She said she made-up a mess of potato salad and brewed a pitcher of tea water, steeped it in the Cuban sun, got it good and sweet, but didn't have much ice. As she talked she kept looking down. Barefooted, her feet were delicate, and tanned, toenails painted red.

"You walk on rosebuds," one of the sailors mentioned. He was the one who had a military fit to his manner, wore his uniform well. "Your feet are like flower pedals."

Lutie blushed, managed to say she got the toe polish from the "*madre* of the house." Magdalena's rouge also brightened her mouth and round cheeks, widened her round eyes. She didn't mention Magdalena's silver comb fastening her dark hair in back, or Magdalena's shell-beads roped round her neck. Lutie felt good about herself, except for the breasts she could hardly carry around, and the flowery print dress a size too small.

The sailor with the guitar didn't say anything. Lutie told him she plucked the banjo.

"What kind of sweet milk you raised on?" the third sailor asked her. He was long in the face, a country looking boy, unsmiling. She imagined him with hayseeds in his receding hair.

"You be raised on sweet talk," Lutie said to him, "I be weaned on corn squeezings."

The Cuban Ramon was standing to one side, listening to the talk as though absorbed in a language lesson.

"I be unmannerly," Lutie said, turning away from the sailors. "Cuban boy be Ramon, son of house. His momma calls him *Chango*, monkey in Cuban. He play like the organ -grinder monkey when he be in mood for it."

"The kid hangs out with our Cuban bootblack, Chico the foot fool," Lovett added. "Fools hang together."

The bronzed Ramon nodded to the strangers, and excused himself in good English. "*El Chango* must swing off and make monkey business in Santiago."

Lutie was the only one to laugh, and the only one to wave him off.

The sailors had pulled up chairs, got off their feet, stretched out their legs. Lutie settled in the rocker, her breasts settling in with her. She took to her fan, a large white fan with an ivory handle. Her eye was on the sailor who thought she walked on rosebuds. He was striding a folding chair, long legs crossed, swinging one foot. He had a big foot.

"You gonna pipe us aboard, proper like?" the sailor with the swinging foot asked Lovett. "Your little lady don't even know our names."

"I do be hankering to make acquaintance with y'all, bless your dear hearts," Lutie spoke up as she kept fanning herself and looking down at her curled-under toes.

"We only be mechanics, mostly screw-ups," drawled the country boy with the long horse-like face.

"The nuts and bolts of the squadron," the good looking sailor with the big feet said.

"Mostly the nuts," the sailor with the guitar smiled.

"Guitar man be bunked over me when I got to stay over in the barracks," Lovett said to Lutie. "Big Bands gonna snap him up soon as he gets his walking papers from the Navy."

The guitar player bowed his head to check out the guitar he'd taken out of the case. Lutie could see the yellow top of his head shaved to an inch of the skin, bristling like a wire brush. He looked up, and said he'd like to pull a few strings to get out of the Navy. He didn't look anyone in the eye, kept his head tilted to one side. Even his smile was slanted.

"You got your eye on *Woogie, the guitar, Woodrow Woods*," Lovett introduced the guitar player to Lutie. "He boogie *woogies* all the time, sets the barracks a-rocking."

"Even when not at his guitar, he always keeps time with a foot," the sailor with the swinging foot spoke up. "He even keeps time with his spoon when he's at chow"

"Like to keep time," Woogie affirmed, tapping a foot, "except Navy time!"

"He looks regulation, but the guitar man's not in tune with the Navy," Lovett said.

"None of us keeps in step with the Navy," the man with the swinging foot thought.

"This old gal likes to keep time with her man," Lutie chimed in, "and keep time with my foot, too, whilst I play me a riff on the banjo."

Lovett next got around to introducing the good looking sailor swinging a big foot. "This pretty boy with the eagle and stripe on his sleeve be Enzo Varsi, petty officer, aviator machinist's mate third class."

Lutie thought he was a pretty officer, first class.

"Varsi outranks us in everything," Lovett said. "A good man, he's too good to be a sailor!"

"And good at making pictures," Varsi said of himself. "The little Lovett woman's pretty as a picture." He dug the stub of a pencil out of his jumper pocket. "Got any paper? Want to put that Madonna face on hold."

"Never had my picture done," Lutie said, getting up to look for paper.

"You got to pick up the handle on this horsey character," Lovett called to his wife as she came back with a pad of paper. "He be a real sketch, name of Eli Dobbins, dead-ringer for a two-legged horse critter!"

"Call me Horse-Face Eli!"

"He got that sad face from a-worry about losing his hair," Lovett added.

"A sad face be off limits on this base," Lutie told him, thinking that Eli Dobbins really did look like a horse, with a long, thin face. His hairline was almost up to the top of his head.

"He's short on hair but long on stories," Varsi had a good word for him as he took a pad of paper from Lutie. "That old boy gives stories away, but bums cigarettes."

"Make men blessed," Horse-Face Eli drawled. "It be blessed to give," and he looked around, begged for the gift of a smoke.

"Bless your dear heart," Lutie said to the guitar player who shook a cigarette out of the pack for the country boy.

"I'll give you a story, if you bless me," Horse-Face Eli said, leaning forward for a light.

"Get a load at this picture before the horse-face saddles us with one of his stories," Varsi spoke up, waving the sheet of paper he'd torn from the pad.

"Never had my likeness made," Lutie said, taking hold of Varsi's pencil-sketch and studying it. She passed it around. "It do be me," she said, standing up. "Leave my picture with you boys, take myself off to mess duty! Tap the beer and roll half an hour around till I be back."

"Save-up my story for you," Horse-Face Eli said as she ran off. "Now, Cowboy Lovett, how you ever rope a filly like that?"

"She be lucky to end up on my line," Lovett said.

"You be lucky to have that curse working for you," Horse-Face Eli said in a cloud of smoke. "Can't remember how you got put under that lucky spell?"

"Got it off a cult-woman," Lovett said. He liked to talk about his curse. "It were said she be a devil-woman, but can't rightly speak to that. Took offense, she did, at me making out with one of her girls!"

"My old Mammy figured my Pappy got a curse like that," Horse-Face Eli said. "He draw females like flies but be rotten in love. Ma had to take a stick to females every time it were a-mating time in the mountains."

"Got no flies on me no more," Lovett said. "Got me a wife."

"Think you broke that curse? Got yourself some good loving with that filly of yours!"

"How do I know it be love?"

"You know you got love if you can't live without it," Woogie said, stroking the guitar strings. "Got love for this little old guitar. Can't live without her."

Lovett shrugged and got up to go outside, check the heat on the patio. It was time to take the air and cover the parrot. Shade had swept away the sunshine and some of the hotness. Lovett got help to set up the portable table under the mango tree.

The sailors took their drinks and smokes outside, set up chairs around the table in the courtyard. An electric light bulb hung down from the tree on a long wire and the men started shining under it. They were getting hungry, started to talk about Navy chow.

"Miss my fatback and greens," Horse-Face Eli got the hungry talk going, "but when I puts on the Navy feed bag I chow down pretty good."

"Navy chow gets peppered with *salt peter*," Lovett spoke with the authority of one who'd drawn the mess duty, "makes a man peter out, but this old boy gets the home cooking and keeps up with home loving."

"*Salt peter* don't make me peter out," Woogie brightened. "Get my tubes cleaned out pretty regular, over in Caimanera." He blushed when Lutie came out of the shadows. She was bearing a plate of chicken, its seasoned and roasted aroma coming with her.

"This cotton-picking gal don't blush at man-talk," she turned on a smile. "Keep shooting the bull while this gal be serving-up the fatted calf." She was beginning to feel at home with the strangers.

"I like the breast," petty officer Varsi spoke up as Lutie bent over him with the chicken.

"Me, too," Horse-Face Eli said, reaching for a piece. "Back to home I was last of the litter, bottom of the totem pole, only got the leftover chicken. Thought the old bird only had a neck and tail till brothers went off!" He smacked his lips, got the breast to his mouth with one hand, swatted flies with the other. "Ever get used to these fly furies?" he asked with his mouth full. "Don't Cubans spray for flies over here?"

"Rather fret over flies than Navy chickenshit," Lovett said, biting a piece of chicken to the bone, stripping off a mouthful of meat.

"Rather swat the breeze with the little lady," Varsi said to Lutie. "Can't you sit yourself down a spell?"

"In Cuba, women don't eat with their men," Lutie said, moving around as she talked, "but I'll sit a spell after I get more fixings on the table." She wiped both hands on her apron and backed into the dark, reappeared with another tray of chicken, and ice tea.

"Tea tastes like piss, no shit!" Lovett said with a spit.

"Mighty fine spread," Varsi hastened to sooth Lutie's feelings. "What's a pretty lady do with herself all day while waiting for her man to come home?"

"Got me the banjo to whack away the time," Lutie said, "and the Good Book," and she looked down at her squirming toes, "and take me little steps, walk me a bit farther every day." She was getting warmed up. "Go to market for the shopping, go to movies when Hollywood pictures be a-showing on the marquee. I be learning to read Cuban from the movie subtitles."

"*Muchacha* be the only Cuban word I picked up, so far," Horse-Face Eli said with a full mouth.

"*Muchacho*, son of house, Ramon, be learning me the Cuban talk and politics, the way Cuba be, and should be."

248

"The little woman gives me the lowdown," Lovett joined in. "A goonie revolution be a- brewing, that be the word."

"You know a different Cuba if you know their words," Lutie said. "Did you know the chairs you be sitting on are female? Cubans think everything be male or female!"

"There sure are some male things hanging around!" Varsi said and got a laugh from all but Lutie.

"Cuban words be sexy," she agreed, not knowing why the men were laughing.

"Their tongue puts them more into sex than us English speakers," Varsi raised his opinion over the laughter.

"Cubans sure be free with sex," Lovett thought, "except where it gets sold in the District."

"Men don't have to get married in Cuba to get sex," Horse-Face Eli found himself saying before realizing a woman was present. He hurried to compliment Lovett on his good wife and life.

By the time Lutie's chicken had made its last turn around the table, the moon and stars had come around. Lutie, who'd gone off with dishes came back to light candles on the table, provide an extra flutter of light.

Woogie had lined up his guitar, his drinks and cigarettes. His bristly blond crew-cut was sparkling in the flickering candlelight as he bent over the guitar. Lutie went back in the house for her banjo, came right back to string along with Woogie and the rhythm of the table talk.

Woogie was tilting his head, listening to the snap of his strings. He liked to look down as he played, liked to toss ideas up as he played. "Do we make music?" he asked, crooning his words, "or does music make us?" He was always saying something unexpected.

"Music makes us," Lutie said, taking him seriously, "makes us feel good."

"Music can talk for us," Woogie let out from the side of his mouth, "but I don't always know what it's saying." He, struck a single chord. "If I knew what that sound meant, I might be able to communicate with God."

"Cuban lady of the house, Tia Magdalena, she talk to God," Lutie sang out, striking her own tune, a familiar spiritual. "Hymns speak to God, I reckon. The Lord is my song."

"Music is the language of God," Woogie said, joining Lutie in a familiar hymn. He changed the tone, sang out to Lutie. "String along with me, my little chickadee!" His fuzzy blond head was nodding up and down, like his foot.

"With a banjo on my knee," Lutie sang back, slipping into Woogie's "country" mood.

"Kick-ass music do put a hang-fire in my windpipe," Horse-Face Eli complained, "chokes me up."

Lutie stopped playing, pressed the banjo next to her heart. "*Country* strumming gives me the homesickness, too."

"I likes to chew the cud about home folks," Horse-Face Eli said, "but the old time music stick to my craw when I be off from home. It don't go down so good."

"You were a-fixing to tell us a story," Lutie tried to change the subject, "before we put on the feed bag. Time you get round to it!"

"You be an angel woman," the country boy said. "I really seen me an angel, back to home, quite a spell ago. She come down from Heaven to save my worthless hide. Weren't no cause for her to do it. I be a rounder, not worth angel spit." He drew the last glow from his cigarette, crushed it in the ashtray. "Got me a story to air out for y'all, soon as I get me a smoke."

"Make it a two smoke story," Woogie said, reaching over his guitar with a pack of cigarettes. "You sure got the bug for storytelling."

"Well, I declare, Lutie said while Horse Face Eli was waiting for a light, "I be known for spinning stories, back to home, more than for my patch quilting."

"Give me some of your angel music to go with my angel story," Horse-Face Eli said to Lutie as he parted his lips for a ring of his smoke that spiraled straight up into the starlight.

Lutie struck a chord on her banjo to get the story going.

"Me and Reb Johnson went off a-fishing one dreary mountain day when it be too wet for working the ground," Horse-Face Eli began. "Cranked up the old Model A, we did, and rattled her down to Abner's Crick. Reb weren't never without a jug of home brew and we be lapping it up all the way down to our fishing hole. Best fishing was out in the shallows by the cypress stumps. We rolled overalls up to kneecaps, waded out in the stream and caught us a mess of catfish, and bloodsuckers, two *feet* of bloodsuckers each, and by that time we'd sucked up the whole jug of Reb's home brew. We be starting to catch a good rain, got fixing to hit the road. Between the two of us I be the one to see most straight, got the call to steer Reb's old jalopy back up to home. Jalopy got no brakes, got to be geared down for a stop, got to be gunned-up for ruts and uphill goings. We'd been getting spells of rain, past couple days, and now it be falling right smart. The day goes dark, sets the chickens off to roosting before their time." He paused to flick the ash off his cigarette.

"Model A got a windshield, but no wipers on the sweep," he started up again. "Had me a deuce of a time seeing up the road, but got along pretty well til I come eyeball to eyeball with that angel woman a-flapping wings on the hood, like a spread-eagle car ornament. I geared down plenty fast. And good thing! Just ahead was a forty-foot drop-off. Rains had tore out the old bridge. Gone another foot and we be goners!" He finished his story and cigarette at the same time.

"Well, I declare!" Lutie said, "You sure was saved! Get yourself born again?"

"Don't know if I be born again, but got my hide saved for a new life in this here man's Navy."

"We all need saving from this here Navy life," Lovett added to the story as he started to roll a wad of tobacco into his mouth. After dinner time was his chewing and spitting time. He could rattle a tin can from six to eight paces.

"Got me a God-saving story worth the telling," Lutie spoke up, touching the strings of her banjo with one hand, her heart with the other. "Maud Simpson's man sure had the need for saving. Old Maud been a-praying for her man since the day she got him to the church. One day after her man was off to chores the words wouldn't come. It worried her a spell, but when her man come home for his noon day victuals she knew why no prayer words would come. She didn't need no more prayers. Her man got saved! She told him so, and he didn't know how in creation she got word he be saved while a-breaking new ground with plow and horse. Maud's man was sure enough saved, and she didn't need to pray no more. He did all the praying from that day on!"

"Far out!" Woogie said, aiming his eyes toward the stars and hitting the melody of Hoagy Carmichael's *Stardust*. "Far out," he kept saying, and humming.

"Farfetched," Lovett spit out, hitting the coffee tin can with a splat.

"Your old man only believes in curses, not blessings," Horse-Face Eli said to Lutie.

"They go together," Woogie chimed in, striking guitar notes out of harmony, "curses and blessings in the Good Book, all mixed up together."

"Bible be a mystery story," Lutie thought," full of clues, but you got to solve it yourself."

"That do put me in mind of a mystery story with a curse and blessing." Horse-Face Eli said.

"Let's smoke it out," Varsi said, leaning toward the storyteller with a pack of cigarettes.

Horse-Face Eli took one, began to move his lips in the light of a match held up. "There be a curse on the head of the no-count *Miller boy*," he began. "He be the devil of all talk in hill and dale." Horse-Face Eli had to stop and wave at the white smoke swirling around his head. "Shoo off, ghost," he said. "This ain't no ghost story. It be the flesh and blood story of the *Miller boy*, bastard by birth and deed, the butt-end of talk on every gossip stump, and every Sunday parlor. Folks keep voices down when running off at the mouth about that *Miller boy*, and the oil lamps get to flicker with so much devilment in the air." He paused to brush away more ghosts. "Devil wrote the book on sin and temptation," he carried on, "and *Miller boy* had learned it all by heart. One summer night, the no-count *Miller boy* went off to a candy-pull at the Harrison homestead, on other side of the mountain. He took that tramp of a gal from across Abner's Crick, he did, and trailed along with the Jones boy and the Randolf girl. Jones boy and Randolf girl stem from good stock, but they let the *Miller boy* and his tramp of a gal trail along with them. It were a good night for company! Wildcats and spooks were out. They all four was tramping along the footpath when

the moon went off and the night were black as the devil's
bunghole. Sudden like, a light cracked open a sliver in the
dark, and all four saw Jesus a-standing there, raising a hand
to bless them. Jesus made his own light. You could see every
feature on the Good Man's blessed face, plain as day. Then
the moon turned on again and Jesus wasn't in the moonshine.
For a heartbeat nobody could get a word out. Then the Jones
boy and the Randolf girl bear witness to a mighty strange
thing. No-count *Miller boy* had the same face as Jesus, the
very same face! You couldn't tell the cursed *Miller boy* from
the blessed Good Man!"

"Shot of white lightening could make 'em see anything,"
Lovett laughed it off.

"But no-count *Miller boy* never done a bad thing after
that."

"Far out," Woogie said.

"Puts me in mind of a tale going round the bottoms where
I be from," Lutie said, "true life story of a swamp boy a-feared
of water. "One precious night, after lamps be snuffed out, the
Ma and Pa of swamp boy hear the back door a-slapping shut.
His Ma and Pa got themselves up and got a look at their boy
a-heading toward the water. They sneaked after their boy to
see what he be up to, and see him sashay right up to the crick
and go straight across the walking log to the other side. He
never done that before. He came back across the walking log
as slick as could be and went back to bed. Same thing next
night. His Ma and Pa got to thinking he were "possessed" by

a water spirit, but it came to pass that they thought he might be just walking in his sleep. Folks planned on waking him up on the walking log so he'd see he weren't afeared of water no more. Next night when he was out a-going cross the walking log, folks called him back to himself. It give him a start when he see where he be! He stopped a-going, tottered this way and that, gave a yell and pitched right into the crick water. That night be on the black side of the moon, and swamp boy weren't seen until next morning, all curled up in the rushes a couple miles down stream. Mystery be what got in him? Good or bad spirits? Folks see him a-balancing between good and bad on that old log on nights the moon don't shine. He be a swamp spirit, maybe good, maybe bad ghost!"

"Sorry, old gal," Varsi said to Lutie. "This old boy don't go for ghosts. Your folks are seeing swamp gas."

"Well, I do declare," Lutie said. "Ghosts don't show up in city lights!" She'd learned over the course of the evening that Varsi came from the big city, Chicago, the toddling town where some of her kinfolk looked for work, back in the days of drought, crop failures, and bank closings. Kinfolk got put down in Chicago as "stump jumpers!"

"The ghosts you country folks see," Varsi talked back, "are spirits in your moonshine."

"In the *stills* of the night," Woogie sang out, striking up a familiar tune on the tuitar.

"Mostly we got witches back my way," Lovett spit out, hitting the coffee can.

"Lovett sure got himself a bewitching wife," Varsi spoke up, and flashed a smile at Lutie.

Lutie started blushing again. She'd been caught sneaking a look at the petty officer. He was pretty, she kept thinking, more pretty than a man should be, and she kept sizing him up, top to bottom. "There be ghosts in Cuba," she stammered out. "Cuban boy, Ramon, tell me ghosts in Cuba abide in trees."

"Never heard tell of tree ghosts," Horse-Face Eli said, "but heard tell of horse-ghosts." He said he was in mind of another story, and another cigarette. He drew an offered cigarette and a light and a breath and spewed out a tale of four unhitched horses "a-galloping up a hill," and they went under a rise in the land and never came up, only the sound of their hoof beats. "Hoof beats still come over that rise on nights the moon don't shine," he came to a quick end. "When folks hear those hoofs a-beating they get to fearing the four horses of the Apocalypse, and the end of the world!"

"Horseshit," Varsi said.

"Gospel truth," Horse-Face Eli swore with one hand raised in the air. "You got it from the horse's mouth!"

"Lord-a-Mercy!" Lutie gasped. "You reckon those white horses can be brought up from the ground?. Cuban boy, Ramon, tell me of Voodoo a-raising bodies from the ground and putting them to work in the cane fields!"

"Don't much hanker to Zombies," Horse-Face Eli said.

"I can really spook you with little gray people from OUTER SPACE," Woogie said, getting in the act.

"You boys sure like ruffing my feathers, making me all goose bumps," Lutie complained with a friendly pout.

"Don't mean to scare you," Woogie kept on, "but I hail from Roswell, New Mexico, and can testify to a flying saucer flipping down in my old stomping grounds."

"It was big news, couple years back," Varsi remembered, sitting straight up. He started to doodle on his pad of paper, passed around a sketch of little figures with big eyes, and heads.

"You must have had a look at the *Life Magazine* spread on those little gray bodies and space debris," Woogie said. "The Army hushed it all up!"

"A sure fire cover-up," Varsi agreed. "Army didn't want us to know about something."

"Lots of holes in the cover-up," Woogie said. "I knew me some folks who bore witness to corpses of google-eyed creatures, and hunks of out-of-this-world wreckage!"

"Government claimed it was just some weather balloons and dummy-bodies," Varsi came up with another recollection.

"What made your little old desert town worth aliens spying on?" Lovett gave another spit and spat.

"Atomic Age began in New Mexico," Woogie replied, "and rocketry!"

"Atomic bomb jitters keep my drawers in a twist," Horse-Face Eli confessed. "Back to home on my side of the mountains, it were thought we be at the atomic bomb bull's eye."

"My hometown started building underground classrooms for school kids," Woogie continued. "Roswell was one of the first towns to start digging-in for the Atomic Age."

"Lord-a-Mercy," Lutie said, looking up at the stars, "them mushroom clouds and flying saucers make my head spin, they do."

"It's a *far out* world up there," Woogie said, following Lutie's eyes to the stars. "Maybe we got enemies up there?"

"A war of the worlds would sure extend our enlistments!" Lovett worried.

"No such thing as aliens from other worlds," Lutie finally had to speak up. "No other world in Creation."

"Weren't your angel messengers of the Lord from another world?" Varsi asked. "Could they have been outer space aliens with wings?"

"Maybe your Roswell aliens be God's guardian angels looking out for us?" Lutie asked of Woogie.

Varsi said something about Lutie having the look of an angel. "Could our little hostess be an angel-alien come down to look out for us?"

"You got yourself a batch of pretty words," Lutie said, looking down at her bare feet. "You got a pretty story for us?"

"All my stories are in pictures," Varsi said, ripping a sheet of paper off his pad. "Picture this, our hostess as a boy." He ripped off another sheet. "Picture our host as a girl."

"Picture do me up good," Lutie said, holding Varsi's drawing to the light, passing it around. "Short hair and flat chest do me up good." She smiled to think that the pretty officer had been looking at her all this while.

"Only had to round off the squares and put curls on the blockhead," Varsi said of Lovett's picture he was passing around.

"Scary, picturing me as a woman," Lovett thought, flipping the picture back at Varsi.

"Picture that army man, George Jorgenson," Varsi said. "Now that's a scary story. He went to Denmark for the cut that turned him from *George* to *Christine*!"

"Sure riled up the base when it came out in *The Indian*," Horse-Face Eli said, "made for a lot of jokes in letters to the editor."

"It be more creepy than funny," Lovett thought, chewing the words around.

"Why'd a man do a crazy thing like that?" Woogie wondered, his hand striking dissonance out of his guitar.

"To make money," Varsi bet, "selling the story all over creation."

"Wouldn't take a million bucks for my stud-piece," Horse-Face Eli brought up.

"That Jorgenson fella wouldn't miss it," Varsi pointed out, "claimed he always *felt* like a woman."

"This boy only wants to feel a woman," Horse-Face Eli thought.

"If I turned into a woman," Varsi said, "I'd take on the whole fleet, wait on the dock for ships to come in."

"You might even fall under the Lovett Curse," Woogie said with a laugh and more dissonance on the guitar, "but draw men to you like flies."

"My Curse ain't no joke." Lovett talked at the same time he was juicing up his mouth, spitting again.

"Let's cut the crap," Woogie said, strumming-up a country tune, "sing out to the moon."

"Ain't I told you, foot music do make me want to *dos-a-dos* round back to home?"

"My guitar's got some Cuban strings that won't strike a note of home sickness," Woogie said, changing the beat.

"Too fast for my little hands," Lutie protested, trying to keep up.

"Time's going too fast," Varsi noticed, checking his watch. "Time to be heading back to the Rock."

"Our Petty Officer sure holds to course," Woogie groaned, "but he keeps us in line for the Good Conduct Medal." He struck up a different tune, nodding at Lovett and Lutie. "Thanks for the memories."

"Come back round, hear?" Lovett said, getting up. "Want you all to come back round, like hands come back round the clock!"

Lutie was sorry to see the sailors get ready to go, but she felt an itch to get between the sheets with her man, their body parts striking sparks. She didn't want to think of the morning when her man would have to take off for the base, like his sailor buddies were doing now.

■■■ ■■■ ■■■

Days came in and out like the tides of Guantanamo Bay. Another morning rolled in at the squadron personnel office, but it wasn't like all the other mornings! Rumors of peace were in the air, talk of an armistice in Korea, and airman Lake Lovett was absent at muster!

The personnel officer went out on the line to check for the missing man, and mechanics from the workshops on the hangar deck were coming up to check on the scuttlebutt of peace. The heat of the day was starting to come up with them.

"No official word on the armistice," Tork kept sending the men back down to work

"Peace won't make us no difference," Tork mentioned to Roy Boy as they prepared for the work of the day. "We'll have to let our enlistments run out, same as ever." He started to put together the *Plan of the Day*, bearing down on the typewriter keys to make deep impression on the stencil.

"Won't make us no difference in the plan of our day, or plan for our lives," he mumbled under his breath.

"Make a difference to the men in Korea," Roy Boy thought, crossing himself. He was always crossing himself. "Phone's ringing! Want me to get it?"

Tork got up and took the phone. It was a call from the Tower ordering a change in the plan of the day. Liberty call was cancelled! Cuba was off limits until further notice!

"No liberty for today," Tork said to Roy Boy.

"Don't make me no difference," Roy Boy said. "What's up?"

"Unrest in Cuba!" That's the only explanation Tork got "Have to change the damn plan of the day!" He pulled the stencil out of his typewriter, started to wonder how he could get word to his *mamacieta* in Caimanera, rolled another stencil in place, began pressing down hard on the typewriter keys to make a good impression. As soon as he finished, he ran off a number of copies, sent Roy Boy out to distribute them. The personnel officer, Lieutenant Gordon, crossed paths with the yeoman striker.

"Line chief's got the whole day shift on the alert for our missing man," the personnel officer reported to Tork. "Ring up the barracks, get the master at arms on it!"

"Liberty's been cancelled," Tork told the officer. "Trouble in Cuba."

"Keep me informed," Crash Gordon said, throwing up his hands. He closed himself off in the inner office.

Tork got around to phoning the barracks, rounding up the master at arms, getting him to run a bed check, get on the search for Airman Lake Lovett.

Tork realized all at once that the man absent without leave was the "square" who dragged a pretty little wife over to Cuba. What if Lovett got himself written-up as a deserter? What if the book was closed on the Korean War but the Navy-hating Lovett got sentenced to an extended term, in the brig? What would happen to his pretty little wife stranded across the bay?

He rang up the Tower, wanted to find out if anyone at headquarters had gotten word on what was going on over there in Cuba? The yeoman on duty only knew liberty was cancelled, but the ferry was running from Caimanera, most Cuban workers were on the job as usual.

Tork was hanging up the phone when an oversized sailor ducked through the doorway, let his seabag slide off a shoulder and crash to the deck. He slapped his sealed record and transfer orders on the counter, looked down on Tork.

"Reporting for duty," he said. "Johnny Island, here, Parachute Rigger second class."

Tork got up, greeted him at the counter. "Been on the lookout for you," he said. "Squadron's short-handed in the Parachute Loft."

"Just got dropped off," he said in a voice that didn't seem big enough for his body. "See that carrier in the bay, just got me in from a tour in Korea!"

"We got a rumor the war's over," Tork said. "You got any word on it."

"Got the word for a couple of days," the big man said, "but it won't stop the Cold War, make a difference." He leaned his elbows on the counter. "What's the duty like at this shithole?"

"You're in time for our busy season," Tork mentioned as he looked over the man's orders. "Summer shakedown time for the fleet."

"Thought I was in for a rest," the new man grumbled. "Well, shore duty's still a break. Maybe I'll get a bunk big enough to hold my feet? I'm six-six, known in this man's Navy as Big Six!" He straightened up, all the way up

Tork's eyes followed him up, way up, the way he looked up to adults as a kid. He wondered how Big Six could keep his balance. By the time his eyes got all the way up to the big man's face, there was less to envy. He had a big nose, out of line, and a thin mouth twisted in a sneer.

"Not sure about bunks long enough for you," Tork said, "don't even think we got chutes big enough for you."

"Don't ride chutes, just pack 'em," the big man said, "but wanna tuck my feet in at night."

"Master at arms will get you squared away in the barracks soon as I can get wheels for you," Tork said, going back to his desk, reaching for the phone. "Men gonna be glad to see you," he looked back. "We need a rated rigger to fold the silks, weave the shrouds."

"I let the men down good and easy," the big man talked down at Tork, "long as they cut me plenty of slack."

Tork began taking a dislike to the towering hunk of man, more so when he caught a whiff. Every inch of Big Six smelled like a sweaty foot!

"Wheels on the way," Tork turned back to the parachute rigger and hung up the phone.

"Got our parachute rigger," Tork said to Lieutenant Gordon as he barged back into the office.

"We got a tall drink of water," the officer observed, looking the man up and down.

"Tall drink of water carries the name of Island," Tork reported, "Johnny Island."

"No man's an Island," the Personnel Officer said, stretching his literary imagination. "No man's an Island in the Elizabethan time of John Donne, but all men *are* islands for Nineteenth Century Matthew Arnold, all estranged by a salty sea!"

"Could I get your signature on this man's orders?" Tork asked, not commenting on the nature of Man.

"I'm with Matthew Arnold," the officer thought while crafting his signature on the orders. "We're like islands, set apart in a common sea!" He paused for another thought. "I guess men in Naval Air are set apart like clouds."

"Right on, Sir."

"Good to have an Island in our midst," the lieutenant grinned at the new man. "We already have a Lake, but he got away!" The officer turned to his yeoman. "Anything on our missing man?"

"No sir. Think he might be caught in that ruckus over in Cuba."

"Maybe not. Look up the procedures for desertion in Navy Regs."

"He's not a deserter yet, " Tork said, knowing the regulations. "You have to prove intent to desert, but he's absent without leave. It's all in the new *Manual for Courts-Martial*."

"I'll check with the Old Man on what action to take," the officer said, closing himself off in his office again.

"All officers in this outfit crazy as that dude?" the new man wanted to know, leaning down on the counter again.

"Lieutenant Gordon's got some kind of degree in English Literature," Tork explained, "but he's a degree or two better to work for than some officers. He's not regulation! Good pilot, too. Can't figure why he's got *Crash* for a call name."

"*Crash* Gordon for your pilot sure would make a man want a good parachute," the parachute rigger said without smiling. "So, how's the duty here?"

"Not as taut as the heavy cruiser I came off," Tork said, "easy-going on saluting and laid back in the barracks."

"How's the chow? I'm fed up with powdered milk and shit-on-a-shingle."

"Three squares a day and a flop! Can't ask for more than that, and popcorn and outdoor movies. We got swimming,

267

golf, bowling, horseback riding, and our own baseball team. We got it all, but monotony rides the hell out of your nerves. We call it the Rock down here, like Alcatraz, I guess. You can't get off."

The phone rang again. "What's up?" Tork answered. "Got our missing man on the other end of the line," he yelled to Roy Boy as an aircraft engine was starting to sputter down below. "Listen up! Our man Lovett's stuck over there in a revolution!"

"How about that," the parachute rigger mumbled, looking down. "I get shore duty and there's no shore to go to."

"How about that," Tork said, hanging up the phone. "Our boy thinks he can get back tomorrow. The revolution ran out of gas."

"Guess I'll be getting some liberty after all," the parachute rigger looked down. "Say, what's holding up my wheels! Need to settle in, get a shower and a change of gear." He scratched himself. "Got me a skin condition, makes me smell *revolting*, like Cuba."

"Cuban sun won't be good for the itch,' Tork said, thinking the awful smell might be permanent, "but might sweat an inch or two off your height.'

"Let me take the load off till wheels turn up," the big man grumbled, coming around the counter without invitation and dropping himself in a chair under the revolving ceiling fan. His legs stretched all the way across the room, all the way to the file cabinets. "You old enough to be in the Navy?" Big Six asked Roy Boy.

"Old enough to be drafted," Roy Boy said, not liking the tone of the question, or the odor of the new man. "Joined Navy to keep out of the Army."

"Army wasn't for me either," Big Six said, "Rather have a bunk and hot rations than a pad on the ground and K-Rations."

"Navy's home to me," Roy Boy said. "Never had me a real home"

"Never had me a real home," Big Six found something else in common with the kid. "Liked to get away, run around, race cars. My old man finally gave me the boot. Had to live out of a locker in the railroad station, sleep around, wake up with a different broad every morning. One day I woke up in the Navy, got me a real Old Man, just as bad as the one I left behind!"

Roy Boy looked up from his desk. "Never had me an old man, except in the Navy."

"No mother, no father, just his Uncle Sam," Tork spoke for Roy Boy.

"Tork's got a preacher for a father," Roy Boy told the parachute rigger. "He had it good."

"My old man turned me off religion," Tork said, getting busy at his typewriter.

"Racing cars, that's my religion," the big man said as he aimed his crooked nose up to the fan for air. "This old boy worships speed.   Got my civilian kicks driving race cars, *winding up* and *spinning out.* Had more guts than brains."

The aircraft engine on the hangar deck below sputtered out, as did the loud talk. The overhead fan kept wind-milling around with its monotonous swish.

"Old Man thinks our boy might not have to be written up at all," the personnel officer sounded off as he reappeared He went on to say a board of inquiry might be required to rule on the airman's absence.

"Heard from Lovett," Tork told the officer. "He managed to find a phone over there in Cuba, claims there's a revolution. He couldn't get transportation back to base."

"He give you any idea what's really going on over there?"

"He heard tell of an attack on some army barracks in Santiago," Tork said, "and it turned Cuba upside down, brought out the men on horseback."

"They're hot blooded over there," the officer thought, looking around. "Why's the parachute rigger still hanging around?"

"No transport yet," Tork replied. "You might like to know our new man's into race cars, and racing."

"He'd make a hell of a pilot, if he could fit the cockpit," Lieutenant Gordon smiled, looking the new man over again. "How's he going to fit the bunks?"

■■■ ■■■ ■■■

Lutie was falling in and rising out of sleep, dreaming she was on a Ferris Wheel, waking to the touch of a another body. Pressed like a flower in book, she dreamed marriage put her in a holy book, but she couldn't read the mind of her man. Sometimes she felt like a wife put aside, sometimes like a centerfold playgirl. In and out of sleep, she dreamed and thought. Sometimes she was going around with her man on a Ferris Wheel. He was a sailor on leave, in need of mothering, but tried to make a mother out of her, right on the top turn of the Ferris Wheel. She held him off, all he way down, held him off, all the way up to the altar.

She sensed she was in her own bed, warm and soft as butter, trying to separate herself from the cream of dreams. Was she waking up in her old swamp house, under the pine smelling boards of the attic? Was she in bed with the older sister, in the house filled to the rafters with other sisters and brothers? Pa was hard as hickory on the girls, soft as coon skin on the boys. The boys were good for nothing but pestering her and hiding from the sheriff. Ma was the second-string wife. Pa had an older set of boys from a wife who died a-borning the last of them.

She came alive to herself in bed with her husband, married-up to the sailor boy who took her up and down and around on the Ferris Wheel. An airman, high up in the world, he fished her out of a stagnant swamp life, carried her off, fish out of water, to a strange land. Something else was trying to surface in her mind. She was in a cold sweat, coming up with daylight memories, soldiers with drawn sabers galloping through the streets, driving people off, chickens and pigs.

Tia Magdalena barred the old plank door, kept at her shrine and beads. The son of the house was missing in Santiago, captured, tortured, killed?

Lutie could hardly picture the son of the house lifeless. He was bronzed like a statue, immortal like a statue, but the mother feared he was stone dead, said he'd gone down with a man named Castor, or Castro. The name stuck in Lutie's mind like *Castor Oil* used to stick in her craw.

■■■ ■■■ ■■■

Lovett caught his breath in the dark, gasped into consciousness, got the feeling of a body in bed with him. What woman was he waking up with this time? He choked on the thought of being married, stuck in a permanent one-night-stand! Marriage got him out of the barracks at night, but got him a new commanding officer. Instead of a hardship discharge, he'd gotten himself a hardship marriage, a lifetime enlistment, no calendar date for release. His dream of desertion came up, the scheme of changing his name, losing himself in the Cuban crowd. Awake, he didn't want to live out his life in Cuba! Asleep again he took a bus to Havana, got a commercial flight to the States, lived out his life in the back woods. Awake, he knew he'd need a passport to get out of Cuba!

He was already a deserter, hadn't been able to get transportation back to base! The Cuban upheaval made the decision for him! Desertion would get him a bad conduct discharge, and out of the Navy. It might come with brig time, and a lifetime of disgrace? He turned over in bed, and back again. He was wide awake, suspended in time between day and night and between Guantanamo Bay and Cuba. He had two lives, one on and one off base. Each day was two days, one in Naval Air, one in Cuban dust. Two lives in one, and two days in one! Too much!

He rolled over, and back again, thought of the night he rode the Ferris Wheel with a girl from the Arkansas bottoms. He hardly knew the flighty girl he was going around with. He felt her all the way up, and all the way down, and got stuck in marriage.

Digging up a wife before knowing her is like digging a well from the bottom up! You get to know the bottom first, have to take the rest, whatever surfaces. The little wife messed with him, like the Navy, chewed him out when he wanted to do his own thing, chewed enough out of his ass to bait a bear trap! He guessed he'd never know love.

■■■ ■■■ ■■■

A rap at the door struck thoughts of love out of Lovett. The rap bolted Lutie straight up in bed. A streak of light came and went with the opening and closing of the door, a cry of help in between. It was a man's voice, the sound and accent of Ramon. A shadow ducked under the bed, and the bed took a shake, settled down.

The door banged all the way open and a beam of flashlight shot through the room, ricocheted around. A stream of Spanish poured out of a man standing in the glow of his own light, a man in khakis, a man of short and stocky build, bushy mustache.

Lovett leaped naked out of his side of the bed, switched on the overhead light with one hand, shielded his private parts with the other. Grabbing for pants heaped on a chair he fumbled for his wallet, showed the man in khakis his Navy I.D. card, and more of himself than he wanted.

The intruder took his eyes from the I.D. card to look at the girl in bed. Lutie had raised herself up behind a gossamer sheet, clad in a pajama top. The man in khakis made himself known as a *gendarme*, and let his eyes down long enough to check Lovett's identity card, his picture, rank, and serial number. He saluted, backed out without searching under the bed. His footsteps sounded on the paving stones outside, and pounded off with the boots of others.

"What in hell's that all about?" Lovett growled at the young man coming from under the bed.

"Salvation from Hell," Ramon breathed hard to get the words out.

"Lord-a-Mercy," Lutie managed to speak up.

"What in the cornbread hell's going on?"Lovett wanted to know, belting his pants together, mumbling all the while.

"Freedom went down," Ramon gasped, catching his breath in spurts, quivering in his military jacket. "We shoot up the

Moncada Army Post in Santiago, don't get soldiers to fall out against El Tyrant! They keep loyal, turn guns on us, and dogs."

"How'd they know to look for you here?" Lovett wondered. "If they didn't catch you on the spot, how in the cornbread hell they get the lowdown on you here?"

"University students make the danger lists, guilty of knowing too much."

Another knock at the door sent Lutie under the sheets and Ramon under the bed. The door flew open and Tia Magdalenan breezed in. She was holding herself together in a flimsy robe, her white-streaked hair undone and hanging loose over her bulk of a body.

"*Policia*, they go," she was able to say to the Lovetts, just as Ramon appeared from under the bed. She kissed him on both cheeks, one after the other, and he smoothed her hair, spoke to her in Spanish, sweet sounds. Lutie interpreted something about hiding in the mountains.

"The boy of the house, Ramon the monkey, is the revolutionary," the young Cuban man confessed in English to the Lovetts. He lay a hand on Lovett's shoulder. "*Gracias* for saving my skin! One more salvation, *por favor*. This message for Angel, your Cuban bootblack. Please to deliver."

"The shoeshine boy's a revolutionary?"

"Just *simpatico*," Ramon said, looking away, "your shoeshine boy has nothing but chains to lose, and shoes to gain."

"We call him Chico the Foot Fool."

"Maybe he be a fool in the foot, not in the head!"

"No time to fool around," Lovett got to thinking about the military police. "I take the note, you take a powder."

"No more revolution for now" Ramon said, turning away.

The Cuban mother sputtered in Spanish, steered her son through a flood of words to the door, looked back, "peace be with you," she said in English.

Part II: TIME ON THE ROCK

Peace rose over Cuba with the dawn. Guantanamo City and Caimanera were drowsy under the sun again. Across the bay, the naval base rose up to its usual level of spit and polish. Peace in Korea was confirmed. There was no formal celebration. Ferryboats brought Cubans back to work, liberty boats took playful sailors the other way.

No charges of unauthorized absence were brought against Lovett, only another entry in his service record, another frown from yeoman Tork. Peace in Korea only let an inch out of the Navy belt, a little letdown in regimentation. Half an hour came off the work day, liberty call came half an hour earlier. Holiday Routine was set for the whole weekend.

Lovett had his own holiday routine in Guantanamo City, didn't get anything out of the weekend letdown on base, except for the times he pulled weekend duty.

The rains came. Wind in the bay snapped warship flags to attention. There were fewer ships. Dark mornings kept dissolving into rains that washed out the watercolor mountains on the Cuban horizon. The sun sometimes broke through, and ships in the bay stood out bright against the gray steel-plated clouds. Days began and ended with the sound and smell of rain. The rain made its own music, syncopated drum beats on corrugated rooftops. The air bore the salt aroma of the sea and the sweetness of the flowering earth. The world was all aslant through jalousie windows half closed against the rains. The base was awash in water and mist, indistinguishable from the bay.

The rainy season murmured on and on, and rain shrank the outside world, even made a man feel smaller. It was "down time," nothing much for the pilots to do but log in flying time for extra pay. Nothing for the men to do but keep a few aircraft in the "up" status . Spirits went down in "down time." Boredom cranked-up. Time seemed to stand still. Men were in each other's way, at war with each other, and the Navy. The big guns still pointed out, but the hostility was within.

■■■ ■■■ ■■■

Came the crash! Line Chief Riley broke into the Personnel office one morning, waved his arm with all the hash marks on the sleeve. "Get a line on the Tower!" he ordered Tork. "Get the Tower to signal that damned plane down, a F8F-2, side number UL-20!" He ordered the Tower to call it back!

His sunburned face was wrinkled in a mask of terror. "Call it back!"

Yeoman Tork knew the line chief was not to be questioned. He grabbed up a phone, dialed McCalla Tower, repeated the chief's orders, came back at the Chief with a question from the Tower. "Why was the plane cleared for take-off?"

"Pilot didn't know the plane was still *down* for a tune-up, not ready for air time."

"Tower's calling the aircraft back," Tork reported to the chief.

"Who's the pilot?" Lieutenant Gordon asked, bursting on scene. "Who's up in the air?"

"Ensign Dutch Decker's on the squadron flight schedule," the chief said.

"The Flying Dutchman has contacted the Tower," Tork repeated information he got over the phone. "His engine's cutting out! We're to get all emergency stations on the alert!"

Lieutenant Gordon passed the word over the hangar *teletalk*, stirred up action in the hangar deck below.

"Pilot's stalled at about three hundred feet," Tork repeated word for word the message he was getting from the Tower. "Pilot reports putting the mixture control into lean but engine won't pick up. Pilot's doing 120 knots, heading into a salt flat, dropping the flaps, raising the gear, trying to pull a tail first landing in the *Hicacal* area!"

"He's a damned good pilot," Lieutenant Crash Gordon said, driving a cigarette into his mouth, flashing his lighter, "damned good!"

"Got the shoulder harness, safety belt and protective helmet," the chief surmised, "might come out of it with just a few sore points."

"He's down," Tork relayed from the phone, "slid straight ahead, no turn over. He secured the cockpit. He's out of the aircraft!"

"Thank the Good Lord!," Roy Boy looked up from his typewriter and crossed himself.

"What's the story on this?" Lieutenant Gordon asked the Chief. "Didn't your people do a plane check?"

"The plane was down for a shop work order. Pilot in a hurry, didn't check it out, not properly, only called up the Tower for taxi instructions."

"What you mean he didn't check it out properly?"

"Crew said he only glanced at the *B Sheet*. There were engine discrepancies noted, but he must have figured the night crew took care of 'em. Mag check gave him sufficient *rpm's* to take off, so off he went." Chief Riley caught his breath. "Coming on duty this a.m., I found the work order, note attached, *work not completed*. Ignition harness still needed a change." He sank his face into the mop of a handkerchief. "Distributor leads were only finger tight," he mumbled. "Night Maintenance was in a hurry, shouldn't have left the plane out on deck!"

"Why didn't our day crew catch it?" Lieutenant Gordon wanted to know. "A pilot would calculate a plane on the line is cleared for flight."

"Damned careless of day crew," Chief Riley agreed, "but pilot should have performed more than a turn-up!" Chief Riley wanted to cover for his men. "You know Dutch Decker's a cowboy in the saddle!"

"Well he's down. All's well that ends well," the personnel officer said with a Shakespearian flourish of his hand.

■■■ ■■■ ■■■

Men on the hangar deck below had been scrambling to their emergency stations. Lovett and Varsi hunkered down at the big wheel of deflated fire hose.

"A lot of good this hose will do on a plane way out on a salt flat," Varsi said to Lovett.

"Just something to keep us busy," Lovett complained, sweat burning his eyes.

"We got to keep sharp," Varsi thought. "That's the hell of plane maintenance! A bad work day for us and a life lost for somebody else."

"You be taking the rap," Lovett said, trying to cover his own guilt, "for letting that pilot wind up and take off!"

"You were first on line, supposed to check the night crew's work order," Varsi said.

"You be the senior man!" Lovett kept up, wiping the dungaree sleeve across his eyes.

"Well, let's hope the Dutchman makes it?" Varsi groaned to himself.

"Don't see no smoke over at Leeward," Lovett squinted.

The two men lay low until the emergency drill was called off. They hung around for their downed pilot to return. He came back in a pickup, got a cheer from all the crews standing by. The Commanding Officer in khaki shorts was on hand to put an arm around the "flying Dutchman," and lead him off.

Later in the work day, Dutch Decker's banged-up plane got dragged back to the hangar. A quick check came up with propeller damage, a dent in the port wing tip, damage to the underside fuselage.

"Well, there's more sweat for us," Lovett grumbled.

"Something to do," Varsi said, "something to keep our hands busy, our skills sharp."

■■■ ■■■ ■■■

The days got to rolling round again in their appointed hours of work, watches, and relaxation. No charges were brought against Lovett for not checking the night report, but he got a lowered mark on his efficiency report, and another bad look from Yeoman Tork. The aircraft casualty was a mark against the whole squadron and rated a routine investigation by Wing.

The season for shakedown cruises came round again, and more ships were coming out of World War II mothballs, no letup in the Cold War. Squadron pilots were back up in the air, running patterns for gun crews on ships to track. Plane crews worked overtime to keep the planes up. The days flew by.

The Cuban heat bore down. There was no air conditioning on base. Off duty enlisted men eased out of the steaming barracks to "air out" in the nearby "Beer Garden." It was open to air on all sides, loosely thatched on top. By the time the stars of the Big Dipper showed through the loosely matted overhead, the beer was really pouring! Operated by Cubans, the "Beer Garden" featured *Hatuey*, a beer stronger than American brews. Called the "one-eyed Indian," *Hatuey* half-blinded the sailors and put some of them on the warpath with each other!

Men without a taste for beer, or out of money, were stuck in the barracks at night, filled their empty hours with poker or shut-eye. Only a few squadron mates had an escape hatch, like Lovett, a "home away from home." Lovett commuted back and forth to Cuba every night, except when he drew the duty. He then racked-out in the barracks, in his own bunk, across from Big Six. Nobody wanted to bunk near the parachute rigger, but those who did got used to the rotten smell. It wasn't from lack of soap and water. He was always toweling off all six feet six inches of himself, showering morning and night. Word was that he had a chemical condition, took pills for it. Pills didn't "cut the mustard."

Woogie Woods bunked over Lovett's usually empty rack. His guitar picking struck some sour notes and no one wanted to be around him either.

"Black Bill" Lighty, the only African-American in the squadron, racked-out across from Woogie, in the bunk over Big Six. He could put himself in a Yoga trance and not complain about the ripe smells from below, or the sounds across the way. He also had the annoying habit of doing pushups between bunks, hundreds of them to keep from "thinking about sex!" He was happy in his out-of-the-way corner of the barracks.

Up and down the rows of bunks, life was laid-back, and sweaty, language guttural and gritty. Talk was up front and to the point, like full frontal nudity. The ugly sound of "fuck"described every person, object, and function, but the word went in and out of minds without a thought. Spoken words were simple, whole-grained, unrefined, only as deep as the grunts that came with them. Sometimes a word hit a nerve and triggered a fight, especially around the smoking table where men gambled at poker.

Most men got out of the barracks on Saturday nights, gambled with their health in the bars and brothels of Caimanera. The "liberty hounds" came dragging back to base, tails between their legs, drunk and wobbly. Speaking in profane "tongues," they staggered up the hill from the boat shed and got serenaded at the front stoop of the barracks by the guitar and voice of Woogie Woods.

"No life to sire in wombs of hire, no life to sire." It was one of Woogie's most repeated ballads, and he always stayed up to give it to the liberty hounds. "No life to sire in wombs for hire."

And the Saturday nights played on and on, until the screaming blues on base hit a high note! The bugle sounded reveille one Sunday morning, loud and clear, but hardly anyone stirred in the upper starboard wing of the AV-51 Barracks. Holiday routine was the order of the day on Sundays.

"DROP YOUR COCKS AND GRAB YOUR SOCKS!" It was the roaring voice of the Chief Master-At-Arms, first class boatswain's mate, Popovitch He was built like a tug boat, low in the water, built for pushing and shoving. Known as "Popeye," he was a salty old seaman, a swaggering dead ringer for *Popeye the sailor man.* He walked and talked like the comic strip character, walked bowlegged on account of his "big balls," showed gigantic forearms whenever he skinned down to a skivvy shirt. He liked to puff on a corncob pipe whenever the smoking lamp was lit, tell about "getting shot out of the water" at Pearl Harbor. On this particular Sunday morning, Popeye was lit-up with rage!

"Heave out and brace up," he bellowed. "Hit the deck, you sleeping beauties!"

"Ram spinach up your ass," came back at him from the rows of bunks, and "blow it out the other end!"

"Now hear this," the master at arms hurled back. "You assholes got your keels running low in the shallows!"

Men with an eye opened could see him sputtering, saliva spewing. This wasn't a routine Sunday! They began falling out, in various stages of undress, falling into ranks, dressing up their lines. Lovett was groping around with them. He'd been in the duty section the night before, had to hit the sack in the barracks instead of bedding down with his Lutie in Guantanamo City. He was trying to square himself up in line with the others. Reveille had taken him by surprise. Blinking open his eyes, he had a hard time remembering where he was, then got to wondering where he'd laid his shaving gear, towel and shower clogs. There was something else he was forgetting.

"Now hear this," Popeye was snorting at the undressed ranks lining up in front of the bunks. "You assholes can draw your rations, but get your tails back to barracks for muster at 1300!" He took a big swig of breath, set his jaw, stuck it out. "You put on plenty of steam last night, will get your stacks blown good and proper after dog watches!"

"What's up?"

Top brass investigation at 1300!"

A murmur went up and down the ranks, questions came back down the line.

"You swabs were too hung over to remember going overboard," Popeye jawed it up! "Went amok last night! One of you beauties really went by the board, knocked a petty officer off his block!"

"Was it me?" Lovett asked himself, now half sure of the answer when the master at arms was calling out his name, "Lake Lovett, front and center!" The dead ringer for Popeye was sputtering and resetting his jaw.

Lovett's legs moved him forward but his memory took him back. He'd been on the Night Check, he remembered, hit the sack in the dark, ahead of the liberty party. He got roused out of sleep by drunken bodies bumping into bunks, clanging locker doors. Trying to get back to sleep, after the drunks settled into a loud-breathing stupor, he remembered the sound of a trickle next to his rack. There was a body mistaking the foot of his bunk for the Head! Someone was taking a leak on his bunk! All hell broke loose in Lovett's mind. Other shapes and shadows came piling up in the dark of memory. A body went down, bunks got jarred out of alignment. A flashlight stabbed at the dark, cut Johnny Island out of it. He was laid out, all over the deck!

Lovett stopped looking back as he noticed the empty bunk of Big Six and approached the master at arms. His bare feet carried him up front, up to the big folded forearms of "Popeye."

"What I done this time?" Lovett pretended to be innocent at the same time he was concocting an alibi. He could argue he wasn't the only one to put the lumps to the parachute rigger! He could argue that Popeye had it "in" for him, ever since he played around with the old boy's wife. Not a skinny dame like the comic strip Olive Oyl, Popeye's wife was full bodied and loaded for action. Lovett didn't know who she was when he bowled a few frames with her, went round with her at the roller-skating rink.

"You slip your cable?" the boatswain's mate screwed up his face at Lovett. "Forget you got put on report last night?" He was throwing out his jaw, daring Lovett to take a poke at it.

Lovett squared himself at attention, his mind doing an about face, looking back again, remembering the hitting and stomping on Big Six. He started to feel the sore knuckles that affirmed the blows that took Big Six down, and kept him there. The big guy had to be pulled by the bib of his uniform to the shower stalls, his heavy, slack body polishing the deck all the way. Night lights in the Head showed him up in a deathly glare. White as a ghost, he was scabbed with blood and vomit, had to be stripped down, rolled into the showering water, mopped dry, pulled back to his rack.

Flashbacks came and went through Lovett's memory. It was Woogie and Black Bill who got him to help swab up their area. The three of them were emptying a bucket of slop when the master at arms came storming into the picture. He sure wasn't happy about getting called out of bed in civilian housing to calm stormy waters in the barracks. He grabbed at the first man he saw.

"This *cullud* boy don't start dis trouble," Black Bill spoke up in his most subservient voice.

"You standing here, ain't you!"

"Yas, suh," Black Bill said, not looking the boatswain's mate in the eye. "Jus' tryin' to clean up dis mess."

"I'll clean up on this blockhead troublemaker," Lovett remembered Popeye recognizing him. "Get your square ass over to the MAA shack!"

"Can I get dressed," Lovett remembered asking.

Flashlight in hand, the master at arms gave Lovett a light back to his locker. The barracks lay still as death when the flashlight probed through the funereal darkness. Awake or not, the men were lying low, sleeping off a drunk or praying to stay out of trouble.

"Get going,"Popeye sputtered. He held the light for Lovett to spin the combination lock.

"You gonna hold a fuggin' locker inspection on me?"

Lovett remembered he should have opened the locker instead of his mouth. He got hauled right off The Assistant Duty Officer at the MAA Shack let him off the hook, for the night, told him to report back in the morning. The morning had come, and Lovett was remembering the night, wishing he could forget.

"Get your ass in the uniform of the day," Popeye looked Lovett up and down on this Sunday morning. He walked bowlegged, following Lovett to his locker.

Getting into uniform, Lovett slipped a word to Woogie. "Got to face the music," he said, "and not your fuggin' guitar."

"We all be facing the music," the guitar player whispered back.

"Do me a favor, old buddy," Lovett asked. "Get the word to my woman. She was meeting me for lunch at MATS."

"She'll get the word."

Lovett looked back, noticed the empty bunk where Big Six used to lay. There was blood on the mattress cover. Work shoes big as gunboats were at rest under the bunk, one shoe on its side, a gigantic tongue gagging out of it. Lovett took the sight of a big empty shoe with him, couldn't get it out of his head.

"Heads up," the master of arms was clearing the way through the barracks.

■■■ ■■■ ■■■

After the master at arms marched Lovett out of the barracks, the men put their heads together, scraped up pieces and bits of memory. Nobody seemed to know what really happened, but everyone wondered if there would be a murder rap if "Big Six" never came out of his coma? Who'd take the rap? All hands harbored a little guilt for stirring up the "rough weather," and a few others remembered their lightening strikes at the parachute rigger, but the most of them hadn't lost their appetites and took off to chow down.

Woogie hung back, planned to look for Lutie and pick up a hamburger and fries at MATS. He liked to lay around in the stillness of the Sunday barracks, liked to strum his guitar, strike up a new tune. As he plucked the strings he watched the clock go round, rolling away more of his Navy time.

Noon time took him to MATS, the Quonset hut out by by the squadron runway. MATS wasn't under air station jurisdiction. It served as terminal for all military and civilian air transportation. The Quonset hut was set up with chairs and couches for tired men and dependents to wait on planes, and chairs and tables in the "grill room" for men tired of Navy grub. There was a jukebox with platters that would spin with all the tunes of home, country, swing, pop, blues, and jazz.

As Woogie turned up at MATS, somebody's nickel had spun a Doris Day number around on the jukebox turntable. It was a song Woogie wished he'd written, a melody and lyric about a secret love. Doris Day's loving voice was going around and around, as if in a rut, like his Navy life. He was not in groove with the Navy.

"Your man can't make it," Woogie said, finding Lutie at a table by the jukebox. He slouched down beside her.

"Lord a-mercy, what he done?" Lutie was hot and flustered, fanning herself with a folded menu.

"Got himself on report, brawling in the barracks."

"Well I declare, he be mighty touchy these days!"

"He wants you to know he can't get here, might be in for some restriction!"

"Woe is me," Lutie fluttered her menu fan. "Losing my man when I find me knocked up with my man's child!"

Woogie leaned forward, surprised "You in the family way?" Lovett hadn't mentioned it. He always wondered how she could manage her own life in Cuba, couldn't imagine her handling another life. He got a cigarette to his lips as quickly as he could, flicked his lighter, settled back in his own smoke, said Lovett was a lucky man, but thought he was truly cursed.

"Almost lost the little critter this very day," Lutie said, trying to get comfortable in her chair. "Cab over in Cuba flipped a wheel! Waited, I did , in sun and sand with whore-women. Whore-women lifted skirts way up to make shade for me. It be a humiliation."

"Whores wanted to make you feel cool?"

"Make me feel shameful, like one of 'em!"

"Maybe those whore-women feel sorry for a woman who gets with child?"

"Do I show?" Lutie fluttered her menu.

 "No way! When's the coming-out party?"

"Springtime I reckon. My sailor boy lay the keel. He better be round for the launching!"

"With a smashing bottle of champagne for the christening!"

"Got me a doctor on base," Lutie said, relaxing again, "a braided lieutenant commander!"

"That's rank enough to keep an airman's wife in line,"Woogie said, blowing his smoke away from Lutie.

"Keep falling out of line," Lutie looked up at Woogie's smoke dissolving in air. "Been out of sorts, full of the miseries, falling down miseries, and slobbering on my dickey, and forgetting stuff."

"You're just playing the pregnant blues."

"Sometimes I wake up on the floor, can't figure how I got there."

"Wish I could lift you up in song," Woogie said, "left my guitar behind."

"Baby blues got me off the banjo."

"What you gonna do, all alone in Cuba?"

"Don't know how I can live without my man, not for more than a night, not since I be with a man."

"How are you fixed for money?"

She hadn't thought about that, sank into gloom. Woogie ordered up two hamburgers and fries, and a thick milk shake, with an egg.

■■■ ■■■ ■■■

What shook up the barracks and put the parachute rigger in a coma? The commanding officer would have to answer for it, report the incident to the Commander of the Utility Wing. He set the Personnel Officer on a fact finding inquiry, appointed him head of an official board of investigation. Yeoman Adam Turner was assigned the clerical detail. Testimony was gathered from twenty eye-witnesses. They were advised of their rights, their testimony taken under oath, all in accordance with the new Code of Military Justice.

It was found that John L. Island, PR2, departed the Guantanamo Bay Naval Air Station at 1730 on 7 November 1953 for authorized liberty in Caimanera, Cuba. He was seen at the Gladys Bar where he consumed approximately fourteen bottles of Cuban beer. He showed up at the State Pier in Caimanera at 2230 for the liberty boat departure. He complained to the shore patrol of feeling ill. He required help getting into the liberty boat. He could not sit up straight in the stern sheets. He was not able to get out of the liberty boat without assistance. He got back to Barracks AV-51 at approximately 2330. Stephen Lyon, airman known as "Slick," was the Barracks Fire Watch and helped Parachute Rigger Island to his bunk, left him there in full dress. Lake Lovett, airman, occupied the lower bunk adjacent to Island. He heard a noise like water splashing, approximately 0030, on 8 November 1953. He claimed Island was urinating on his bunk, and he jumped up, and may have hit him. Woodrow Woods, airman, occupies the bunk over airman Lake Lovett. He reported that Parachute Rigger Island had fallen in his own urine and vomit. Some unidentified man in the dark kicked Island in the hind-end, not in the head. Airmen Woods, Lovett and Lighty dragged Island to the showers, cleaned him up. He might have bumped his head on the cement ledge in the shower stall. Island was dragged back to his bunk, and the mess around it swabbed-up. Joseph

Popovitch, Chief master at arms, AV-51, was called to the scene. He put Airman Lovett on report for insubordination, and suspicion of hitting John Island, PR2.

The official inquiry found that Island got out of the rack, began throwing up, spitting blood. Yeoman Striker Roy Chipman woke up and reported it to the MAA shack. The Dispensary truck was summoned, and Island taken away on a stretcher.

Phil Donaldson, hospital corpsman third class, was on duty at Sick Bay when Island was admitted. Island complained of nausea, headache, and could hardly walk or talk. He was lethargic, had signs of intra-cranial injury with lacerations on front and back of the head. Skull x-rays behind the right ear showed no fracture. There was a contusion of the sacrum. A spinal tap showed bloody spinal fluid. He was put on intravenous glucose and saline. He was in a coma next morning, admitted to the sick list, transferred to the U.S. Naval Hospital for further diagnosis and treatment. Since then, Parachute Rigger John L. Island is in and out of comas. Prognosis is guarded. Lake Lovett, airman, has been confined to barracks during this investigation.

The opinion of the Board of Investigation as to the circumstances attending the illness or injury of John L. Island is that his condition could be the result of intoxication, illness, or injury on the night of 7 November 1953. None of the individuals associated with John L. Island the night of 7 November 1953, and the morning of 8 November 1953, had malicious intentions. The illness or injury resulting in Island's hospitalization was incurred in the line of duty, and was not the result of his misconduct.

It was recommended that the squadron institute a policy of instruction for all hands, particularly Officers and Petty Officers, in the care and handling of individuals apparently in a drunken or unconscious condition. It was also recommended that all persons returning from liberty in a helpless or unconscious condition be admitted to Sick Bay. Further, it was recommended that Lake Lovett, airman, be assigned a special court-martial in accordance with his alleged offense of insubordination.

■■■ ■■■ ■■■

"You've heard the board's findings, opinions, recommendations," the Commanding Officer noted in his address to the men at a morning muster. "It's a sad day when men of the best Navy in the world go to war against each other! The hot war in Korea is over, but the Cold War won't go away. It's a war between different ways of life, between democratic freedom and Communist dictatorship, a war between good and evil!"

A war between freedom and dictatorship, Lovett was thinking as his body stood ramrod stiff. It was his freedom on the line!

A war between good and evil, Woogie was thinking as he held his place in line next to Lovett. It had the makings of a blues ballad, a marriage between good and evil, a good girl and a man who did her wrong. Good and evil, left and right, a marching cadence of rhythms went through his head.

A war between love and hate, Horse-Face Eli was thinking. He'd just gotten a *dear john* letter from his girl. She'd written him off. She returned his love with hate.

A war between men and women, Tork was thinking, a war for equal rights. The woman he shacked-up with in Cuba had no equal rights. His girl back home said there could no love between men and women without equality.

A war between the old and young was going through Popeye's mind with the war between good and evil. The young punks coming along didn't have respect for their elders or the old ways!

A war between black and white, Black Bill was thinking.

A war between rich and poor, Lieutenant Gordon was thinking, Communism on his mind.

There's a war going on in each of us, Enzo Varsi was turning over in his head, between the good in us and the bad.

Private thoughts were marching through the ranks of separate bodies and minds. It was Roy Boy who was wondering how God kept in touch with so many different thoughts. There was an ocean of white hats bobbing around in a sea of problems, and only one God.

"Nobody's got problems but me," Lovett was saying to himself, thinking of his confinement to base and a court-martial and brig time. In the meantime he'd been assigned a "shit detail,"a work party cleaning out underground bunkers on the Leeward side of base, bunkers abandoned after World War II. They were strung with cobwebs and deep with bat droppings. It was a real *shit detail*, and he was thinking of getting back to it.

"You men are on the good side of this war," the Commanding Officer broke into each man's thoughts, "should not be at war with each other!"

What you supposed to do when a drunk wants to pick a fight? Roy Boy was asking the commanding officer in his mind. He never drank, never got in trouble, but drunks always wanted to take him on, beat him up.

"Think we should put booze off limits?" the Commanding Officer asked the lined-up men, "and liberty in Cuba?" He paused, expected some answers.

"Men can't fly without getting gassed up now and then," one of the line chiefs dared to speak up. "Lower the boom on men who can't hold their liquor, not on the whole outfit."

"I go along with that," the skipper said, folding his arms, "but who do I crack down on when the barracks gets out of line?"

No one spoke out. Eyes looked straight ahead, blank blue and brown eyes, green and gray, as if there was nothing to see.

"My board of investigation recommended only one man for a court-martial," the commanding officer finally resumed. "Should one man take the rap for all?"

Roy Boy thought of Jesus, but had to keep his hands down, couldn't cross himself.

The Commanding Officer paced back and forth, not waiting for an answer. "So be it," he said.

"How be the parachute rigger?" someone in the ranks wanted to know.

"Word is our man's out of danger," the squadron's Old Man said, facing the men. "Latest diagnosis has him down with encephalitis, a condition that could have come from that blow to the head! But let me knock some sense in you liberty hounds. Encephalitis could be fingered by a lady virus over there in Cuba, or come out of some dirty bottle."

The men were looking straight ahead with their vacant eyes, but Cuban women and whiskey glasses started filling their minds.

"Encephalitis is an inflamation of the brain," the Old Man interpreted his men's blank stares. "It causes confusion, a disturbed behavior, a coma." He looked up and down the lines, seemed to be looking for more questions, then asked the personnel officer to "carry on."

The personnel officer dismissed the squadron, except for "Airman Lake Lovett!" He was to report to the personnel office.

The hangar deck was starting to hum with activity as Lovett trudged up to the personnel office, much slower than the time he remembered taking Lutie up.

"You're off the shit list," Yeoman Tork told him as soon as he let himself in the office, "but the lieutenant wants a word with you."

"Lovett! The Old Man's dropped your special court," the personnel officer told him, "dropped the charges of causing serious bodily harm, but the insubordination charge holds. He's giving you another month of restriction, and docking you another month's pay."

Lovett looked down, squeezed the white hat between his hands. Restriction was just another kind of wait, he thought, just waiting for his enlistment to run out, but his little woman couldn't wait so well, alone in Cuba.

"You can appeal to the Old Man," the personnel officer said, "but I think you're getting off pretty easy."

Easy for him to say!

■■■ ■■■ ■■■

Lovett didn't know what to say! What do you say when crew members embarrass you with a handout? Men in the barracks had picked up a hatful of cash for his "little woman," handed it to him on a Sunday afternoon. Lovett choked-up, finally got out some thanks before the men broke up, went back about their business. Lovett lay back on the rack, watched the men over the angle of his upright toes. How different they started to look, not like a zoo of pacing animals. They were still caged, growling, snapping towels and insults at each other, but they didn't look so angry, and not so ugly. Lovett felt like part of the pack for the first time. A Prisoner-At-Large, he thought of himself as a "P.A.L."

His squarish feet brushed against each other as he looked over them at the men. The brawny sailors were starting to look like Teddy Bears! He wondered how much each man put in the hat. He wondered if he should give the whole hatful to his wife? He could use cash for himself, cigarettes and beer, and hamburgers and milkshakes for Lutie when she met him at MATS. She was giving him a hard time. The Navy doctors said she had "epilepsy," the *falling sickness*. Pregnancy might have triggered it. A battery of tests was fired at her, and a barrage of prescriptions. She was given a fighting chance to carry off the pregnancy. He wished the Navy doctors would scuttle it.

He let his mind slip in and out of thoughts of pregnancy, epilepsy, and fatherhood while contemplating the mattress above that sagged down like a pregnant belly. The guitar player with the crewcut had just hoisted himself into the bunk. He was complaining to everyone that the sun burned him off the pier. It was his favorite place, alone, on a Sunday afternoon. He could strum his guitar and watch for the friendly dog-fish flapping around.

The pregnant bulge in the mattress above made Lovett thinking about a hardship discharge. Navy WAVES had a song about "getting pregnant" and "getting out!" A pregnant wife with epilepsy might pull it off for a man!

■■■ ■■■ ■■■

Lutie was aware of her bed shaking as she came out of sleep, fearful of the dark and dreading the coming of another day. She was quivering with the fright of strange noises. She knew there was a small iguana that came out of the patio drain at night, rattled around, and a prowling cat that sometimes overturned a flowerpot   Sometimes there were faint echos that never quite materialized, the sounds of the house ghosts!

Tia Magdalena told her not to fret about the "ghost-spirits." They came with the bricks and mortar of the house, stuck in between worlds. Tia Magdalena's big house compound had been a field hospital in the Cuban War of Independence. Some Cuban patriots gave up the ghost in this old house, were still on duty. Their footfalls made the house creak, but they were only playful boys, would be old men if they hadn't shaken off the flesh.

Tia Magdalena once confided in Lutie that she'd seen a uniformed spirit on guard at the foot of her bed. He was assigned the spirit watch, when she was widowed, a ghost who would only do his duty. Now a ghost was keeping Lutie at attention most nights.

At an unfamiliar sound she sat all the way up in the dark, drawing the sheet up with her. She looked down at her bare parts shivering and shining white in the ghostly streaks of light. Ghosts were not to be afeared of, she told herself. They were like guardian angels. She remembered making room for her guardian angel in the bed she shared with a sister. There wasn't much room for the three of them.

Awake, she was more afraid of being without money than alone in bed with ghosts. Tia Magdalena had been setting her a place at table, held up on the rent, but advised her to go home, let her own people take care! Lutie didn't know how to get back to the Arkansas bottoms! The Navy would only pay for one trip home a year, and she'd been her man's dependant for much less time than that. Home had no money to fetch her back. She couldn't even get a letter from home.

She'd had a sneaky thought of getting money off sailors, like the Cuban bar girls, but she didn't think the Good Lord would go for that, unless she had nothing at all to eat. God forgave folks for anything if they had nothing to eat. God gave the first man and woman animals to eat when they were hungry and cast out of Paradise.

The pretty man named Enzo Varsi came to mind when she thought of making money off the sailors. He'd paid her a visit just before she'd gone to bed this very night, "took time" he said, "on a short weekend liberty to look her up." He wanted to know if she needed a body to keep her company. She thought he wanted to take liberties with her body, and when he said he only wanted to be "at her service," she thought he meant "service," like a bull! He never made a move on her, just sketched her picture as she rocked in her chair and loneliness. Varsi said he'd put her on canvas someday! She didn't know if he meant putting her in a painting canvas, or a canvas bunk. She knew sailors sometimes called their bunk a canvas. A "canvas back" was another name for a "rack sack."

Lutie remembered putting the pretty officer off, saying she was sick, pregnant sick. She let him go, and now she was alone in bed, afraid of being with ghosts and an unknown child.

■■■ ■■■ ■■■

Low in spirits, Lovett found himself stranded in the barracks on another Sunday, sunk in the rack, depressed as usual. Lying face-up, he could only think of the pregnant mattress and fatherhood. He turned away. The next bunk was barren, Big Six still fighting for his life in the base hospital. Lutie had looked the big guy up on one of her routine appointments. She got to see him in the "dirty surgery ward," bedded in a long corridor of lined-up cots. He wore a "turban of bandages," and his head was in the clouds. Making no sense, he kept mumbling "chute up and fly high," over and over, "chute up and fly high," like a broken record, over and over. His mind was stuck in a rut, and Lutie didn't think the big guy would ever come back to the barracks and "knock anybody's block off."

"Got a cigarette?" A voice shook Lovett out of the doldrums. He got a look at Horse-Face Eli bending down at him in the lower bunk.

"You back in the harness?" Lovett wanted to know, punching-up his pillow and pulling out a pack of *Lucky Strikes*. Horse-Face Eli took one and stuck it in his mouth, forgot to ask for a light.

"Bucked that old gal off my back," Horse-Face Eli said.

Everyone had the word about his "Dear John" letter. The girl who kicked him out of her life wasn't one of the bodacious barefoot gals from his storytelling. It was his "city filly of unbridled passion," the girl he met at "Great Lakes," near Chicago. She wrote of being tired of waiting for him, had found a "somebody a sight better." She wanted her picture back, the professional photograph of her looking over a bare rounded shoulder. Squadron mates rallied round the downcast boy. Woogie Woods dedicated a country tune to him, sounded it out around the barracks, "send my saddle home, Baby. No more bridal paths, Baby!"

"Sent her saddle home," Horse-Face Eli said, nodding thanks as Lovett flicked up a light for his cigarette.

Woogie hung his crewcut head over the upper bunk, singing, "no more bridal paths, Baby."

"I'm back on my feed," Horse-Face Eli said, looking up. "Put that filly out to pasture. Just got me nothing to do."

"Saddle up one of your kinfolk stories," Woogie suggested, "make our downtime giddy-up!"

"Got me a love story, but Lovett won't know about love!"

The word of a Horse-Face Eli story got out among the stragglers in the barracks and they began to rally around Lovett's bunk. Two men who'd been shuffled-up at poker around the long smoking table gave up their seats to find a place around Horse-Face Eli. The dancing fool, Slick, answered the call on the double, came two steps forward, one step backward, dancing to his own mambo beat. Enzo Varsi came stomping around in his shower clogs, securing a towel around his middle as he came. Black Bill Lighty rose out of a Yoga trance. Even Roy Boy, down on his bunk, elbowed up to attention.

"Lay it on us," came Woogie's voice from the pregnant bunk above Lovett, and his legs came hanging over the side. Empty bunks all around that corner of the barracks were filling up.

"Anybody got a cigarette?" the storyteller asked, surveying his audience. "Can't get my story up the stack without a little smoke."

Packs of cigarettes were held out.

"Reckon I got me a love story that might pass inspection," he said, fingering a cigarette out of someone's pack, and a second one to roll up in the sleeve of his skivvy shirt. He waited for a light.

"Got to leave out the sexy part," Horse-Face Eli started, "don't want to get a rise out of you horny boys," and he let out a sigh with his smoke. "Let's just leave the cuddling part out of the story and start with a neighbor fella on my side of the mountain falling for a bodacious gal from the dale. He wanted to team up with her, permanent like. Along come a slick city dude, tickled that gal's fancy, got her to kick the traces and run off. Mountain boy took to his shotgun and blows her away. Folks figure a man got a right to shoot a two-timing wife, but that gal weren't his legal woman, not yet, so the folks had to lay the jailhouse blues on our lover boy. By and by he gets himself out of them jailhouse blues, but can't shake the female blues. He got to brooding like a setting hen and lay a half-cracked story on the neighbors. Claimed, he did, his gal come back up from her gunning down, come back to spook him. Preacher-man put a hex on that a-meddling ghost, but can't shoo her off. Neighbor fella gives up his old ways, lets the liquor take his farm down. Folks get to fretting for that neighbor man, get to poking round about his diggings. They got sight of a woman gallivanting behind his shutters, a female woman like the one he shot full of holes. Folks sashay around to pay him a social call, don't find no sign of no woman, only a man-mess all around, until they get spooked by a female voice coming through a wall. Folks skedaddle, don't come back no more, not till the old fella lie on the death bed!"

Horse-Face Eli sucked the life out of his cigarette and buried in an empty shoe polish can. He slowly unrolled the cigarette he had up his sleeve, waited for someone to hand him a light.

"Tell us," Varsi said, sliding a bare foot back and forth in his shower clog, "after your neighbor fella gave up the ghost, did he show up again, like his woman did?"

"His spirit never come back up," Horse-Face Eli was sad to say, "but the woman ghost wouldn't go way. She show up in the pine-framed mirror that be a-hanging in the old boy's Sunday Sitting Room!" Horse-Face Eli lowered his voice. "Folks saw her in the looking glass, don't see their own reflections, nohow. They had to break the mirror in pieces, still couldn't get all the pieces of her face out of sight."

Someone asked the storyteller if he ever wanted to take a gun to the two-timing gal who shot him down with a "Dear John."

"You missed the lesson to my story," Horse-Face Eli looked up sadly. "You can't kill love!"

■■■ ■■■ ■■■

"We can use a laugh," Woogie announced from his upper bunk. "Chico the Foot Fool's on his way up!" Woogie had caught sight of the Cuban shoeshine boy before his shoeshine song could announced him. "You are my sun*shine*, my only sun*shine*, Chico be your shoe*shine*, your only shoe*shine*." Chico, the shoeless shoeshine boy, showed up in the upper wing of the barracks.

"No shines today?" Woogie spoke for the group of men still gathered around his bunk for the Horse-Face Eli's story. "Got no inspection coming up."

"Could the shoeshine boy *hablar* with the sailor-men and polish up the English?"

"Make yourself to home," Lovett spoke for the men sitting and standing around his bunk. "We just be killing time."

"How you kill time?" the shoeshine boy wondered in English. He crouched down in a space on the edge of the bunk where Big Six used to lay most of his body. "You strangle time twixt hands of clock?"

"To kill time is to waste it," Lovett explained, "like we have to do in the Navy."

"Chico make time live!" He stuck out his legs, stared at his bare feet, wiggled the toes. He introduced one foot to the other, "foot meet foot,"and he nudged the feet together. "See, they make love!"

"Wish I was foot loose and fancy free," Woogie laughed, looking down from the upper bunk

"Wish I could get my feet out of the Navy," Lovett said, rubbing his toes together as thought they were making love.

"How about some music for the feet?" Woogie suggested from the upper bunk. "Lovett, hand me up my guitar? I'll make time run fast with the Texas two-step."

"Foot music won't leg us out of the Navy," Lovett complained. "Maybe Black Bill's hypnotism can take us out of this damn time."

Everybody knew Black Bill could play tricks with the mind. Everybody knew he could work miracles with time. He could plant a "wake-up call" in a man's head that would automatically wake him up for the mid-watch. In the wink of an eye he could make a man forget, or remember, or just go to sleep. One time he put a man out, made him rigid as a footbridge between two bunks.

"Not jived-up for it," Black Bill said. "Yoga got my mind all emptied out."

"You got to empty-up the Horse-Face mind," someone suggested. "Get that *Dear John* woman out!"

"Got her out," Horse-Face Eli was quick to interrupt, "every frigging hair of her head off my mind."

"Try one of those out of body experiences on us," someone came up with another request. Everyone remembered the time Black Bill put "Slick" under the influence and took his subconscious mind to the poker table, told him to take a look at all the hands. When Black Bill brought Slick back to his old self, faraway from the poker table, he could name some of the cards in all the poker hands!

Black Bill remained folded in the lotus position.

"Can a body really get out of itself?" Enzo Varsi wondered out loud.

"Black Bill took me out of body," Slick said.

"What if you can't get back in your body?" Horse-Face Eli wanted to know.

"Getting out of your body would be a good break," someone laughed.

"Got me the body of a stud!"

"Could you put me in a different body?" Enzo Varsi asked Black Bill.

"Pretty boy don't like his body?" Black Bill wondered, looking up. "Want a trade?"

"Not with a man," Varsi said. "Want to see me in the skin of a woman, get the feel of it."

"We'd all like to get a feel of a woman," Black Bill said, "but hypnotism only has the power to persuade, make suggestions."

"Navy got us all hypnotized," Lovett suggested, "got us in its power."

"World around us hypnotizes," Black Bill agreed, "makes us do what it wants," and he was thinking of being hypnotized into a "black boy."

"A good story can take us out of body," Horse-Face Eli suggested, "take us into the head and body of other folks, take us out of our own boredom."

"You boys got yourselves hypnotized into boredom," Black Bill thought. "Time you made your own minds work for you, did some reading." He was reminding himself of the way he got into reading. He wouldn't have anything to do with it at first. He didn't want to run off and be alone. You had to be alone to read. He liked the black print in school books, but not the white voices that came out. After a black teacher got to reading to him, the printed words began to sound black, and they started to take him places, even into the world of white folks.

"Put Lovett under," Horse-Face Eli broke into Black Bill's thoughts, "get inside his head and take the curse out!"

Most all the men knew about Lovett's "curse." He tossed it in the ring whenever sex came up in a "bull" session. The "curse" was just a lot of "bull," most guys figured, and laughed it off.

"Hypnotism can't cast out demons," Black Bill said in all seriousness.

"Praying can!" It was Roy Boy intervening from a couple of bunks down the row.

"This black boy don't know about praying."

"Roy Boy's a born-again Christian," someone brought up, "and looks like he just got born."

"Get into Roy Boy's mind," Lovett suggested to Black Bill, "see if there's anything there."

"None of that voodoo on me," Roy Boy called out, hunching himself down.

"Could Black Bill's hypnotism take me back in time?" Horse-Face Eli asked.

"You got all your past times stored up in you," Black Bill said, "just need the right button to push."

"Can't rightly picture my Old Grand Pappy Harrison," Horse-Face Eli said, "would like a gander at him, back when I were a pup."

Black Bill unwound himself out of the lotus position, gained his feet. "Let me put my mind to it," he said, "and yours." He looked Horse-Face Eli in the eye, told him to look within, asked him what his old Grand Pappy looked like?

"Grand Pappy be all crunched up in store-bought overalls," Horse-Face Eli said in a voice more slow than ever, "be all wrinkly in face, bald head smooth as baby's ass. He got his reading spectacles pushed way up on the old crinkly brow. Grand Pappy, he always ask me where his spectacles be? I tell Grand Pappy I don't rightly know, pretend to look for his specs, don't let on they be cocked on his old forehead. Laugh, almost pee in my pants. Make Grand Pappy spitting mad when I lets on where his specs be hiding on him!"

"What your Grand Pappy do for a living?" Black Bill probed.

"Grand Pappy hunt and plow and plant, make corn seed into powerful moonshine, get more gallons to the acre than any other dirt farmer round about! Grand Pappy raise other things too, like me. I grew up with no electricity, no party-line tellyphone, no inside crapper. Water pump outside, too. but that homestead be the best roost I ever got, till the Navy."

"Was your Grand Pappy ever in the military?"

"Spanish-American War, I recollect. Had his whole regiment strung out in three photograph pictures pieced together, had it a-hanging in the Sunday Sitting Room. He'd a-show you a tiny figure in the middle of it, claim it were him in fighting trim."

"What else you got to tell us about your Grand Pappy?"

"Picture him skinning bark off hickory logs, warming 'em in the coal stove. Hickory logs keep feet like toast on frosty nights, but log get cold by daylight Grand Pappy kicks old log outa bed, shakes house and everybody up! Can hear it now, rolling round, waking me up."

"Roll Grand Pappy around in your head," Black Bill suggested, "and wake up with him."

Horse-Face Eli came out of his faraway look, nodded his head like a horse, said he remembered his Grand Pappy with reading specs pushed up over his eyes.

"Why do we forget so much?" Varsi wondered. "Why's it so hard to remember?"

"Forgetting's easy on the brain," Black Bill figured. "If we carried around in our heads everything that ever happened yesterday, it would take all today to remember. Our brains would get packed up!"

"We pack some memories in our muscles," Woogie thought. "Sometimes I forget a piece of music, but my fingers don't."

"My legs have trouble remembering how to walk on land, after a spell of sea duty," someone remembered, "but the knack comes back."

"My hands forget the feel of a woman," someone complained. "How's that for a bad case of memory?"

"Hope I can dump every chickenshit memory of this here Navy," Lovett grumbled

"Anyone else for a memory trip?" Black Bill looked around.

No one spoke up. Most men hesitated to let themselves go, let themselves fall under the power of someone else. That's what they hated about the Navy.

"Could you take my body back home?" Lovett broke the silence.

"Could hypnotism get me *into* your Navy?" the Cuban shoeshine boy spoke right up.

"This old boy can only take you in and out of yourself," Black Bill said. "Hypnotism's not Black Magic."

"Chico got the black magic with the shoe polish," the Cuban bootblack said.

"I could use a touch-up," Roy Boy called over to Chico and felt around under his bunk for shoes.

"Chico can put shine on Roy Boy's shoes, and face. Got letter from the Cuban friend!"

"From the convent virgin!" Slick let the world know, and danced around Roy Boy's bunk.

"Nobody gives that yeoman kid the time of day," Woogie said from his upper bunk, "but he's the only one of us making time with a good Cuban woman."

Roy Boy's "female mail-order affair" wasn't news to anyone. The Cuban shoeshine boy set him up with a convent girl and was carrying their letters back and forth. Sometimes the letters were taken off Roy Boy and passed around for laughs.

"There's a woman for every ugly one of us," Black Bill said to Woogie, "even for the kid."

"How's *your* woman?" Woogie looked down from the rack above Lovett.

"Little woman's filling out," Lovett said, without looking up.

"That little old gal don't need any filling out," Horse-Face Eli said with a poker face. "She already got a pair that can beat any other two of a kind."

"And she's got a full house," Woogie piped up from his perch on the top bunk, "full with child." He swung his legs back into the rack and the mattress sagged back down in the middle.

"She be getting her pregnant ass on base tomorrow," Lovett mentioned. "It be time to get her feel-ups at the quack shack."

■■■ ■■■ ■■■

Lutie got sticky hot in the taxi ride to Caimanera, didn't chill off in the open ferry boat that churned her across the open water of the bay. She even got more heated as she walked from the ferry landing to the bus stop, brooding. Pregnancy was an "epidemic" on base, she'd been told by the base doctors. Too much "*down*time" for shore duty sailors with their wives. She was the only off-base pregnancy.

Dreading the thought getting checked-out by the doctor's eyes, she was enjoying the sailor eyes as she walked to the bus stop. Their whistles put a swing and a bounce in her step, and a swirl to her skirt.

Thinking of seeing her man at MATS before the check-up she felt a load on her mind, like the loads native women carried around on their heads. Her head was burdened with pregnancy and epilepsy. A seizure could make her miscarry, she'd been told, or go belly-up dead. She might bring forth some kind of monster creature. It was hard to carry all these thoughts on her mind.

Less heavy were the words Tia Magdalena had with God. God told her the little American woman would bear a golden child. God's word was not enough for Tia Magdalena. She took Lutie to a Santeria woman on the outskirts of town .The "truth-sayer" cooked up a "potion," and lay down some laws. Tia Magdalena wasn't "set on Santeria ways," but God told her that the table of the world was set with many ways to live.

Lutie wondered what she should tell her man when she found him at MATS? No need to burden his head with doctor and God talk. Restricted to base, her man was already way off keel. He was like her baby, she smiled to herself. Baby wanted to be delivered from my belly. Husband wanted to be delivered from the Navy!

As she walked and thought and kicked a stone along, she wished she didn't have to lug a heavy body along with her thoughts, two bodies in one! She wished she could be as light as a thought, think herself all the way to MATS without an effort. A final step carried her into the shade of a tree by the bus stop. A post oak bent its crooked branches over benches where sailors and Cuban workers were waiting for their ride. One of the dusky Cubans in the shadow of a broad–brimmed hat stood up to give Lutie a place to sit. He was humming *la Guantanamero*. Lutie joined him with the words she'd learned from Tia Magdalena's son. "I want to play out my destiny!" All the Cuban workers joined her in Spanish or English, "play out my destiny." They carried on until the battleship gray bus came along to carry them off.

Lutie chose a seat by an opened window where she could catch the air stirred up by the bus. The breeze twirled strands of hair around her thoughts that were filled with the Cuban melody of destiny. MATS was her destination on the bus. Where would pregnancy take her? All the while *destiny* was flying around in her head the naval base was passing her by, one gray building after another. No ships were anchored in the bay. The sky was blue as the bay. The sky's round dome was mapped with clouds of islands and continents. The whole sky fit in her head.

Her destination arrived, the Quonset hut housing MATS! Stepping off the bus her outstretched leg would have lifted the spirits of any sailor standing by, but she was alone, and the bus left her in a swirl of gravel dust.

Inside MATS, she was soothed by a sizzle of hamburgers and the voice of Doris Day. Lutie bet it was her man who pumped nickels in the jukebox. She saw him close to it, sitting alone, a square hulk, one leg crossed over the other, a black shoe keeping time to the *Secret Love* of Doris Day.

Lutie eased into a chair next to him, happy to get off her feet, get to open and close her legs under the table, get aired out.

"Here I be," she said, "your not so secret love."

"Here I be, no secret love for the Navy, counting the days till I get out."

He was wishing his Navy life away, same as ever.

Part III: AFTERLIVES

Lovett came back to his Navy life in a different body, square as ever, but a cane to help it along. He came back to his old squadron's first reunion, came back in a different century, a different world. It was harder for him to understand the world, and harder to get around in it.

Lovett found old sailors becalmed in a Miami hotel lobby, but couldn't recognize a face. The men were of his vintage, old enough to have been pressed into service during the Korean War and get bottled-up at Guantanamo Bay. They were well aged.

The square of Lovett's body seemed to have squared in size. The square of his head seemed smaller by contrast. The hair of his head was mostly missing, all but two wispy wings of gray crossed together over the top. Somehow there was enough of his youth in him to get recognized by friends of his youth.

"What in blazes brought Cowboy Lovett to a Navy roundup!"

A few other old boys standing nearby expressed surprise, too, and gathered around. They seemed to remember how bad the Navy shoe pinched Lovett, how taking orders got him bent him out of shape.

"This boy be his own skipper nowadays," Lovett let them all know, "be in command of my own life, except for the little woman." He'd come back in a different body but with the same wife. She was close to his side, like a crutch. Her hair was cut short and dyed blonde, but she was still round and recognizable. It was observed that she overfilled a cocktail dress, spilled a little over the top.

"Can't believe you're still winging it with the old blockhead," someone addressed Lutie.

"How's our little mascot you delivered to the naval base?"

"Lake Junior's all grown up and flown the coop."

The men grouped around Lutie were sorry to learn that their mascot wasn't likely to make the reunion shindig.

■■■ ■■■ ■■■

Reporting for "reunion duty" after so many years, the men mustered their memories. Most of the men had gotten mustered out of the Navy as soon as they could, but held their time in the Navy high. They no longer bitched about the Navy, only about their health and the world they were in. They'd all worn out and outgrown their bodies, and the world had outgrown them. They were even out of sync with each other. It wasn't easy to make connections, not until they found the cash bar, and got mixed and blended back together.

When old sailors get together, cocktails and memories get stirred up. Memories distilled out of the wild oats of youth improve with age, especially when mixed with a jigger of bravado and a dash of wishful thinking. Tales tapped out of a common experience came out in different ways, but the only *proof* was in the whiskey.

The driftwood days of Guantanamo Bay were littering the shores of everyone's memory, but mostly empty shells that only held echoes. Their prime had passed and Cuba had passed into Communism. New wars in Afghanistan and Iraq had taken the place of their war in Korea. Guantanamo Bay had been converted into a prison camp for terrorists. Some of the old boys thought "Gitmo" always was a prison. Others remembered it as a shore duty paradise. They all remembered soft or hard times on "the Rock."

Reunion talk came around to life *after* the Navy. For many old boys, life began after they got their honorable discharges. They'd taken their lives to all parts of the country, had become prosperous and leaders in all walks of life, and were blessed with well appointed children and grandchildren. They were all better liars than flyers.

There was talk about the missing members. Some of them would turn up at the "Welcome Aboard" reception in the hotel "Cabana Room." Well over a hundred squadron mates, and their mates, showed up for beer, pizza, sea stories, and dancing.

■■■ ■■■ ■■■

The "kid yeoman," remembered as "Roy Boy," was pointed out to Lovett and wife as a Catholic priest in the Miami Diocese! He'd aged well in the cloth, hung on to a young face that didn't match the gray of his hair and sideburns. Not wearing the collar, he'd surprised everyone as "Father Roy." Now he was surprised to see Lovett and Lutie still together, "one in body and soul," and remembering Lovett's curse, he asked if Lovett knew love, found God.

"Is God lost?"

"You'd get to know love, if you know God," the priest said, and apologized for talking "shop."

"Bless your dear heart," Lutie said to the priest.

Father Roy was one of the organizers of the reunion and had to move on, greet others.

It was hard enough to think of Roy Boy as a priest, but Lovett was much more surprised to find the squadron push-up and Yoga man, "Black Bill," a "preacher man." He called himself "The Right Reverend Bill Lighty," wore the collar and air of an evangelist, but looked pretty much the same. Only a few tight rings of gray curled around the dark shine of his temples.

"Have you run into Roy Boy of the personnel office?" Lovett asked the Reverend Bill Lighty. "He's a Catholic priest, by God!"

"We all be our own priests," Black Bill said, his eyes still probing with a penetrating force, reminding Lovett that they were good for putting men into a different state.

"Black Bill was a good hand at hypnotism," Lovett introduced Lutie to his dark and wiry-haired squadron mate.

"Not into hypnotism these days, " Black Bill said, "and not into Black Bill!"

"He's just my plain Bill," the woman by his side spoke up and moved between the two men facing each other off. "I'm the preacher's wife. Last time he got anyone hypnotized was when he put me in the marrying mood." She looked a little younger than her husband, and a shade lighter, and she flashed a brighter smile.

"My wife, Ruby," the Right Reverend William Lighty introduced her to the Lovetts, "the jewel of my life, mother of a pair of pearls."

"Sure got a shiny sparkler on her finger," Lutie noticed. "It got me hypnotized."

"Gave up hypnotism when I got the Word," Lighty said, as if starting a sermon. "*Hypnos* had something to do with sleep in the Greek. Got me a call from Jesus to wake folks up."

"My old man could use a wake-up call," Lutie said of her husband. "He's square-shaped like a book, but don't have a word of the Good Book in him."

"Could put the Good Word in him," the preacher offered, "but won't do him no good if he don't know the Lord." He turned to his wife, told her "this here boy's the one with the storybook Curse."

Ruby smiled, looked Lovett up and down, spoke up, said her "Bill" never talked much about the Navy, or any squadron mates, except for the man with *the* Curse. As she talked she was thinking he'd lost it.

"His real curse was the Navy," Lighty kept talking. "He cursed the Navy with every breath."

"Now he bad talks his own body," Lutie said. "It won't let him do what he wants."

"But don't want myself out of this old body," Lovett said, "my hitch's not up."

■■■ ■■■ ■■■

The squadron was no longer a body of one. Maybe it never was, but all the pieces were scattered around the hotel "Cabana Room." The Lovetts and Lightys strung along together, lined up for pizza and beer, came across an empty table where they could get comfortable with themselves and the past.

Just as they put their faces together, a horsey face showed up. Lovett and Lighty had no trouble recognizing "Horse-Face Eli." The old boy had outrun his youth, but not the face and nod of a horse. His hairline had gone over the top of his head, making it look longer. Except for the glasses he'd pushed up on his forehead, he looked more like a horse than ever. He'd ambled over to their table with his can of beer and slice of pizza, asked if he could "team up!" The men at the table introduced him to their wives. He said he was all alone, his "yoke mate" gone off to "greener pastures." The wives bemoaned his loss. The men only asked him to hang out with them.

"Been lapping it up since the sun be over the yardarm," Horse-Face Eli said, "off my stride, got to get me off my feet." He pulled up a chair.

"You still live in a book house of stories?" It was Lovett wanting to know as he clicked beer cans with the newcomer.

"Got me a stable full," Horse-Face Eli said, getting comfortable in his chair

"Look who's moseying our way," Black Bill said.

Everyone t the table looked up at a swarthy man with a woman in hand.

"Ahoy, all hands," he said. "Remember me, Carmine Marino, spaghetti boy, lover man, grease monkey?"

"You hung on to your gladiator shape and Roman nose," Lovett noticed

"Hanging on to the wife of Enzo Varsi, a *paisano* you boys used to hit it off with."

"I'm Zoe Varsi," the woman introduced herself, "and think I recognize Lovett and Lutie from the skeches Enzo made!"

Lutie remembered Enzo, the pretty petty officer who made her feel good, and made good pictures. She surveyed the woman who was that pretty man's wife, calculated her lush brown hair was dyed, or a wig to match her outfit.

It came to Ruby Lighty at the same time that the woman was of good taste, a diaphanous scarf tucked at the neck of her brown suit.

Horse-Face Eli noticed she wasn't wearing a ring.

Lovett thought her face, under powder and rouge, had a remarkable resemblance to the man she married.

"I'm Enzo's widow," she added as everyone was looking her over.

"Bless his dear heart," Lutie cried out. "What happened to your man?"

"A long story, a meaningless ending!"

"He was my Italian *paisano*," Carmine Marino slipped in as soon as he could.

"Carmine's an actor," Zoe Varsi said of her guide, "still on one of those TV afternoon soaps."

"Well, I declare," Lutie said. "Maybe I see that face on the television box."

"I kept hanging in there, aging with the show," Carmine Marino was quick to respond. "My character never gets killed off." He seemed anxious to get away. "Got to tune myself out, get back to my table. Stand watch over this pretty lady!" He backed off. "See you around."

"Enzo always talked about the Lovetts," Zoe Varsi said as she was helped into a chair.

"Enzo would want you to have these sketches," and she patted her handbag. "I came all the way from Chicago to keep him on the squadron roll call." She pulled sheets of sketch paper out of her handbag, passed them around the table.

Lutie saw herself as a young woman in Cuba, hardly recognized herself but remembered the artist, and his big feet.

Lovett looked at his picture and remembered his thick hair parted in the middle.

"Hard to recognize my young self," Lutie said to Zoe Varsi, "but you sure look like I remember the artist, a lot like him."

Lovett and the other men nodded in agreement. The widow was embarrassed, said something about years of marriage casting couples in the same mold.

Lutie said she was glad "none of *her* man's looks rubbed off on her," and she gave Lovett a friendly pat. He didn't take offense. His mind was imagining Enzo *in* Zoe! It made him smile.

Lutie thought out loud that Enzo always made her feel "pretty."

"He was an artist, wanted to make the world pretty," Zoe Varsi said, " but couldn't make a living with paint and brush, made do with square and compass as an engineer."

"My man squared himself with the world as a grain inspector," Lutie bragged.

"Sometimes the world goes against our grain," Black Bill said.

"A man has to work so hard at making a living he misses out on living," Lovett thought.

"Sure puts me in mind of a country boy I heard tell of," Horse-Face Eli pondered, "worked like a horse, didn't know who he be by time to go out to pasture."

"That's my Enzo," the widow thought, "worked hard, ended up with Alzheimer's, didn't know who he was, or the woman he married."

"Life's a waste," Lovett suggested. "First half of life a man has to fill up with learning, second half it all leaks out, goes to waste."

"Life's not wasted if we fill up with the word of the Lord," Bill Lighty broke in, reminding everyone at the table they had a preacher in their midst.

■■■ ■■■ ■■■

"Remember Crash Gordon? How's it going?"

The old personnel officer appeared at the table where the Lovetts and Lightys were huddled together with the Horse-Face widower, and the Enzo Varsi widow. The man had a quiver in his hand, and a woman in hand. She was shaded under an enormous hat.

"You called me the *Lady of the Lake*," Lutie looked up, remembering.

"English 101," he said, smiling at everyone around the table. "This old pilot landed up as a professor of English, and got grounded as professor emeritus."

"I'm Mrs. Professor Emeritus," the wife broke in, smiling under the brim of her hat.

"Catherine Gordon," her husband introduced her, "same name as the mother of the Romantic poet, Lord Byron."

"Mother of three sons," she said, "but no *Childe Harold*."

"I'm Zoe Varsi," the widow identified herself. "The personnel officer might remember Enzo Varsi, mechanic, third class petty officer."

"Names and faces don't match so easily in the sunset of my point of view," the old lieutenant shook his head, thinking out loud. "Zoe and Enzo, the names make a rhyming couplet!"

"Not in rhyme anymore," the widow shook her head, "Enzo passed on."

The personnel officer said he was sorry for her loss, and his "flippant remarks." He also apologized for his bodily tremors, the beginning of "Parkinson's." Only his body of literature, he managed to say, was still in good shape, and he and his wife had to move on, greet others.

■■■ ■■■ ■■■

No one at the table recognized Woogie Woods when he appeared at the table with a rope-like mustache over his mouth and a ponytail swinging in back. He asked Lovett if he remember the sag in the mattress over his head in the barracks. Lovett managed to stagger to his feet, swing arms around the old guitar player. They hugged awkwardly, backed off to get a better look at each other.

Woogie thought Lovett was still square, but his "big wings of hair had folded-up like planes at rest on a flattop."

Lovett thought Woogie had gone from "bristly crew-cut" to "bristly unshaved."

Woogie still talked with his head aslant as he said he liked the looks of "the little Lutie woman." He grabbed her up. "You feel like a woman's supposed to feel," he said, swinging her around in his arms.

"Don't play me for the fingerboard on your old guitar," Lutie gasped, laughing as she came back down on her feet.

"You used to be regulation," Lovett said to Woogie, "right out of the book of regs!"

"New regulations," Woogie grinned, "out of the counter-culture book." His thin-lipped smile stretched out the scrawny mustache. "Tried to hook up with the hippie generation."

No one liked the ponytail, no one around the table, and they let him know. Horse-Face Eli even came up with "Horse-Tail" as a better name for Woogie.

"We'd make the front and back-end of a pony act," Woogie laughed back He sat down, went on to let everyone know he'd flown high on the airwaves after squadron days and had his own radio show, *Boogie With Woogie*! He filled everyone in on his career. The flip side of his musical career, the private side, turned out to make the most impression. Over the years he'd "picked a wife for every string of his guitar," said he was "all strung out!" Marriage, he thought, was a grab bag. A man never knows what he'll come up with!

"Come up with any more little gray aliens?" Lutie asked, remembering Woogie came out of Roswell where flying saucers had spun legends.

"Only come up with gray wrinklies claiming to be Navy buddies," he said, waving a hand around.

"You and me were plucking buddies," Lutie reminded him, "banjo and guitar."

"Got any more pluck in you?" Woogie asked, not waiting for an answer. He said his combo was lined up for the reception dance and she could "string along."

"First off," Lutie said, "my banjo be back to home."

"Banjos are easy to pick up, like wives," Woogie shot back. "I could even pick you up a new husband." He winked at Lovett.

"No new man for this old gal. Takes too long to break a man in."

■■■ ■■■ ■■■

When Woogie's combo raised "Anchors Aweigh," sailors and wives got the dance underway. The music quickly picked up the swing of the Big Band Era.

"Music of our age," Black Bill said.

"The Big Band*age* for the hurts of wartime," his wife showed her lighter side.

The music swung Bill Lighty and wife onto the dance floor. Lovett begged off, said he only had one good leg. Horse-Face Eli also held his seat, claimed his feet only touched the *barn floor* to country music. He was sorry he couldn't give the ladies a turn around the floor, but could spin a good story for them.

"Got a story about my Enzo as a sailor?" the widow asked. "I'd love to hear about him in the Navy."

"Your boy wasn't good for a story, never got *off base*," Horse-Face Eli was sad to say. "Good boys don't make good stories."

As he talked, the old squadron mates went flying by with their wives, tipped wings to each other as they danced circles around each other. It seemed like a squadron review to Lovett, but he couldn't line up some of the old faces going by with faces that used to answer to muster at Guantanamo Bay. Those he recognized were caricatures of their former selves, appearing one after another, as if in the separate panels in a comic strip.

All the while, Lutie kept wondering why her man never kept up with any of those naval characters, not a letter or phone call in all these years. She found herself on the lookout for Yeoman Tork, the man who called her "Miss Liberty!" She remembered him at work in khaki shorts, and in dress whites on the ferry boat to Cuba. He kept a woman over there.

She was still looking for him when Bill and Ruby Lighty came breathless back to the table. They crashed in happy smiles. Another couple approached the table, a bowlegged man with a squadron souvenir cap cocked sideway, and dragging a woman behind him.

"Look alive!" the man's gritty voice commanded. "Here's Popeye the sailor man, and his woman!" He talked out the side of his mouth, kept the other side gripping a pipe.

Lutie thought the "sailor man" standing over them really might pass for the comic-strip character, but he had more bulge to his belly than to the biceps and forearms. "Glad to meet a sailor man called Popeye," she said, looking up. She thought the woman beside him was more fleshy than the Olive Oyl of Popeye fame.

Lovett had put it behind him but couldn't forget his fear and dislike for that man. Popeye had shrunk with age but was still a tugboat of a man, built to push people around.

"These here swabs gave me a hard time," the bowlegged sailor said to the woman at his side. He let everyone know she was his wife, "Grace Popovitch."

"Take the load off," Horse-Face Eli invited the old boatswain's mate and wife to sit down. He was quick to remember the ruckus in the barracks, but vague about the details.

Lovett harbored a special uneasiness for the boatswain's mate, remembering that loose canon he had for a wife. The woman with him must be a later wife. She never gave Lovett a second look.

"Never wanted my aching eyes to get a look at you swabs again," Popeye was saying out the side of his mouth, "but the eyes don't have it no more" He pulled up chairs for himself and wife, got right down to making sure the ladies knew he'd been shot out of the water at Pearl Harbor, said he was sleeping-in that Sunday morning, getting blasted up on deck, an eyeful of the "rising sun on Jap aircraft wings." He asked everyone what they were "up to" on that Pearl Harbor day?

The women claimed they were too young to remember. The men said they didn't have radios back then, didn't get the word until Monday morning, at school, and there was special assembly. Popeye's wife said she wished her "old sailor man" didn't remember Pearl Harbor at all! The memory of it still woke him up, she said.

"I remember Pearl Harbor," a voice came crashing down. "Remember this old boy?" A giant of a man was towering over the table, looking down, half his face hidden by a trim beard that came to a point at the chin. "We got some old rigging to weave up, after all these years."

Lovett cringed at the newcomer. It was the parachute rigger, and the stinking memory came with him, but not the smell.

Lutie had to stretch her neck to take him all in. "Big Six!" she gasped out loud, remembering how she used to think his name was "Big Sex." She remembered visiting him in the naval hospital when he was like a vegetable.

"Chute-up and fly high," he saluted them.

"You had that stuck in your craw," Lutie recalled, "time I visit-up with you in Sick Bay. Chute-up and fly high, you kept a-saying, like a broken record. Thought you flipped your lid."

"You were cracking up, back then" Popeye supplied, shooting smoke out the side of his mouth.

"Back in the groove now," the tall man thought, looking down as he swung an empty chair over to the table. He sat on it backwards, hung his arms over the top. "Play it safe and live it up, that's the spin I put on life these days."

"Big Six be our old parachute rigger," Bill Lighty said to his wife, Ruby.

"I'm Zoe Varsi, Enzo's widow. You still go by the name of Big Six?"

"Suits me!" He went on to say he wasn't quite six feet six anymore, but the name "puts me in mind of the good old days."

"Those bad old days look better nowadays," Lovett said.

"Good old days had you with a baby," Big Six said to Lutie. "I got out the infirmary when you went into labor."

"Well I do declare," Lutie said. "You sure got your memory back, after all your head trouble."

"Got my head screwed back on straight."

"And you dropped a healthy colt," Horse-Face Eli said to Lutie. "Remember his christening at the base chapel, and his first steps on base. I could tell a story about the time he were a toddler a-watching planes warm up. Scared his hair, he said of the backwash."

"Well, bless your dear heart," Lutie said. "That little boy don't have hair to scare no more."

"You still have the falling sickness?" Big Six asked of Lutie.

"Well, I do declare," Lutie said, "you sure got your thinking cap on. Got me all doctored up, thank ye kindly."

"We all be fallen," Bill Lighty said. "You saved?" he asked Big Six.

"Parachutes save," Big Six said.

"Who packs your chute in life, pulls your strings?"

"I'm a free man," Big Six scoffed, holding up his hands to show no strings attached.

"You had plenty of hang-ups, back in the barracks," the preacher recalled, "had yourself loaded down with anger."

"Learned where to put my anger," Big Six shot back. "I'm a psychologist."

"Psychology gonna let you down like a parachute."

"Psychology keeps me up, got me in the counseling racket, and I'm still in practice, hundred bucks a throw."

"In old days you be into car racing," Lovett remembered, hoping to change the subject. "Got me a flashback of that picture on your locker door, snapshot of you in goggles, alongside a racing rig."

"This old boy sure was hell on wheels," Big Six recalled himself, resting his bearded chin on the back of the chair, "but that's a lot of laps back."

"Slipped your cable one time in the barracks," Popeye reminded him, pulling the pipe out of his mouth, "and ran aground, got yourself that berth in Sick Bay."

Lovett didn't like the way the talk was going, squeezed his hand around the cold can of beer, got a grip on himself for a confrontation with the parachute rigger. "Who knows what really happened way back then," Lovett managed to get out. "Memories come back like old movies on the TV. You can't quite remember if you saw the flick or not?"

"We misremember," Big Six granted, "but the past is there if you know what buttons to push. In my business I help people push buttons, remember, and *forget*."

"Hypnotism can work for you like that," Bill Lighty said, "but prayer works better!"

"Think I heard tell about a big six-six man almost killed in the barracks," Zoe said. "What's that all about?"

"That's an old story," Horse-Face Eli said, "not worth the telling."

"Story's about me," Big Six said, "but memory's knocked out of me."

"All of us had a lot of hard-knocks on the Rock," Lovett spoke up, relaxing his hand on the can of beer but shaking his head at Varsi's widow. How could she have a handle on that incident so long ago?

"You got a better memory than most of us," Big Six said to Varsi's widow, "and you weren't even there."

"My man was."

"Why you not be a-dancing with your woman?" Lovett asked Big Six, hoping there was a wife to take him away.

"No wife. Had one, but she couldn't keep up."

"Marriage be no joyride," Lutie tried to find something to say. "Had me some rough rides with my old man." She gave him a pat.

"The *Old Man* is our sin-self," Bill Lighty slipped in a preacher's word. "The *New Man* is the born again man."

"That's the signal for this old man to hit the silk," Big Six said, standing up, all the way up. "Moving on!"

Lutie followed him up with her eyes. "Time for this little gal to hit the bed sheets," she said, lowering her eyes to address her husband. "How 'bout you, Old Man?

"It's *Stardust* time for us all," Ruby broke in, calling attention to the Hoagy Carmichael tune in the air.

It was a good night, they all agreed, and promised to see each other in the morning. The Lovetts stopped at the front desk on the way to their room, found a message from someone called Ramon Manrique.

"Who's he?" Lovett wondered.

"The Cuban son of the house?" Lutie reminded him.

"Your rebel boy! What are the odds we'd run across him in Miami? What are the odds?"

■■■ ■■■ ■■■

"You think our lives are in the cards?" Woogie Woods asked in the middle of a poker game. He was tapping his cards on the table, keeping to the tempo of a melody he was humming.

"Life gets handed to us," the old officer with Parkinson's said from the other side of the table, "and we have to make the best of it."

"Let the cards talk," another poker player insisted. It was the old pilot known as Ponzio, remembered as a high flying pilot, now hunched over the poker table as a pilot grounded for life. The cigar screwed in the side of his frown kept a tight grip on every word his lips shaped. "Get the action going!"

What in deuces you getting at, our lives in the cards?" It was Slick Lyon, the game sponsor. "The winning hand's in the cards."

"And our fortunes are in our *hands*," Dutch Decker contributed.

Old squadron mates were strewn around the table in Slick Lyon's hotel suite, the "Lyon's Den." They'd gotten together after the reception to relive the poker of their naval days.

"Life's not in the cards for a seagoing sailor," Slick grinned "It's between the *decks*."

"You always got a joker up your sleeve," Woogie said to Slick, still keeping time with the tap of his cards. "Got *La Guantanamero* stuck in my head, that old Cuban song about destiny."

"Got your destiny in the palm of my *hand*," Slick said, throwing a chip in the pot.

"I'm folding," Woogie sighed in tune with *La Guantanamero*, letting go of the cards he'd been tapping.

"I'm calling," Slick said.

The hands around the table went down, and Slick pulled in the pot. "Been getting the *Lyon*'s share," he made a pun on his name. "This boy thinks destiny's not in the cards, it's in the way we play them. Look at me. I parlayed a common deck hand all the way up to a big dealer in Cadillacs!"

"You hit the jackpot," Woogie agreed, starting to deal the next hand. "But you got to hand it to me, too, a lowly grease monkey getting to the top of the charts in the music game!" He dealt the cards slowly, said he was "played out" from making music all night. The cards fell slowly from his fingertips. Even his ponytail was frazzled, coming undone.

"You enlisted men did all right with the hands you were dealt," the old pilot, Dutch, granted as he picked up his cards, one at a time, "but you can't make anything out of a junk hand."

"Destiny's not in our cards," said the man with Parkinson's, the professor emeritus, Crash Gordon. "The fault, dear Brutus, is not in your stars, but in yourself. Shakespeare had all the good plays!"

"Sometimes good hands don't play well," Woogie said, dealing out the last card, "like hands in marriage."

"Never took a chance on marriage," Dutch mentioned, more interested in his cards. "Good pilots don't take chances."

"Can't draw a full house without marriage!"

"How 'bout the full house we drew at the reception tonight?" Dutch Decker was trying to change the subject.

"The Varsi widow was queen of the draw?" Slick looked up from his cards. "Sure would like to see what she's got!"

"You already got the queen of the draw," Big Six broke into the conversation. All six feet six of him came uncurled up at the far end of the table. He sat up, fingered his pointed beard, his "Freudian touch." He liked reminding the poker players he was a psychologist.

The mention of the "queen of the draw" reminded all the men around the table of Slick's wife, a second wife, half his age. She'd just taken herself off to bed in the next room.

"Got me a winner of a wife," Slick agreed, taking a quick read of his cards, and the faces of others. "But when you draw a wife out of a younger generation, you don't live in the same world. No matter, though, in the same bed."

"The Varsi widow's shoes might look good under my bed," Dutch was reconsidering, along with his cards.

"Feet too big," Ponzio assessed, screwing the cigar in his mouth.

The air was too heavy with smoke and tension to hold anymore talk. Chips clicked, heads nodded, smoke spewed. Finally, someone said life was in the choices we make, not in our cards. It was Truett, known as "True," a first class grease monkey in everyone's memory.

"If I were you, True, I'd choose to be with my pretty wife instead of us bums," Woogie said.

"Christy wants me to make my own choices," True said of his wife. "She has a mind for free will!"

"I choose to raise," Crash Gordon spoke up.

"What choices did enlisted men have in the Navy?" Woogie wondered out loud. "We had choices made for us!"

No one called him on that, but Slick chose to call the game. He laid down another winning hand.

"Could have taken it," Ponzio spewed out. He showed everyone the hand he'd given up on.

"Full many a great hand is born to blush unseen," the professor emeritus made a play on Gray's *Elegy*. It was his turn to deal. He passed out cards with a shaky hand, one at a time, all around the table.

"It sure would help my game if I could see everybody's hand," Slick noted, sorting his new hand. "Back at Gitmo, Black Bill put me in one of those trances and my out-of-body eyes got a peek at all the poker hands!"

"Never fell for that out-of-body crap," Big Six sneered. "You guys set us up."

"From my sunset point of view, we'll all be getting an out of body experience one of these days," Crash Gordon said, turning everyone off. "That's in the cards for sure!"

"Well, that old Varsi boy got his out-of-body experience," Slick reminded everyone, "but sure left a great looking widow's body behind."

"Big feet!"

"Not a hair on your ass if you don't make a play for her," Slick said to Dutch. Slick was a former enlisted man but no longer afraid of talking up to officers.

"You think I lost every hair on my ass, too!" Dutch took a swipe at his bald head.

"Think I got you all beat," he added.

"This boy don't believe anything he can't see," Slick said, calling the game. "Show me what you got."

When the cards came down, spread out for all to see, Slick had the best of them, hugged in the pot.

Dutch, the old pilot, let the cuss words fly.

"Sit on your hands," Slick suggested to him, "and just contemplate your "*naval*" origins!"

"We had a belly full of that at the reception," Big Six sounded off from his end of the table, and he gave a "Freudian touch" to his pointed beard.

It was Slick's turn to deal. "Sure was good to see Cowboy Lovett and his woman," Slick said, tossing cards around the table. "That old boy was lucky in women. I'm lucky in cards."

"You're lucky in love, too," Ponzio said, gripping the cigar in his teeth as he talked.

"Puts me in mind of the Lovett Curse," Woogie said as he scooped-up his cards. "It was in the cards for that old boy to be lucky with women, unlucky with love! He sure played his cards right to get that woman of his."

"His curse was a load of crap," Big Six thought, stroking his beard, "and we all knew it."

Slick asked him how Lovett could have won that woman on his own.

"Found a woman as empty headed as him," Dutch intervened, tapping at his bald head for emphasis.

"You still giving that old boy flak," Crash Gordon wondered, "for letting you go up in that plane that wasn't readied?"

"Was your crackup an accident, or in the cards?" Woogie asked.

"It was an accident for me," Dutch decided. "Lovett didn't have a full deck, accidents were in the cards for him."

"Maybe our lives aren't in the cards," Crash Gordon said, shaking his head. "You can cheat at cards! Can't cheat life, not out of the last draw."

■■■ ■■■ ■■■

"Thought you were dead," Lutie said when she saw her "Revolutionist Ramon" in the hotel lounge. Airmen were down in a business meeting, a good time for Lutie to set up a meeting with Ramon. She would have recognized him right away, even if he hadn't told her on the phone to look for a man in a navy blue suit, "white hair and black tie."

"Dead to the old life," he said, hugging her to him for a moment. "Alive to *La Causa*!"

"Causa what?"

"Cause of the free Cuba! You helped me stay alive for *La Causa*," he reminded her in perfect English.

Lutie blushed at the memory of Ramon seeing her in a pajama top.

"Your man got a vital message to the shoeshine boy," Ramon kept talking. "Poor kid! He made a torch out of himself for *La Causa*!"

Lutie's blood ran cold at the recollection of the shoeshine boy. The report of him burning up in the streets of Caimanera unnerved her years ago, and today.

"He was a martyr," Ramon said.

"We thought he be crazy," Lutie said. "Martyr mean crazy?"

"No matter, not anymore," Ramon thought.

They sat down together, sank into the cushioned seats, came to rest together, touching. Lutie avoided his eyes, looked up at the crystal chandelier sparkling in the sunlight.

"I was one of the first to follow Castro, you know," Ramon started telling Lutie. "I was one of the bearded ones, came to power with Fidel, broke with Fidel over power, got myself out of Cuba with just my skin, and the olive greens on my back."

"Get your old Ma out, too?" Lutie asked, looking down.

"*Madre* now talks to God, full time," he said, crossing himself.

"Tia Magdalena always gave me the good word from God," Lutie remembered, looking away.

"You were too young to be a wife, and mother."

"We all get over being young."

"Tell me about getting over it."

"My man got himself out of Navy blues but couldn't get blues out of him, had himself a hard time in civvies. He took the G.I. Bill for a free ride in the agriculture and mechanics college, got to know the inside and outside of seeds, sprang up into one of them grain inspectors."

"We know what a seed of grain will become," Ramon said, "but what is a child man supposed to become?"

"Lake Junior be a Golden Child, like God said he would be, but he went from child to man before I could stop it, and lost his shine. Grew up, he did, in New Orleans, near Westwego where my man worked at the grain elevator. Grain elevator blew up, grain dust be like gunpowder, you know, and this old girl almost lost her man. Did lose my Golden Child! Had the seed of his daddy in him and don't pay his folks much heed. Boy don't intend coming to this here squadron shindig, not even to see old sailors boys who made him a mascot."

"We never know how we'll turn out."

They sat together in silence. After awhile Lutie complained that her grain inspector was "going to seed," crippled-up with arthritis, and other "miseries."

Ramon said something about the fruit of the grain being best just before it goes bad. He contradicted himself, said old age is just plain bad! He said his whole life hadn't turned out the way he planned.

Lutie asked if he got "to write stories the Heming Way?"

"Not an author," he said. "Couldn't even author my own life story." He went on to talk about "the cream of Cuban exiles" going from the top to the bottom in Miami. When he got to America he had to "kill for a living in a slaughter house, sweep the blood and bone pieces off the killing beds." He said he read for the law at night, made it as a lawyer, and a *politico.* He said his words got beamed back to Cuba on *Radio and TV Marti.*

Lutie wanted to know if he got into marriage. He said he'd gone to "seed" with an American woman, raised the "American family, a boy and a girl." He was an American himself! "Ramon," he said, "is now Ray, only a little light of Cuba still in me!" In retirement, he was a volunteer at the Cuban Research Institute by day, and played dominos and chess with Cuban exiles by night.

"A miracle we found each other!" Lutie thought, "two pins in a haystack!"

"Got word of your reunion at the Research Institute," Ramon said. "Miracle was my memory of your squadron's name, the *Mallards*. It came up when one of your old Mallards, named Turner, was at the Institute to look for a woman he left behind in Cuba."

"Well, I declare," Lutie said, remembering that Tork's real name was Turner. "That old boy did have a woman in Cuba, but I never got a look at her."

"Not likely he'll find his woman," Ramon said. "The Cuba we carry around in our heads is lost baggage."

"Lots of lost baggage turning up at this here reunion," Lutie said. "You be the best of it."

■■■ ■■■ ■■■

"What's Ramon like?" Lovett asked Lutie as he was undressing for bed.

"Not much better looking than you, even with his clothes on," Lutie smiled, looking him over.

"Had a hunch you fancied that Cuban dude." Lovett thought. "Never figured Doris Day was the only gal with a secret love!"

"Reckon you be jealous. You must love this old gal! God be a jealous God."

"Not jealous," Lovett insisted, "and this old boy got the curse, can't know love!"

"Maybe you got a secret love for the Navy," Lutie said. "You been a-loving the reunion."

"Navy looks better through wrong end of binoculars."

"Those times be so far away, it seem like a dream," Lutie looked away, turning to the mirror for a look at herself. "If you could turn hands of clock back round, would you marry up?"

"With who?"

"Why you never sweet talk this old gal?" Lutie looked herself up and down in the mirror, extended a leg, stretched and flexed a foot. "Ain't I the flame in your old heart?"

"Want me to burn up?"

"Ramon say your shoeshine boy burned up for the Revolution, not for being gay."

"Don't want to give it no mind!"

"Don't you put your mind on that Varsi widow?"

"Now who be jealous? Put the blame on the curse."

■■■ ■■■ ■■■

"Damn her to hell!"

Lovett's words leaped out of the dark. The king-size hotel bed quivered under him.

"You having yourself a stroke?" Lutie gasped, coming awake under Lovett's shadow.

"Maybe it were only a bad dream," he managed to get out. "Don't you fall back off to sleep, hear! Don't leave me alone! Hear!"

"Lord a-mercy, what in Creation got you in such a stew!" Lutie could feel the touch of his heat, and pulse. Snapping on the bed light, she could see the terror in his face.

"That Varsi woman had the hots for me," Lovett was able to get out.

"In your dreams!"

"The Varsi widow were no woman! She were Varsi made into a woman!"

"Well, that sure do take the frosting off your dream cake!" Lutie got wide awake. "Get yourself one of them pain pills."

"What makes a man want to get into a woman's body?"

"You ought to know!" Lutie rolled over toward him. "Don't fret your old head over a dream."

"What makes a man want to change bodies?"

"You ain't been so happy in your old bod."

"Wouldn't trade my man parts!"

" Don't pay it no never mind. Why you try to make sense out of a dream?"

"Don't seem like it were a dream! You ever figure on changing your pretty body?"

"Changing it into a heavenly body," Lutie was quick to reply.

■■■ ■■■ ■■■

The body of poker players got itself together for one more session in Slick Lyon's hotel suite, right after the banquet.

"Attention all hands," Woogie said with authority, dealing out the cards as quickly as he could, spinning them around the table. He was feeling more lively tonight. "Let's get this last flight of poker off the ground."

"Deal me the good life tonight," Crash Gordon spoke up, "if you still think our lives are in the cards?"

"I've shuffling our lives up," Woogie said, "dealing out reincarnations."

"I'm coming back in spades," Slick said, glancing at his cards and smiling.

"Far out!" Woogie said to himself, grinning at his hand.

"Cut the bluffing," Ponzio snarled. He screwed the cigar around in his mouth. "Let the cards talk."

"Count me in,"Dutch Decker said, spinning a chip on the table.

"Only need one more card," Slick announced, drawing one from the dealer, "to make my life complete."

"I'm good," True said, not taking another card. "Looks like our last night's gonna be my good night."

"Farewell to arms, and wings," Crash Gordon said of the reunion, and folded. He looked around. There were more poker players in Slick's suite than the night before. A new face at the table was Carmine Marino, the airman who'd come back as a daytime star of television. He didn't talk much, said he liked to get his words from scripts.

The old boatswain's mate, Popeye, had barged into the game, made room for himself at the table, made more talk and smoke go round.

The yeoman Tork had been talked into the game. A retired high school teacher, no wife in hand, twice divorced, he got lined up.

More chips were in the pot tonight, more hands around the table. Slick's young wife was still up, dealing out the sandwiches she'd ordered-up from room service, huddling around each of the men, one at a time, lingering longer around Carmine Marino. She'd seen his character on television, said it was a "treat" to view the "illusion in the flesh." He said she should have seen him in the flesh as a young sailor. He had wavy black hair, a head full of ringlets in the shower. Now his hair was thin and streaked with gray.

Popeye thought Slick's wife was a "trim little craft," and she let everyone know she was a "model" before coming alongside a sailor. She had to get him "overhauled," keep him "shipshape!" His squadron mates thought he looked like a wax statue of himself, tight of face, dyed of hair, sealed and preserved in a jazzy Playboy smoking jacket.

The cards kept flying, and talk, and smoke.

"Wish we could fish-up the old skipper's daughter for our poker pool," Slick raised the idea, and his bid.

"She'd make a good catch for you," Crash Gordon said to Dutch. "Only a schoolgirl when we were flying high at Gitmo, she got herself grown-up, divorced, and available."

"As queens follow kings, she's in the cards for Dutch," Woogie said.

"She's the daughter of the squadron," Dutch said, "our Old Man's kid, too young for me." He was the master of ceremonies at the banquet and introduced the commanding officer's daughter. "She almost talked our Old Man back down to earth again," he granted, "made the skipper seem almost human!"

"The old girl really kept her figure," Slick's wife mentioned, showing a crack of cleavage as she leaned over the table. She neatly stacked the chips in front of her husband, and bid everyone a good night.

"Talk about queens following kings," Dutch said when she was gone. "Slick, you sure dealt yourself a good hand in marriage."

"The Old Man's daughter would be a good bet for you," Crash Gordon kept thinking.

"Our Old Man's little girl found herself an old boyfriend," Dutch announced, "an enlisted man! Seems like the two of them are picking up the cards where they left off."

"That leaves you with Varsi's widow?" Slick said. "She's on her own, a lonely queen of hearts."

"If you really want a *stacked* deck," Woogie raised his voice, "you got to deal with Lovett's little woman."

"What in the blue blazes did she ever see in that square-ass?" It was Dutch Decker shooting down Lovett again.

"Guess it was the curse," Tork reminded everyone. "Wonder if he ever ditched it, got to know love with his little woman? Wonder if any of us got to know love?"

"Guess most drew bad hands at the marriage game," Woogie thought, looking around. "Got the idea a lot of our marriages folded. Got you all beat, have a straight, five divorces in a row, and a sixth one on the way."

"Divorce was unheard of, back when we were kids," Tork mentioned as he dropped out of the game. "I was a preacher's kid, used to figure marriages got dealt out in heaven."

"You believed in a cruel God," Woogie thought, looking up from his cards.

"I believed in a cruel God," Horse-Face Eli said, "every time I looked in the mirror, until I got to be a man. God evened me up in the end!"

"You'd be a winner at *stud* poker," Slick quipped, "but bet you're sitting on the short stack in this here deal."

"I be calling you on that," Horse-Face Eli challenged.

"Let's see what you got!"

When the cards went down Slick had the best of them, again! "I'm not playing for the money," he apologized as he raked up the chips, "don't need all these American eagles, only play for the love of the game."

"What's this thing called love," Woogie asked in a singing voice that carried the Cole Porter tune,"this crazy thing called love?" He was dealing out the next hand.

"What's this crazy thing called life?" Crash Gordon asked, picking up his cards with a shaky hand. "What's it all add up to?"

"Life's defined by biologists as anything that grows and reproduces," Tork spouted. He was still a teacher at heart.

"That makes sex the defining thing in life," Slick looked up from his cards and panted lustily

Popeye said sex was worshiped in ancient Pompeii. He talked out one side of his mouth, puffed smoke out the other. "Had me some liberties in Naples, home port for the 6th Fleet," he piped up. "Round the Bay lies the old wreck of a buried city, Pompeii." He stopped talking long enough to square his jaw, make sure everyone was listening. "Vendors peddled key chains hung with the *Flying Phallus*. Old Romans worshiped a cock and balls with wings!"

"What the hell do young airmen worship?" Slick looked around with a grin pasted on his face.

"I've got you all by the balls," Woogie claimed, and called the game.

All hands went down, but Carmine Marino came up with the best of them. As he pulled in the pot he said the old Roman gods always dealt Italian boys the "sexy hands."

"Time to give our cards a rest," Slick said, tapping his cards on the table. "We got to hit the *deck* pretty early for the memorial. A lot of old hands to remember!"

▪▪▪ ▪▪▪ ▪▪▪

"Taps in the morning," Lovett reminded Lutie when they got back to their hotel room after the banquet. He had "Taps" on his mind for the morning memorial service, but "Taps" was for the night. "Taps in the morning," he said to Lutie. "That's a laugh!"

"Taps for all of us, one day," Lutie thought, closing the door and leaning against it as if to hold out the angel of death.

"You fixing to lecture me on the afterlife?" Lovett asked, sliding off his tie, swinging out of his sport coat.

"You know all there be to know of a seed of wheat," Lutie thoght, "but don't know a crumb about the Bread of Life!"

"The seed has it all, all that was, all that will be."

"It do say in the Good Book that a seed of wheat got to fall to the ground and die before it rise up again."

"If you got to live another life, would you marry up with this old boy?" Lovett was remembering his wife's question of the night before.

"If you knowed what love be, you not have to ask me that," Lutie said. She looked at herself in the mirror, pushed up the bodice of her cocktail dress. "This old gal do got a lot, and loves her man with all she got!"

"And the old gal's got a lot of life in her," Lovett said, thinking of all the life he'd let fly by.

"Your old Ma gave you life, but no notion of the afterlife."

"Reckon we be in the *after*life," Lovett thought. "Afterlife, that be *after* the good life!" Supporting himself on the bedpost, he kicked off his shoes, stepped out of his pants. "Been out of the good life for along time," he said, sitting on the edge of the bed, having trouble reaching down to his socks. "Maybe I be right with the Lord if I be right with my bones."

Lutie bent down to pull off his socks. "You gonna leave your old bones one day," she said, massaging one of his feet between her hands, "and fly up on the wings of eagles."

He told her she was already getting one of his feet into heaven!

"Got to get 'em both there, if you reckon a-taking this gal across to that other side."

"We come a long way together, since Cuba," Lovett thought, laying hands on her head.

"And this here Navy wing-ding sure has been a long time a-coming," Lutie concluded, standing up. She reached behind her back to unfasten the dress, let it slip off the curves of her shoulders. "Seem like we be different folks back then," she said, holding her dress up, "all them galaxies away. Seem like that girl you married outlived herself, came back a ghost."

"You scared of your own ghost?"

"Scared you might not like the shape of things," and Lutie disappeared in the bathroom. "Do my hair in the morning," she was saying as she reappeared in a wrap-around robe.

"Be goodbye to everyone after the memorial service tomorrow," Lovett said with a grimace. He was trying to hoist his bad leg into bed.

"Life be one *goodbye* after another!" Lutie was saying, helping him get both legs between the sheets. "Goodbye, Goodbye, Goodbye! Folks always be moving on. What be the *good* in goodbye?"

"Why you think Varsi's widow said her goodbyes so soon?" Lovett wondered as he struggled to get settled down.

"Reckon she got tired of nobody knowing her," Lutie said, bending over him, smoothing his pillow, "and tired of some old boys wanting to know her too good!"

"She took a fancy to you," Lovett said, "like Varsi did."

"Spooked me, she did, after that dream you lay on me," and Lutie said, "If she be a she."

"Everybody hides a thing or two," Lutie was thinking, "but not you. You ain't the best bargain on the lot, but I sure got me a square deal when I got you."

Lovett got the itch to scratch at the lie he'd been hiding all these years. He'd always been a "babe magnet," but conjured up his curse to trick girls out of marriage. Girls wanted love more than sex.

"Got me a confession," Lutie said before Lovett could make his own confession. "This gal be guilty of hiding something.

It were little old me a-planting the seed in Varsi's widow to
ask you to stand up for her man at the memorial."

"Suppose you reckoned I'd have to come up with a prayer
for Varsi?"

"Prayed you had a prayer in you," Lutie said as she swished
around the bed, turned back the covers on her side. "Reckon
you don't have a prayer, bless your dear heart! It be your
curse." She slid into bed, turned away, kept talking. "Seems
like you still believe in your old curse, and don't know you
ain't got it no more. You got to know heaps of love from this
old gal!"

"Reckon I shook off that curse when I found you."

"Can't find love," Lutie thought with her back to him.
"Got to give love. Love and charity go together like ham
hocks and eggs." She reached out to switch off the bed lamp.
The hotel room sank like an anchor into the dark. "Sometimes
this old gal thinks you hooked up with her just to get out of
them nights in Navy barracks."

"Got yourself another think coming," Lovett heard his
voice going around in the darkness, and Lutie's voice coming
round back, "think you need your sleep."

For awhile Lovett lay awake in the dark and silence, thought
he was back in the barracks at Guantanamo Bay, stacked-up
with squadron mates, wrapped-up in their breaths, but not
their thoughts, wrapped up in himself alone.

He came back to himself in his Miami hotel room with
Lutie, came back to an aching body unable to turn over in

bed, came back to a wife who'd been questioning his love. How could she not know how much he always loved her? She didn't even know how much he looked for meaning in life, if only a grain of truth! He could read the DNA code of life but not the patterns of living. He couldn't read the minds of others, and nobody could get inside his mind!

That be the story of my life, he said to himself, the curse of my life. Nobody ever really got to know me!

CPSIA information can be obtained at www.ICGtesting.com
Printed in the USA
LVOW090350051011

249093LV00001B/120/P